PRAISE FOR KERRY LONSDALE

Everything We Keep

A Top Amazon Bestseller of 2016 and *Wall Street Journal* Bestseller

Amazon Charts Bestseller

Liz & Lisa Best Book of the Month Selection

POPSUGAR and *Redbook* Fall Must-Read Selection

"This fantastic debut is glowing with adrenaline-inducing suspense and unexpected twists. Don't make other plans when you open up *Everything We Keep*; you will devour it in one sitting."

—*Redbook* magazine

"Aimee's electrifying journey to piece together the puzzle of mystery surrounding her fiancé's disappearance is a heart-pounding reading experience every hopeless romantic and shock-loving fiction-lover should treat themselves to."

—POPSUGAR

"You'll need an ample supply of tissue this one . . . From Northern Cali s a heart-wrenching story about fat ant."

—*Sunset* magazine

"Gushing with adrenaline-inducing plot, this is the phenomenally written debut every fall reader will be swooning over."

—*Coastal Living*

"A beautifully crafted novel about unconditional love, heartbreak, and letting go, *Everything We Keep* captures readers with its one-of-a-kind, suspenseful plot. Depicting grief and loss, but also healing and hope in their rawest forms, this novel will capture hearts and minds, keeping readers up all night, desperate to learn the truth."

—*RT Book Reviews*

"A perfect page-turner for summer."

—Catherine McKenzie, bestselling author of *Hidden* and *Fractured*

"Heartfelt and suspenseful, *Everything We Keep* beautifully navigates the deep waters of grief, and one woman's search to reconcile a past she can't release, and a future she wants to embrace. Lonsdale's writing is crisp and effortless and utterly irresistible—and her expertly layered exploration of the journey from loss to renewal is sure to make this a book club must-read. *Everything We Keep* drew me in from the first page and held me fast all the way to its deeply satisfying ending."

—Erika Marks, author of *The Last Treasure*

"In *Everything We Keep*, Kerry Lonsdale brilliantly explores the grief of loss, if we can really let go of our great loves, and if some secrets are better left buried. With a good dose of drama, a heart-wrenching love story, and the suspense of unanswered questions, Lonsdale's layered and engrossing debut is a captivating read."

—Karma Brown, bestselling author of *Come Away with Me*

"A stunning debut with a memorable twist, *Everything We Keep* effortlessly layers family secrets into a suspenseful story of grief, love, and art. This is a gem of a book."

—Barbara Claypole White, bestselling author of *The Perfect Son* and *The Promise Between Us*

"*Everything We Keep* takes your breath from the very first line and keeps it through a heart-reeling number of twists and turns. Well-plotted, with wonderful writing and pacing, on the surface it appears to be a story of love and loss, but just as you begin to think you've worked it out, you're blindsided and realize you haven't. It will keep you reading and guessing, and trust me, you still won't have it figured out. Not until the very end."

—Barbara Taylor Sissel, bestselling author of *The Truth We Bury* and *What Lies Below*

"Wow—it's been a long time since I ignored all of my responsibilities and read a book straight through, but it couldn't be helped with *Everything We Keep*. I was intrigued from the start . . . So many questions, and Lonsdale answers them in the most intriguing and captivating way possible."

—Camille Di Maio, author of *The Memory of Us*

All the Breaking Waves

AN AMAZON BEST BOOK OF THE MONTH: LITERATURE & FICTION
CATEGORY

LIZ & LISA BEST BOOK OF THE MONTH SELECTION

"Blending elements of magic and mystery, *All the Breaking Waves* is a compelling portrayal of one mother's journey as she grapples with her small daughter's horrific visions that force her to confront a haunting secret from her past. Examining issues of love, loss, and the often-fragile ground of relationships and forgiveness, this tenderly told story will have you turning the pages long past midnight."

—Barbara Taylor Sissel, bestselling author of *The Truth We Bury* and *What Lies Below*

"With a touch of the paranormal, *All the Breaking Waves* is an emotional story about lost love, family secrets, and finding beauty in things people fear . . . or simply discard. A perfect book club pick!"

—Barbara Claypole White, bestselling author of *The Perfect Son* and *The Promise Between Us*

"A masterful tale of magic realism and family saga. With its heartfelt characters, relationships generational and maternal, and a long-ago romance, we are drawn into Molly's world. While her intuitive gifts may be ethereal, her fears and hopes for her daughter and personal desires are extraordinarily relatable. Woven with a thread of pure magic, Lonsdale crafts an intriguing story of love, mystery, and family loyalty that will captivate and entertain readers."

—Laura Spinella, bestselling author of *Ghost Gifts*

Everything We Left Behind

Amazon Charts and *Wall Street Journal* Bestseller

Amazon Editors' Recommended Beach Read

A Liz & Lisa Best Book of the Month Selection

"In this suspenseful sequel to *Everything We Keep* . . . readers will be captivated as the truth unravels, hanging on every word."

—*RT Book Reviews*

"A stunning fusion of suspense, family drama, and redemption, *Everything We Left Behind* will hold the reader spellbound to the last sentence."

—A. J. Banner, #1 Kindle and *USA Today* bestselling author of *The Twilight Wife* and *The Good Neighbor*

"Love, loss, and secrets drive Kerry Lonsdale's twisty follow-up to the bestselling *Everything We Keep*. *Everything We Left Behind* is an enthralling and entertaining read. You'll be turning the pages as fast as you can to see how it ends."

—Liz Fenton and Lisa Steinke, authors of *The Good Widow*

"While *Everything We Left Behind*, the long-anticipated sequel to *Everything We Keep*, is page-turning and suspenseful, at its center it is the story of a man struggling to discover the truth of his own identity. A man who is determined above all else to protect his family, a man who is willing to risk everything to find out the truth and to ultimately uncover the secrets of his own heart. For everyone who has read *Everything We Keep* (if you haven't go do that now!), this is your novel, answering every question, tying up every thread to an oh-so-satisfying conclusion."

—Barbara Taylor Sissel, bestselling author of *The Truth We Bury* and
What Lies Below

"With one smart, unexpected twist after another, this page-turner is as surprising as it is emotionally insightful. *Everything We Left Behind* showcases Kerry Lonsdale at the top of her game."

—Camille Pagán, bestselling author of *Life and Other Near-Death
Experiences*

"Told through a unique perspective, *Everything We Left Behind* is a compelling story about one man's journey to find himself in the wake of trauma, dark secrets, and loss. As past and present merge, he struggles to confront fear and find trust, but two constants remain: his love for his young sons and his need to protect them from danger. This novel has everything—romance, suspense, mystery, family drama. What a page-turner!"

—Barbara Claypole White, bestselling author of *The Perfect Son* and
The Promise Between Us

EVERYTHING
WE GIVE

ALSO BY KERRY LONSDALE

The Everything Series

Everything We Keep

Everything We Left Behind

Stand-Alone

All the Breaking Waves

EVERYTHING
WE GIVE

KERRY LONSDALE

Published by Lake Union Publishing, Seattle

www.apub.com

Amazon, the Amazon logo, and Lake Union Publishing are trademarks of Amazon.com, Inc., or its affiliates.

ISBN-13: 9781503902312
ISBN-10: 1503902315

Cover design by Damon Freeman

Printed in the United States of America

For my readers:
Because of you, Ian has a story.
#grateful

CHAPTER 1

IAN

Almost any guy can credit at least one woman who influenced the man he is today. I have two. One adores me and the other deserted me. Both have shaped me. And both have made a lasting impact on my photography.

Because of my mom, Sarah, I gave up my aspirations of becoming a photojournalist. It's not easy for me to admit, but it's difficult to pursue an assignment through the Associated Press when you can't bring yourself to snap a photo of a human being suffering. But thanks to my wife, Aimee, opening my eyes to the more idyllic side of humanity, my photography no longer focuses solely on nature and wildlife. It has evolved to include a human element, and has been featured in magazines the likes of *Discover* and *Outside*.

Despite the yin and yang effect these two women have had on my life and the trauma that set me on a career path I hadn't intended to take in my youth, I still arrived at my original destination: that of an award-winning photographer.

As for the women? I love them both.

I remove the last of my photos, this one titled *Synchronicity*, at the Wendy V. Yee Gallery to make room for my friend Erik Ridley's upcoming exhibit. The image is of an *aloitador*, one of several horse handlers, launching over a sea of wild Galician horses packed into the village's *curro*, a small, circular arena. Dusty and sweaty, his arms defined with sinewy muscle, the Spanish horse handler has one goal in mind: land on the horse's back and manage it to stillness.

I captured the shot last July at the *Rapa das bestas*, an ancient "shearing of the beasts" ritual that occurs annually in the northwestern region of Spain. Wendy describes the photo to prospective buyers as a riveting example of man in sync with beast. It's one of many I submitted to *National Geographic* last month when Erik heard of the magazine's interest in publishing an article about the *Rapa*. Erik introduced me to the photo editor, Al Foster, and I've just concluded a call with him. Al accepted my proposal. My work will be featured in an upcoming issue, and if I'm lucky, I'll nab the issue's cover.

Dream. Come. True.

I fist-pump the air, then lean *Synchronicity* against the wall with the other photos to be boxed and held in storage during the special exhibit.

"That's the last of them," I tell Wendy, making my way over to her desk. Her assistant, Braxton, is still out with the flu so Wendy had called me to help prep the gallery for Erik's showing by taking down my work and putting up his.

Wendy and I have known each other since our time at Arizona State University when we both realized we weren't cut out for photojournalism. Wendy discovered she was better at selling photos than developing film, and my inner demons still waged their war. Landscape photography was safe and I was good at it. Besides, a waterfall had yet to lunge at me and smack the equipment from my hands.

Wendy looks up at me from where she leans over her desk. "I have one more for you." She points her pen at a photo I'd hung on the far side of the gallery, a monochrome in gray of an Indonesian palm forest.

Swooping patterns etch numerous acres across the panoramic shot. The design is almost beautiful until you realize forests have been decimated to supply the demand for palm oil, as noted on the placard Wendy had me post alongside the photo. Erik's work is edgy in his attempt to portray the harsh reality of destruction happening to natural environments from the impact of human consumption. The upcoming exhibit, a photographic retrospective, is daring compared with previous shows Wendy has hosted and exactly what she wanted when I referred Erik to her.

"The show must make an impact. I want visitors to feel the devastation Erik portrays, but we must still strike a balance in its presentation. I'm thinking more color." Wendy jiggles the computer mouse. The monitor brightens, displaying Erik's portfolio. She scrolls through his work, chewing her lower lip, her gaze darting over the thumbnail images. "This one." She clicks on the image, an aerial of a white farmhouse drowning in an expansive cornfield, combines slicing through the rows like an alien invasion. Knowing Erik, I'm sure the corn is genetically modified.

"Do you mind replacing the monochrome with the farm? Switch them for me; then I'm done with you."

"Yes, ma'am." I give her a mock salute, find the framed photo in storage, and dash across the gallery in a sudden rush to get out of there. Aimee's waiting for me at the café. I work with a smile.

"You're cheerful. What's gotten into you?"

"I—" I stall, and my grin widens. I point pistol-style at Wendy. "I'll tell you tomorrow." I want to share my news with Aimee first. She'll be thrilled.

As I take down the monochrome, I think about how we should celebrate, and I get an idea: cocktails and dinner at La Fondue. *Parfait!* It's been a few months since we've had a night out together. Dinner should help us get back to the way things were before June. It's time we celebrate us, which makes me think about *how* we'll celebrate, especially after we put our four-year-old daughter, Sarah Catherine, to bed. My entire body buzzes.

Hmm. Maybe I can convince the in-laws to keep little Caty for the night.

I text my mother-in-law, Catherine Tierney. Caty's with her now. Hopefully she can stay. I have plans, mature-audience-rated plans, for Aimee and me.

Slipping my phone into my back pocket, I hang up the white farmhouse photo. The scene transports me back to Idaho where I grew up in a similar house. My dad owns the land, which he inherited from his father. But he doesn't work it, never has. He leases the acreage because he's rarely home. I don't think he wanted to be home, at least not while I lived there. As a sports photographer, Stu Collins chased the next great Hail Mary pass.

I finish up, put away the tools, and join Wendy at her desk. I check my tactical wristwatch, a recent birthday gift from Aimee. Erik has a meeting with Wendy and he's late. I was hoping to catch him before I left.

"What time did Erik say he's coming in?"

"He's not going to make it." Wendy types some notes, her goth-painted nails a stark contrast to the cream linen sheath she wears. They blur across the keyboard. "*Mercury News* sent him on assignment to cover the damage from the Big Sur wildfires. He called while you were outside on your phone. He says he owes you a beer, and he's bringing me a bottle of Domaine Chandon."

"Make sure he does. Don't let him back out on that."

She shoots me a look as if she would ever let that happen. She pauses in her typing and pencils a note in a ledger. "As much as I would have loved Erik to hang his own photographs, I prefer you. You have a good eye for placement." She looks at the farmhouse on the wall. "Much, much better. OK, you can go now, shoo-shoo. I have a sale to make." She glances over her shoulder.

Behind her in the one corner she keeps reserved for her represented artists, no matter the exhibit, a young couple bickers over an image I shot last year in Canyonlands National Park. Their voices have risen above the instrumental jazz softly playing in the background. The man says the photo is his favorite here. His friend—girlfriend, wife?—objects. The color scheme is wrong. It's not contemporary enough for their newly furnished living room done in dusky blue.

"Show them *Nightscape*," I suggest to Wendy. The photo is a duotone of the San Francisco skyline.

Wendy nods. "I was thinking the same thing."

I kiss her cheek. "Great working for you today. Next time I'm charging for my time," I tease.

"You already do. You get a nice payment from me every month."

She's right about that. Wendy sells almost every photo I bring to her.

I leave the gallery and walk the two blocks in October's temperate air to Aimee's Café. The scent of roasted coffee, cinnamon, and baked goods wafts over me when I open the door. I inhale deeply. God, I love that smell.

I ignore the cursory glances from patrons when the bell above the door alerts them I'm here, and I especially ignore the oil paintings on the wall that butt up against my photography like the person in line who has no concept of personal space. Paintings done by Aimee's ex-fiancé, James Donato.

I don't mind they're up there. They don't bother me. Not really.

Actually . . .

They do. They really, really do bug me.

Five years into our marriage and she still hasn't taken them down.

I honestly didn't care about them and why they were still taking up prime wall real estate until June. After living in a dissociative fugue state, James returned with memories of, and emotions for, *my* wife still

5

intact. But Aimee made her decision. James needed to understand that. She left him. She moved on. She chose me.

Then I remember that they kissed.

I bite down on my teeth.

I want those paintings out of here even though I've held off mentioning that to Aimee. Because James's artwork seems to make her happy.

Happy wife, happy life.

I force myself to relax, even broaden my smile. I wave at Trish, who works behind the counter, and go in search of Aimee.

"She's not here," Trish calls after me.

I stop and swing around. "Where is she?"

Trish shrugs. "She didn't tell me. She left a couple of hours ago."

I rap my knuckles on the wall in thought. I'll call and tell her to meet me at home.

"Let her know I'm looking for her if she comes back," I say and leave the café.

On my way to the car, my phone rings. Erik's mug lights up the screen.

"You owe me," I answer.

"How does it look?"

"Spectacular. I'm a genius with a hammer and nail. Hanging your sorry-ass photos is exactly what I wanted to do on my afternoon off."

Erik laughs. "Better you than me."

I met Erik several years ago at the Photography Expo and Trade Conference. He started out as a photographer with the Associated Press, traveling to war zones and areas of extreme poverty, but the confrontations he witnessed and suffering he documented took their toll. Quitting while he was ahead, and still in possession of his life and sanity, he now freelances. Together we found a means to an end. I respected his photojournalistic skills and Erik has long admired my nature and wildlife imagery. We became mutual mentors and fast friends. Erik's the guy I call to meet me for beers at the end of the day, or for a round in the ring at the gym when I need to work off the edge.

"Thanks for everything, man. Beers on me when we meet up again," Erik offers.

"Beers on you for the next month."

Erik chuckles, a deep rumble. "I suddenly find my calendar full. Not sure when I can see you."

"Nice try, Ridley." I glance left and jaywalk across the street. "You still in Big Sur?"

"Nope. Driving home."

"How was it?"

"Horrible. Lots of burned acreage. Too many homes lost and people displaced. But hey, I got a call from *Sierra Explorer*. They're sending me to Yosemite next week. It's for an online piece about the dangers of hiking along Vernal Fall. Nothing new, but with those kids going over the edge last month, there's been a brouhaha to restrict the number of hikers and move the fencing for the viewing platform back. Guess who's writing the piece? Reese Thorne. Have you heard of her?"

I groan before I can think not to.

"Uh-oh, not sure I like the sound of that. She was at ASU same time as you. Something I should know?"

"Nope."

"Do you know her?"

I hesitate. "I know of her. She's drawn to important stories. Her readers love her and her articles have won awards."

"But . . ."

I don't want to tarnish his first impression of Reese, but I feel he needs to know what he's getting into since his photos will be attached to her article. "Let's just say in this new age of reporting where readers favor opinion over fact, Reese has thrived."

"Yeah, that's what I heard. I just thought you might know a little more about her or had worked with her in the past, back at school or something. We're spending two days together."

"I'm a landscape photographer and she's a journalist. Better chance she's been on the front lines with you than the backwoods with me."

Erik laughs. "True. Speaking of landscapes, I'm going to stay a few extra days and take some nature shots for my portfolio. Do you mind looking through them when I get back? I'm sure I could use more pointers. You have a critical eye."

"Sure. Anytime."

"Great. What about you? Have you heard from Al about the Rapa piece?"

"I'll take a rain check on answering that question," I say, arriving at my car. I tap the key fob, unlocking the door.

"That can only mean one thing, but I'll hold off the congrats for later. I want details when you're ready."

I sink into the driver's seat. "I'll bring you up to speed when you buy me that beer."

"You're killing me."

"Gotta get home to the wife, my friend. Chat later."

I end the call with Erik and speed-dial Aimee. I'm sent straight to voice mail. "Hey, Aims, honey. I've got some great news. Call me back." I text the same message.

When I arrive home, I park the Explorer in the driveway of our one-story 1960s ranch. The house is beyond old and in need of a remodel. But, hey, it's home. We sold my condo and Aimee's downtown bungalow to give us just enough of a down payment so our mortgage didn't slice a jugular in our monthly cash flow.

The investment was worth the life savings, blood, sweat, and signing over the parental rights of our firstborn. Kidding. But we live in the same neighborhood as Aimee's parents, something we both want for Caty. I don't have extended family, and what family I do have—a missing mom and estranged dad—is seriously messed up. For Caty to grow up by her grandparents? It means everything to me.

Besides, we aren't in too bad of a financial situation. Aimee has been scouting locations for a second and possibly third coffee shop because the flagship store has consistently performed well. My photos move fast when on display in brick-and-mortar galleries. Through my online gallery, I've acquired international clients with money to burn. Interior designers have sought my work to display in hotels, resorts, and restaurants in five different countries. This *National Geographic* assignment will be the caramel syrup on top of my portfolio sundae. I'm rocking the photography world.

Cue another fist pump.

I punch the air and let myself into the house and my phone pings with a text from Catherine. She attached a video of Caty dancing with the caption: Caty's happy dance. We'll keep her for the night. Have fun!

Great news for Aimee and me. We have all . . . night . . . long to ourselves. My mind dives under the sheets in our master bedroom and I grin.

Thinking of Aimee reminds me: I haven't heard from her. This isn't like her. She's usually quick to respond.

I frown, scratching my jawline. Where is she? She didn't mention any appointments today. Or did she? I must have checked out of our conversation when she chatted my ear off at four-freaking-thirty this morning. Those crack-of-dawn wake-ups kill me. I don't know how she does it five days a week. But I start my day with her anyhow. I treasure those intimate moments with her as the darkness of night shifts to the gray of dawn.

I call her again. I go straight into voice mail again. Strange.

I roll my shoulders, loosening the apprehension that wants to settle there. I shower—hot date tonight—and when I don't find a message or call notification from her afterward, I call her again. Uneasiness break-dances as I wait for her to pick up. I hate that feeling, especially when I land in her voice mail. Again. Damn.

I have good news I'm dying to share.

I want to talk with my wife.

I want to see my wife.

Visions of twisted metal, broken glass, and busy emergency rooms snap in my head like a camera flash on sports mode. I swear at myself, angry my mind even goes there. But the possibility of losing her, whether by accident or by choice, drives my thoughts in that direction. They've been taking that route often these last few months.

I call Aimee's friend Kristen Garner. She could be visiting with her.

"Hi, Ian," Kristen huffs into the phone. A very pregnant Kristen at nine and a half months. She and Nick are expecting their third child and the squirt is already overdue.

"Is Aimee there?" I ask, shooting past the small talk.

"No, she's not."

"Have you heard from her recently?"

"Not since yesterday. Is something wrong?"

"She wasn't at the café when we were supposed to meet and she's not answering her phone."

"When did you last hear from her?"

"This morning before lunch." I glance at the time. It's almost six.

"I'm sure she's fine. She could be shopping or something. Maybe her phone died."

I should have thought of that. I pace the master bathroom thick with steam, a towel wrapped low on my hips. "You're probably right." But unlikely. She doesn't ignore my calls or let her battery die.

I wipe condensation from the mirror with my forearm. Water beads on my skin. I blot my chest with a hand towel. The bathroom smells of aloe vera soap and the wooded spice of my shampoo.

"Do you want me to call Nadia?" Kristen offers.

"Nah, I'll buzz her." After I get dressed. My good news has made me overly anxious. Aimee will call soon enough. She'll walk through the front door at any moment.

I call La Fondue and sweet-talk the hostess into a reservation. She puts a table for two in my name for eight thirty.

After dressing in dark washed jeans and a fitted black button-down, I try Aimee again. This time the phone rings and rings. I disconnect and bring up the texts I sent earlier. They've been read.

Say what?

I tap the corner of the phone against my forehead, trying not to read into this.

Admit it, Collins. You're reading into this.

I rely on instinct to deliver the best moments to photograph. That award-winning instant captured in time. Right now, my instincts are telling me something is wrong.

I type out a short text—Are you hurt?—then tap the back key, editing my message to Are you OK?, else I sound overly dramatic. I don't want to jump to conclusions. I send the text and immediately three dots appear underneath. Her response comes an instant later. A simple word that has a knot expanding in my throat.

No.

No? That's it?

I wait for the three dots to jump around on my screen again, hoping for an explanation to arrive. Something more than a cryptic no.

A minute passes and still nothing. My thumbs fly over the keyboard.

Where are you?
Do you need me to come get you?

And before I can think not to, I send the text I'd originally drafted.

11

Are you hurt?

She doesn't reply and my damn nerves go haywire. I stare hard at my phone, willing a text from her when it dawns on me.

Idiot.

I launch the Find My Phone app, pushing aside the first thought that pops into my head—*stalker*—and quickly pinpoint that she's at her friend Nadia Jacobs's flat. Has she been there the entire time? Hopefully, I think on a relieved breath.

I call Nadia and she immediately answers.

"Ian." She sounds relieved to hear from me.

"Put Aimee on. I need to talk with her."

"Hold on."

I hear a muffled noise as though Nadia's walking into another room. I expect Aimee to get on the phone, but it's Nadia who speaks. "Aimee—"

"Where is she? Why didn't you give her the phone?"

"She said she's leaving shortly. She'll meet you at home. But, Ian, I'm really worried about her. I haven't seen her like this in a long time."

"Like what? I haven't seen or heard from her since this morning. I'm in the dark here, Nadia. Other than one text, she's been ignoring my messages and calls. What's going on? Is she hurt?"

"Physically, no. But James said something to her that's really upset her. She won't tell me what, though."

"*Who* said something to her?" My voice is as cold as the chill that's settled in my chest at the mention of his name.

"You didn't know? James. He's back."

CHAPTER 2

IAN

James is back. Again.

Can't the guy stay away?

I scowl.

"Did she go see him?" She did in June when James briefly returned to California.

"Yes," Nadia says, and I'm devastated. I sink onto the edge of the couch in the living room.

Aimee's reunion with her ex had been one I'd dreaded since returning from Mexico more than five years ago when we found James alive but living in a dissociative fugue state. She'd explained to me why she went to see him earlier this summer. She had to say good-bye. I thought that good-bye was for good.

Apparently not.

I'd been in Spain. It was one week before the Rapa started. It was a trip I'd wanted to take since Erik first told me about the festival several years ago. Upon landing, I called Aimee from the baggage claim to let her know I'd arrived. Her voice sounded strained. She blamed it on being tired, as she did again and again with each phone call during my fourteen-day trip. She sounded unenthusiastic and mildly depressed. It worried me. Our conversations felt off, forced. But I know her well. She was hiding something.

It wasn't until I returned home and tucked an overjoyous Caty into bed that Aimee sat me down at the kitchen table. The bottle of vodka and two shot glasses should have warned me this wouldn't be an easy conversation.

"What's going on?" I asked warily.

"I saw James." She then told me everything, and I mean everything.

We'd known James had surfaced from the fugue state the previous December. Kristen had told Aimee about James's call to Nick, Kristen's husband and James's best friend. We knew James would return home. The question was when.

Well, I got my answer over a shot of vodka. He arrived the day before I left for Spain, Aimee told me. After dropping me off at the airport, Aimee had driven to James's house. She hadn't meant to see him, but she couldn't seem to drive away. Then suddenly he was there, on the sidewalk, knocking on the passenger-side window. And she let him into the car.

"Do you love him?" I asked.

"No. Not in the way that matters." Ribbons of tears cut across her cheeks.

"What's the way that matters, Aimee? Do tell. Because to me, love is love." I bit out the words, letting her hear my anger, my shock at finding out she'd kissed him. That James had pulled her onto his lap, and that his hands had been all over her.

"I am not *in love* with him."

I felt my eyes harden, my expression chill, as I looked at her across the table. She was miserable. Her hand shook when she reached for the bottle, only to pull away. She folded her hands in her lap.

The kitchen was quiet; we were quiet, sitting on opposite sides in the dim light. I inhaled deeply and closed my eyes when I asked, "Do you want to be with him?"

"No." She looked at me, appalled. "*No!*" she repeated more firmly. "I love you, Ian. I'm *in* love with you. I'm sorry I went to see him. I didn't mean for it to get out of control the way it did and I can't apologize enough. I'm sorry. Can you ever forgive me?"

I poured myself a shot, then another.

She watched me, and she watched the bottle, the quick pours into my shot glass and my fast empties as I tossed them back. "Say something," she whispered when I finished.

I slowly shook my head. "I don't think I should right now." I excused myself and retired to my office. I told myself I needed time to sort this out. I needed to believe she did love me and wouldn't leave me. But the truth? I didn't need to convince myself of anything. I knew she loved me. I knew in my gut she wouldn't leave me. As to forgiving her? I already had, long before James returned since I knew he eventually would. That's how much I loved her. But it hurt. It hurt big-time.

Over the next few days, we talked about it, and gradually, over the summer, we eased back into a comfortable rhythm, though not quite at the same beat. But we survived James's return. Our marriage was still intact. Or so I thought it was.

"I'm coming over. Tell Aimee not to leave." Whatever James said to her, whatever he *did* to her, I needed to know what happened, right *now*. Not in an hour. Not tonight. And especially not tomorrow. Because the last time James was in town, he kissed my wife.

Scratch that. It wasn't a kiss. It was a hands-all-over-James-would-have-fucked-her kiss had Aimee given him the chance. Had she told him yes.

But she hadn't.

Thank God Aimee didn't go back to him. Thank God James moved to Hawaii.

Then why is he back and what does he want with Aimee?

My wife.

The possessive thought punches through my skull as I hang up with Nadia and grab the car keys. Wondering what James will do and what he did with Aimee this afternoon has me racing down the freeway to Nadia's flat in downtown San Jose.

I jab the code for Nadia's underground parking garage and tuck the car into a guest spot. Within minutes, I knock on her door and she immediately answers as though she were standing on the other side, waiting. She smiles, lips closed and brows raised, and steps aside. I take it as a silent message of good luck. My heart taps a nervous, rapid rhythm against my sternum.

Any man—straight or swinging for the other team—would be captivated by Nadia's auburn hair, jade eyes, and sharp facial structure. She possesses the type of beauty you can't look away from, which is what I set out to achieve in the series of photos I took of her a couple of years ago. They're mounted on the far wall of her open-space flat. I intensified the red of her hair and green of her eyes, a striking contrast to the living space's palette of grays and wood grains.

But I don't see these portraits. Nothing about my surroundings registers. I only have eyes for Aimee. She stands across the room, arms folded tightly so that her fingers dig into her lower rib cage. She stares out the window, a wall of glass looking out to the city's lit downtown. Dusk has arrived, lending just enough light in Nadia's darkened apartment to illuminate the moisture on Aimee's cheeks.

I briefly close my eyes and send up a prayer of thanks. She's here and she's unharmed. Pressure builds in my chest with each rise and fall, pulling me in her direction. I want nothing more than to have her in my arms, to reassure myself that she is mine.

Nadia closes the door behind me.

"How long has she been here?" I ask.

"About ten minutes before you called. I'd just gotten home from work."

Not long then, which means she was with James for at least as long as I tried to reach her. One and a half hours.

I swallow roughly. A lot can happen in ninety minutes.

"Has she said anything since our call?"

"Nothing except that she wanted to collect herself before she picked up Caty from Catherine's house. My opinion? I don't think she wanted to go home to you feeling the way she does."

Which is how? Did she realize she is still in love with James and is afraid to tell me?

Nausea surfs a wave in my gut.

What did James say to her? What did he do to her? I might have met James when he was Carlos a couple of times, but I don't know James. I've never met him.

Nadia adjusts the dimmer light and the flat brightens. Aimee blinks, her eyes adjusting, and wipes her cheeks with the back of her hand. I know she knows I'm here. She had to have heard me knock. I will her to look at me, but she keeps her gaze fixed on the glass.

Nadia glides a hand across my shoulders in a show of support. "I'll be in the kitchen."

I nod, hooking my thumbs in my pockets, and approach Aimee. She turns at the sound of my boots on hardwood and holds up her hand, stopping me. She shakes her head. A prickle of dread coasts down my spine. I stop opposite the coffee table cluttered with magazines, books, and potted succulents. A basket of folded laundry rests off to the side, an odd, out-of-place piece in Nadia's *Home Décor* living space.

"I'm just checking on you. I've been worried."

She glances over her shoulder toward the kitchen where Nadia went. "I don't want to talk here."

I hold out my hand for hers. "Then let's go home. I'll take you." Now that I'm here I don't want to be apart from her.

She shakes her head again. "I'm not ready. You go. I'll meet you there."

"I'm not leaving you until I know what's wrong," I say, even knowing she doesn't want to talk here. "After what happened this summer, I have the right—"

"Ian, please." She groans in frustration and grabs a sock ball from the laundry basket, and for a moment, I think she's going to throw it at me. Instead, her shoulders slump and the sock ball drops to the floor. Her chin dips and it breaks my heart. She looks so sad.

"I want to talk later," she says. "Right now, I'm still . . . processing." Processing *what*?

"Aimee . . ." The not knowing, the uncertainty, it's killing me. *Please don't tell me you're in love with him.*

A tear falls and it motivates me to act. One small drop off her chin and I close the distance between us, wrapping her in my arms. She stiffens and holds her breath. I murmur in her ear, telling her how much I love her. How much I care about her. I press my lips to her forehead and smooth my hand down her hair. Eventually, she relaxes and leans into me so that I'm supporting her weight. Then she cries.

I rock with her. "Baby, you've got to help me. We can't fix this unless you tell me what's wrong."

Her arms rope around me and hook low on my waist. I lean back to look down at her. I can't see her face. "Please tell me why you're sad."

Her breath shuttles out of her. "I'm not sad. I'm angry, or I was before you got here."

"Are you mad at me?"

"No, I'm mad at me. I'm hating myself right now." Aimee leaves my embrace and returns to stare out the window.

"Baby." I follow. I lean my forearm against the glass and study her profile, the faint freckles that decorate her nose like a dusting of chocolate on latte foam. I gently run a finger down the length of hair where it meets her shoulder. "Why would you feel that way?" I ask softly.

18

Aimee folds an arm under her breasts. She knuckles off her tears. I want her back in my arms. I don't like the way she's withdrawing into herself, shoulders stooped and back bowed. I don't like her keeping things from me.

We don't do secrets, not after my tumultuous childhood and what she went through with the Donato family. We agreed to have an honest marriage with open communication. This includes discussing her past relationship with James, despite how much I want to despise the guy. Not that James has done anything directly to me. I just don't like how he treated Aimee, let alone the psychological mind trip James sent her on courtesy of his brother Thomas.

Talk about a fouled-up family. I thought my parents had problems. Screw the cake. James and his brothers take the whole damn bakery in the dysfunctional-family department.

Aimee takes a deep breath. "I was fine while I was with him. We just talked, you know? He told me about his sons and how the three of them are enjoying island life on Kauai. I know how much I hurt you . . . hurt us . . . when I saw him last summer. I told myself I'd never go out of my way to see him again. But he called. He's trying to move past all the shit his brother made of his life, and to do that he felt like he owed me an apology, face-to-face. He said I deserved that much after everything he'd put me through. So I met with him. I was fine while we talked, but afterward? Everything hit me and I started bawling and shaking and, goddammit, I was so angry. I thought I was past all this, what with counseling." She finally looks up at me and smiles weakly, an apology.

"Aims," I murmur. I caress her cheek with the back of my fingers, then let my arm fall to my side.

"Anyway," she says with the flick of her hand, "I couldn't stop crying. I drove around hoping to calm down before I had to pick up Caty, and when I couldn't stop, I found myself here instead. If I came home as upset as I was, I knew I wouldn't be able to clearly communicate to you why I went to see him, and I didn't want you to jump to conclusions."

I rub her back as I listen to her, hating she felt like she couldn't come to me, and hating James more for making her feel this way.

"I don't like how emotional he makes me. It reminds me how I used to be with him."

"And how was that?"

"Naive and immature. Too trusting when I should have been asking questions."

I adored the trusting Aimee and I love the woman she used to be. I especially love the woman she's become while we've been married. Headstrong, confident, and passionate. The best mother I could ask for our daughter, which is important to me.

But stupid me, that isn't what I latch on to. I'm still fixated on my earlier assumption that Aimee realized she still loves James . . . in the way that matters. Despite what she just told me, I can't get the possibility out of my head.

"How often have you seen him since June?"

"What?" Aimee frowns, her expression off-kilter. I arch a brow, waiting for an answer. She tugs at the hem of her blouse. "Just today."

"How much time did you spend together? When did he call you?"

"Jesus, Ian."

Ice rattles in a martini shaker. "Drinks, anyone?" Nadia calls from the kitchen.

"No," I answer without taking my eyes from Aimee's.

"Yes." Aimee sends me a cool look. "I told you, I don't want to talk about it here." She strides to the kitchen bar counter.

I fork my fingers through my hair and exhale harshly out my nose. I trail Aimee to the kitchen.

Nadia slides a dirty martini toward her. Aimee removes the olive-laden toothpick and downs the cocktail. She then reaches for my glass when she notices I'm not drinking it.

"I guess you were thirsty," Nadia quips, toasting with her own glass. "Salute." She tastes the cocktail, smacks her lips twice, and glances over her shoulder at the microwave clock. "I can order in Thai."

"No, thanks. We have dinner plans." I lean a hand on the counter, hook my other in my front pocket, and watch Aimee consume my martini, thankfully at a slower pace than her first drink.

"I'm not hungry." She sets down the stemware.

"All right, then." Nadia drags out the words. She rattles the shaker. "More cocktails?"

Aimee shakes her head and empties the glass. "I'm ready to go home." She picks up her purse where she left it on the couch and goes to stand by the front door.

I sigh. Looks like we're leaving.

"I'll drive." I pinch the bridge of my nose and call up my patience. I'm going to need it tonight before I say something else stupid that pisses off Aimee, especially when I should be doing the opposite: offering her a shoulder to cry on and an ear to listen. "Thanks," I tell Nadia. "I'll bring her by tomorrow to get her car."

"No rush." She lightly grasps my wrist. "You're a good husband, Ian. She needs you right now. She's hurting."

We both are. "I know. And thanks."

I join Aimee at the door. So much for celebrating my best news ever. "Let's go home."

We take the elevator down to the parking garage standing side by side without touching. I want to be angry with her. I want to rail at James for contacting my wife again. But all I feel is empathy for him, which surprises and irritates me.

I understand how James feels, the confusion and disorientation, the need to reach out to Aimee, the love of his life. I get how he doesn't have a sense of lost time, and that, to him, it feels like he left Aimee yesterday.

I spent my childhood amid a similar bedlam. It wasn't a fun place to be.

We reach the parking garage and I fumble the keys from my pocket. They drop on the ground.

"We need to swing by my parents' and get Caty," Aimee says, since she doesn't know about the arrangement I made with Catherine, and it no longer matters. We don't seem to be going out to dinner.

I pick up the keys. "I know," I snap, pressing hard on the fob. The car unlocks, the sound echoing in the cavernous garage, and I jerk open her door. She sinks into her seat with a wary glance in my direction. Mustering some calm, I close her door.

CHAPTER 3

IAN, AGE NINE

Ian watched the bus disappear over the rise of the road before facing the dusty white farmhouse he called home. Parked off to the side was his mom's silver Pontiac station wagon.

He blew out a steady breath, inflated cheeks shrinking like depleted tires. She was home. At least, he hoped it was his mom, Sarah, and not her other, Jackie.

For as long as Ian could remember, his mother had erratic mood swings. She'd forget what she was doing from one day to the next, sometimes from one moment to the next. And Ian would have to remind her. He'd walk her through her tasks as his mom stared at him, childlike, wide-eyed, and bewildered.

It wasn't until a year ago that his dad had tried to explain to him his mom's bizarre, and at times volatile, behavior. She'd gone missing for two days only to return home with her clothing torn and dirt-stained, her cheek slit open and eye blackened. His mom had no recollection of the previous forty-eight hours. She wanted to sink into a hot bath and go to bed, but Ian's dad insisted on taking her to the hospital. Three days later she was discharged with stitches in her cheek and a diagnosis for her mind. Dissociative identity disorder.

Ian didn't really understand what that meant or why she had it. His dad wouldn't tell him. But he did learn other people lived inside his mom. That's how his dad initially described his mom's condition to him. The doctor knew of one, Jackie. He warned there might be others. Ian hadn't noticed yet if there were, but he and his dad were all too aware of Jackie. Jackie had been making appearances since before Ian was born.

The doctor referred his mom to a psychiatrist and prescribed her antidepressants and mood stabilizers, which Ian had overheard her telling his dad she didn't want to take. She didn't like being controlled, and that's what the pills would do. As for following up with a doctor, Ian rarely saw her go and his dad wasn't around enough to make her go. Ian hadn't seen any appointments scheduled on her daily planner either.

A fly landed on Ian's elbow. He shook his arm and scratched at his skin where the bug had made him itch. He opened the mailbox and retrieved bills stamped OVERDUE and embroidery catalogs. He stuffed them in his backpack and slowly walked up the driveway. Gravel crunched under his beat-up Vans. A breeze thick with the smell of fertilizer stirred around him, ruffling his mop of hair. Bangs spilled over his eyes. He pushed them aside and crossed his fingers on both hands.

Please be Mom. Please be Mom, he recited in his head with each step.

He had too much homework to worry about Jackie getting his mom into trouble again. Three months ago, Jackie had withdrawn the cash in his parents' bank account, leaving no funds for the bills. That's why they were behind in payments.

Ian stopped in the entryway, the front door slamming behind him, blown shut by the wind. His mom looked up from her embroidery machine in the dining room and smiled. Ian smiled back and the tightness in his shoulders eased under the heavy weight of his backpack. She was Sarah. Jackie's smiles weren't as nice.

The house smelled musty, the air stale and warm, making his nose twitch. He rubbed around his nostrils and looked at the windows in the room. All four were closed, the curtains drawn. Dirty dishes and half-empty cups, interspersed with teetering piles of team uniforms and Scout shirts, cluttered the table like a city skyline.

"How was your photo expedition?" Sarah asked.

It was great. Yesterday, Ian thought.

"OK," he said out loud.

Ian had spent Sunday morning walking through the fields taking pictures of ants and magpies with a camera he found in his dad's home office. It was much better than the one his dad gifted him on his fifth birthday. His mom hadn't been home when Ian returned for lunch, and she still hadn't arrived by dinner. Ian ate cold spaghetti left over from the previous night, watched an hour of Sunday-night football hoping to spot his dad on the sideline with the other sports photographers, then stayed up late waiting for his mom to come home. He finally drifted into a fitful sleep at three a.m., hiding under his blankets, after he heard the floorboards creak under his mom's high heels. Though, it wasn't really his mom. Sarah didn't wear heels. Jackie did.

His mom glanced at the wall clock. It was 3:45 p.m. "You were gone a long time. Did you get some good pictures?"

"I think so," he muttered. He hadn't developed the film yet like his dad had taught him.

"Hungry? I made a ham sandwich. It's in the fridge."

Ian slipped off his backpack and let it drop to the floor. His mom's gaze followed. Her smile fell.

He unzipped his pack and gave her the mail.

She hesitated before taking the stack, then stared intently at the sealed envelopes in her hand. "What day is it?" she asked in a voice just above a whisper.

"Monday."

Her shoulders dipped. Her gaze swung over the pile of cheerleading uniforms beside her. She embroidered decals for local sport teams and Scout troops. She'd once told Ian the money she made paid for his clothes and sports equipment so he wouldn't have to shop at the secondhand store.

"These are due in an hour. I'm not going to finish on time. I thought it was Sunday." She glanced through the mail in her lap. After the fourth bill, she tossed the lot onto the table, turning her face away as though disgusted by the envelopes' contents. Her head lowered, and long light-brown hair spilled over her shoulder like vertical blinds. For a few moments, she sat unmoving, her spine curved into the shape of a crescent moon.

"I'm sorry, Ian."

"It's OK." He looked down at his scuffed Vans. He should have woken her up before school and told her. But the fear he'd be waking Jackie rather than Sarah kept him from knocking on her door.

Ian shouldered his backpack. "I have homework. I'll be in my room."

He shuffled into the kitchen on his way upstairs. The room smelled of molding bread and sour milk. An opened carton of half-and-half sat on the counter, forgotten. Beside it, his mom's planner lay open to Sunday. Yesterday.

If the heels on hardwood last night hadn't already confirmed it, the planner opened to the wrong date did. Jackie had been the one who came home last night. Ian guessed she was also the one who woke up this morning. His mom must have shifted back to Sarah earlier today. She'd have twenty-four hours of lost memories from the time Jackie was dominant, and no awareness that the date had changed.

Ian flipped the page in the planner. On the line by five p.m., his mom had penciled CHEER SWEATERS DUE TO COACH TAMMY PENROSE. A phone number followed. He left the planner on Monday, then opened the fridge. Fermenting vegetables assaulted his nose. His nostrils twitched and he pinched his nose to stop the sneeze. He grabbed the plated ham sandwich and went upstairs, passing his dad's home office on the way to his room.

He stopped and backed up a few steps.

Pinned to the bulletin board beside the desk was a Kansas City Chiefs calendar opened to October. Red *X*s crossed off the days through the seventeenth. Last Thursday, the day his dad left to photograph the Chiefs game against the Saints. He'd be home late tonight.

An idea formed in his head like an image revealed on instant Polaroid film. Dropping his pack, he set down the sandwich and sat at the desk. He opened drawers, removing paper, a ruler, and pencil. He drew a grid that mimicked the calendar, writing OCTOBER at the top. He added a few more details, then returned downstairs.

In the kitchen, his mom hung up the phone. "Mrs. Penrose gave me an extra day to finish. I have to work late tonight so we'll eat early." She filled a pot with water, intermittently dabbing the corners of her eyes.

"Don't be sad, Mom. You know how you sometimes forget what day it is?" Ian tacked his makeshift calendar to the fridge door with a magnet.

"What is that?" she asked.

"A calendar. Mrs. Rivers makes us cross out the days in our school planners so we know what day it is. Dad does it, too."

His mom traced Sunday's bold red *X*, then made a fist, hiding her finger. She brought her hand to her chest.

"I'll cross out the days on this calendar. That way you'll know what day it is and you can cross them off on your calendar." Ian pointed at the Monday, October 21, square, then tapped the same box on his mom's planner.

His mom looked at him. Her eyes welled.

Ian glanced away, fixing his eyes on the dishes left from breakfast still on the kitchen table. He'd upset her. She didn't like his idea. "I'll take it down." He reached for the magnet.

"No. Don't." She touched his shoulder.

Tears burned his eyes. He pressed his mouth flat. He scratched his head, then folded his arms tightly over his chest.

"I'm sorry I left you alone last night. I'm sorry I keep making mistakes. I'm so sorry."

His mouth twitched. He clamped his lips tighter, holding in the sob. His mom always apologized. He hated how she forgot things. He wished she could be normal like the other moms.

His mom cupped his jaw, forcing Ian to look up at her. He noticed that her cheeks were blotchy and her nose red. "I'm sorry I didn't make you breakfast," she said.

"It's OK."

"No, it's not." His mom lowered to her knees and clutched his shoulders. "I should have seen you off to school. The thought of you waiting alone for the bus . . ." She inhaled deeply. "I'm sorry," she whispered.

Ian was used to feeling alone, something else he hated. He flicked the calendar. The corner caught under his thumbnail. He pressed against the paper's edge until the tender nail bed burned. "What time will Dad be home?"

"Late, after you're in bed. Do you wish he was home more often?"

Ian nodded, his attention on the spot of blood blooming under his thumbnail. He wouldn't feel as lonely if his dad didn't travel as much. But he had to work. Medical bills had to be paid and mouths fed.

Ian could feel his mom watching him, but he couldn't look at her. He'd cry and that would upset her. It might make her shift and forget again. The pain of the paper cut helped keep the tears from falling.

"I'm doing my best to take care of you. You know that."

He slowly nodded even though he didn't always feel like his mom did her best. How could she? With hours, even days, missing from her life, the constant shifting from her to Jackie, Ian felt like he spent more time caring for her. If only she could be normal like other moms. He wouldn't feel so worried all the time.

CHAPTER 4

IAN

Aimee keeps her gaze averted, staring out her side of the front window as I drive back to Los Gatos. She's quiet and feels farther away than the cup holders that separate us. I bet I could touch the wall she's erected were I to reach for her.

That wall's been there since James showed up last June.

I want to bulldoze it down.

I need to know what bombshell the guy smuggled into California.

If the death grip on the purse Aimee holds in her lap tells me anything, she's still processing. Thinking about this afternoon.

Thinking about him.

I force out a harsh breath and promise myself I won't push. She started opening up at Nadia's. She'll talk in due time.

Hopefully sooner rather than later. With the deadline *National Geographic* gave me, I leave for Spain soon. And I'm leaving knowing James is in town.

Swearing under my breath, I rake my hair and shift in the seat, angling my torso so that I'm somewhat facing Aimee. The temptation to hold her hand has me fisting my own. I bite my tongue so I don't blurt out my news to lighten the mood. To say anything that would get her to look at me as though I'm the most important person in her life. I want to be that man for her.

An idea coalesces. I want her to come to Spain with me, and not just because of James. She'll love the wild horses. We could use the time away to get ourselves in sync again. No thanks to James, our marital rhythm has been out of tune since I returned from the Rapa.

Aimee clutches her hands. I give in and cross the barrier. Threading my fingers in hers, I bring our joined hands to my lips. I kiss her wrist. I love the feel of her skin. Soft and luxurious, like the lotion-bottle label says. Aimee worships the lotion bottle in our bathroom and I'm the lucky bastard who gets to feel her velvety skin glide against mine.

I rub my cheek against her hand and when she doesn't pull away, a fraction of the tension tightening my shoulder blades diminishes. She's looking at me. I can feel the weight of her gaze and my body tingles with anticipation. My pulse accelerates. I'm going to take her straight to our bedroom when we get home. This gorgeous woman is mine and I want my hands all over her. I want to feel close to her, seek out that connection that seems to be missing lately. And damn it, I want to make sure she's mine.

I take my eyes off the freeway and look at her. "I love you."

She blinks. The whites of her eyes glow from the headlamps of oncoming cars. Her mouth—those delectable lips I have an overwhelming urge to kiss, and would kiss were I not driving—part to speak.

My breath catches. I know that look. This is it. She's ready to talk. My heart races like a sprinter coming around the last corner before the finish. Maybe we'll work through her reaction after meeting with James before we get home. I hate that she's hating herself. Maybe going out to dinner will make her feel better, get her mind off him. Perhaps La Fondue is still an option. It's only seven-fifty. We have forty minutes until our reservation.

"Do you think we married too soon?"

Boom! The bombshell detonates.

My foot spasms on the accelerator, causing the car to lurch.

That's not what I expected her to say.

Hell no! I waited thirteen months to tell her I loved her.

OK, yeah, so what if the thought of losing her to James when I accompanied her to Mexico to find him was the proverbial kick in the ass I needed to tell her how I feel. I could also care less that I proposed only three months after we returned. We loved each other. We wanted to spend our lives together.

There's only one person who could get her asking such a question five years into our marriage. A question that comes way beyond left field. More like Hawaii.

"What did James say to you?"

"This has nothing to do with James." Aimee slips her hand from mine. I feel the emptiness immediately, a punch to my gut.

"Doesn't it, though?" I squeeze the steering wheel. "The guy shows up. You go see him. You ignore my calls and texts. I can't reach you for hours—"

"It wasn't hours."

"—only to find you at Nadia's bawling. Then you tell me to go home. What am I supposed to think?"

"When you put it that way—"

"What other way is there?" I snap.

Aimee tenses. She stares at me, her eyes big and round, waiting.

For what? I'm clueless. I stare back.

She doesn't say anything. Neither do I.

I don't know what to say. I've got nothing.

Wait. Hold that thought, I've got one thing.

I briefly close my eyes and swallow the anger. "I'm sorry. The last thing I want to do is argue."

We watch each other for as long as I can safely keep my eyes off the road. She chews her lower lip and a horn blares. I swing my head around, switch lanes, and Aimee quietly says my name. "I'm sorry, too. I should have called you."

"You should have come home," I say gently. "You should have trusted me to be there for you."

"I know. It's just I still feel bad about last summer. Underneath all my anger, I was embarrassed." She looks at her hands in her lap.

"Look, I get how the situation between you and James is weird. It was a long relationship with an intense, fucked-up ending that wasn't your fault."

"It was in a way. He clocked the neighborhood jerk when we were kids and I hero-worshiped him for years. I think . . . no. I know, to some degree, I still idolized him even after our relationship changed and we became more than friends. I should have known—"

"No, no, no," I interrupt. "How old were you when you started going out? Thirteen? Don't go blaming yourself. You were a kid." I look askance at her. I've asked the question before, but at the risk of making her more upset, I've got to ask it again. "Are you still in love with him?"

I still cringe at myself once the words are out.

Damn, Collins. What's with the insecurity?

Then I remember how every woman I'd loved has ditched me. The fear Aimee will do the same has got its claws on me.

Aimee fires an exasperated look in my direction. "You know I'm not. But he's part of my past. He helped shape me into who I am today. How do I make you understand?" She thinks for a moment, weighing things in her mind. "How about this? I don't love you less because of James. I just love him differently, and because of my experience with James, I believe I love you more than I would have had James and I never been together. I guess the best comparison is that I feel for James the way you feel for Reese."

"Oh no." I laugh the words, shaking my finger. "Our situations are nothing alike."

"I know you were once in love with her. She's your history, and you've barely told me anything about her."

"Don't turn this back on me. This isn't about me. It's about you and—"

"I'm always sharing my feelings. I always talk with you about James and what I'm thinking. We agreed to be open about our past relationships, girlfriends *and* mothers."

"What has my mom got to do with this?"

"You've hardly told me anything about Reese, not like how you've shared with me your relationship with your mom," she adds, when my cheek flexes from clenching my jaw too hard.

"There's nothing to talk about," I say quietly. About either of them. It took years of therapy for me to be able to discuss my mom without feeling that burning sensation of anger well up like a Yellowstone geyser. Now I just feel guilt and regret, a whole lot of it, too. I know I could have done more for her. But I also could have done as my dad repeatedly asked of me and let her be. She was not my responsibility, but I felt otherwise.

Aimee knows everything about my childhood, the way my dad practically abandoned me week after week, leaving me alone with my mom, giving me no choice but to look after her. I was a kid, for God's sake. I can't imagine doing the same to Caty.

I stomp down the hurt of past memories and focus on driving. The road ahead is straight but our discussion is an old one, spinning doughnuts between us.

I glance at Aimee. She looks stonily at me. She taps the purse in her lap. Annoying little thumps that tighten my back. I roll my shoulders, crack my neck, flip the turn signal, and exit the freeway, easing to a stop at a red light.

"James is in love," Aimee says as the car idles.

"Hopefully not with you."

She makes a noise of impatience. "No, not with me. Natalya. Remember that woman we met with him when Carlos visited my parents' house? Her," she says. "James has been living with her in Hawaii. He asked if I thought him falling for someone he'd technically just met last June was too soon. It got me to thinking about us."

Maybe Aimee and I need to rethink our open-book policy on sharing our innermost thoughts and feelings. She's gutting me.

"I love you, Aimee. I love you so much. You and Caty are my world."

"I love you, too, Ian." She leans over and kisses me below the ear, letting her lips linger. I briefly close my eyes. I needed her touch. I needed to hear and feel her love for me.

Aimee yawns and presses a hand to her stomach. "The martinis aren't settling well. You mentioned something about dinner plans." I frown and she clarifies. "Back at Nadia's."

I shake my head. "It's nothing. We'll get Caty and grab some takeout."

She nods and her gaze turns inward.

"What are you thinking?" I ask as we approach our neighborhood.

"Ah." She rubs her temple. "James asked if I wanted to file charges against Phil."

I cringe, immediately feeling like a cad. "That's why you were upset earlier."

She closes her eyes and nods. "It brought back James's proposal, the assault, and the ensuing fallout."

Before we married, Aimee had told me about Phil's sexual assault. She buried the incident, programming herself to ignore the hurt, at James's request. Out of love for James, which baffled me. The situation sounded as disturbing as the Donato family. How could she have agreed to such a request? But my own mom had made many outrageous requests of me. Except for one, I followed them all.

34

The things we do for love.

While pregnant with Sarah Catherine, Aimee met with a therapist to work through the trauma of James's disappearance, Thomas's machinations, and Phil's assault. I dropped her off at her appointments, even attended a few, and was there to hold her when her hour concluded.

"Where is Phil now? Do we need to worry about him?"

Aimee shakes her head. "I'm of no value to him anymore. He used me to hurt James."

Thank God, Phil's out of the picture. I caress her cheek with the back of my fingers. She leans into my hand. "Do you want to file charges?"

"No, I don't. The last thing I want is to be dealing with any of the Donatos."

"Think about it, I'll support whatever you decide."

"That's what James said. He offered himself up as a witness if I wanted to file charges against Phil. He even offered to turn himself in since he asked me not to file charges initially. I think he's trying to come to terms with his mistakes."

"Is that why he's back in California?" I ask, parking curbside in front of the Tierneys', Aimee's parents' house.

"It's one of the reasons."

Morbid curiosity has me asking, "And the other?"

Aimee's expression turns odd. "He wants to meet with you."

Me?

"What in the world does James want with me?"

My gaze moves beyond Aimee and I lift a finger. "Hold that thought."

Caty must have seen our car from the front window. She bursts out the door, princess skirt flowing and wand sparkling as she waves the glitter stick over her head. She might have my coloring, amber eyes and sandy-brown hair, but her half-moon smile and wild curls are all Aimee.

I leave the car and scoop up Caty before she reaches the sidewalk. "Caty-cakes!" I smack a kiss on her cheek. She smells of peaches and ice cream.

She squeals. "Daddy! What are you doing here? You're supposed to be celebrating. Hello, Mommy."

Aimee joins us. She kisses Caty, then frowns up at me. "What are we celebrating?"

"Umm . . ."

"Does this have to do with the dinner plans that suddenly aren't important?"

I inhale through my nose. "Maybe."

"Tell us, Daddy. Tell us." Caty wraps her arms around my neck and tugs.

I grunt and look at my family. We didn't get off to a great start, but maybe Aimee and I can salvage the evening. "I got a call from *National Geographic*. They're sending me on assignment."

Aimee falls back a step. Her mouth falls open. "Ian, that's huge!"

I beam. "It's pretty damn cool."

"Yay, Daddy!"

"I'm so happy for you."

Aimee's reaction sends a thrill through me. "Yeah, this is a big deal for me."

"For all of us. And you were going to just drive us home and not mention it?"

"Well . . ." I let a squirming Caty slide down my leg. She skips circles around us, waving her wand. Someone's on a sugar high and her dealer stands in the doorway, illuminated by the lit entryway behind her.

"Why are you here? Have you two been arguing?" Catherine boldly asks us, making her way down the porch. "Play nicely and go to dinner."

I waggle my brows at Aimee. "Wanna go play nicely?" Her cheeks flame.

"Really, Ian." Catherine shakes her head.

I dip my chin, hiding my grin. I don't mind Catherine's interference. We're fortunate Aimee's parents care. I wish I could say the same about mine.

Aimee hugs her mom. "We were just leaving."

"Good. Enjoy your evening. I'm keeping Caty for the night." Catherine reaches for her granddaughter's hand.

"Where's dinner?" Aimee asks me.

"La Fondue."

Her gaze smolders, traveling down me, lingering on my abs and other manly parts. Maybe she's changing her mind about playing.

My face instantly warms. I clear my throat, reining in my thoughts.

"That's why you're dressed up," Aimee observes.

I nod. I'd forgone my uniform of faded jeans and V-neck Ts for something nicer. More suave and sexy. I even styled my hair, although one unruly lock keeps landing back on my forehead. I comb my fingers through my hair.

"Our reservation's in twenty minutes."

"Then why are we standing here?" Aimee walks back to her open car door.

"Exactly what I was thinking." Catherine waves good-bye. Caty blows kisses and they go back inside the house.

I join Aimee at the car. "Let's grab some grub."

Once we're outside the restaurant, I turn to her. Hooking my hands low around her back, I peer down into her face. She touched up her makeup on the drive over. Nobody can tell that James—the jerk—had made her cry. I sure can't. I gently kiss her tinted lips, careful not to mess the painted line.

"Are you sure you want to eat out? We can order takeout and have a quiet night in." Her mind has been tossed back to one of the most horrific days of her life. The last thing I want is to force her to put on a smile and be in public if she'd rather curl up on the couch with a box of Kleenex and a pint of Chunky Monkey. Of course, that would only make me want to track down James and shatter his nose.

Aimee blinks a couple of times but smiles. She fiddles with a button on my shirt, her eyes locked on my chest. She lightly scratches her fingernails on the material. Pinpricks shoot outward, rippling across my skin. I cover her hand with mine, holding it against my heart.

"Aimee?" I prompt.

"Yes, I'm sure," she says to my chest.

She might be, but I'm not. I tuck a finger under her chin and raise my brows.

"I'm sure," she says with more conviction, even adds a smile. "Let's eat. We can talk about my day and the James stuff later. I want to hear everything about your assignment." She cradles my jaw and plants a firm kiss on my mouth. She then rubs her upper lip as if wiping off the kiss.

I chuckle and Aimee laughs, apologetic. "I guess that's my cue to shave." I scratch below my chin. I need to trim. My five-day rugged shadow feels more like a short beard, making my face itch.

I think of what Aimee was about to tell me in the car. What could James possibly want with me? I want to ask her, but I don't want to invite him to our table. Tonight is for us, a celebration of our achievements.

Wrapping her hand in mine, I lead the way into the restaurant. We don't eat here often, only on special occasions, like getting THE CALL from *National Geographic* occasions.

Throughout the three-course meal of breads dipped in raclette cheese, venison seared in seasoned oil, and strawberries dipped in chocolate fudge, I tell her about the assignment.

"Al Foster, he's the photo editor Erik referred me to. He loved my shots from the Rapa. He says the ones with the horses in the hills are great, but there's too much happening around them. There're too many people. He wants me to photograph the horses when they're not being wrangled, so he's sending me back to Spain."

Aimee's mouth angles downward. "I still haven't seen your photos from the last trip."

I roll my fondue fork in the melted cheese. "You've been busy," I say, somewhat glum. And we had to confront other, more pressing issues.

She shreds a piece of bread. "Caty talks about them all the time."

"I'll show you tomorrow."

"I'd like that. Early, though, if you don't mind. I have a meeting with the bank first thing and I need to prep." Aimee bites into the bread. "Are you writing the piece, too?"

I shake my head. "Not this time. I'm just captioning photos if they want me to. The magazine's assigning a writer, but I don't know who yet. He'll meet me there so he can hike the hills with me. The editor wants my photos to align with the angle the writer's taking on the article." I lean across the table and brush my thumb across Aimee's chin. "Cheese."

She wipes her chin where I flicked her skin. "It's good cheese." She jabs a fork into another chunk of bread and swirls it in the pot. "I should add a cheese fondue to my menu, maybe for a late-afternoon or early-evening crowd."

I frown. "Great idea, but do you want to serve food that late? You'll have to stay open later." She already spends plenty of hours managing the Los Gatos shop. The two additional storefronts she plans to open will take up more of her time, even without staying open longer hours.

"The Starbucks around the corner added wine and tapas to their menu."

"You're better than Starbucks."

"I know, but . . ."

I cover her hand. "Focus on what makes the café different. Let the other coffee shops chase you, not the other way around."

"You're right." She sips her chardonnay. "You're absolutely right. Sometimes these ideas I get"—she twirls her index finger by her temple—"sidetrack me. I need to stay focused. I've got a lot to do to get the new locations opened." She pushes out a long, steady breath. "So . . . Spain?"

I drink my wine and set down the glass. "Come with me."

Her expression is hesitant. I can see it in the way her gaze flickers over our meal. I try not to feel disappointed.

"When do you leave?" she asks.

"In about a week or two. I have to check the weather reports. It's the beginning of their rainy season."

"How long will you be gone?"

"Five days, a week, tops."

She bites into her bottom lip. "I don't know. That's such short notice."

I look at my empty plate.

"Well . . . maybe if I . . . no . . . that won't work. I—"

I squeeze her hand. "Just think about it."

"I will." She nods and I'm fine with that. We can discuss the details later. For now, the evening is going well, and considering I didn't bring James's name up once since we sat down, I would say our date has been damn near perfect.

I must admit, though, James isn't far from my mind.

What does he want with me? I've never met the guy. I did run into Carlos a couple of times, once in Mexico, and again when he and Natalya had lunch with us at the Tierneys'. That was weird.

I consider asking Aimee. She had been about to tell me in the car before Caty saw us. But she drinks her wine and gives me *the look* over the rim of her glass. All thoughts of "that other guy" go up in smoke.

I'll bring it up in the morning. Tonight's for us.

We return home after dinner, sans kid. Strange walking into a quiet house without having to pay a babysitter or take Caty through her bedtime routine. Thank God, Aimee and I are on the same channel. She turns to me the second I flip the dead bolt, her gaze locking on mine, her hands on my belt. She smiles wickedly and yanks the leather strap from the loops of my jeans. The belt snaps the air and she drops it on the floor.

Damn, I love it when she's hot for me.

Laughing, kissing, and stumbling, we make our way to the bedroom, leaving our clothes scattered, a trail of undergarments and shoes. Lips locked, I lift Aimee in my arms. She wraps her legs around my hips and I walk us to the bed where we tumble onto the duvet. I don't bother yanking aside the cover. That involves too much time with my hands not on her.

I inhale the subtle scent of the perfume I gifted her last Christmas and it sends a rush to my center. I bury my face into the crook of her neck and gently scrape my teeth along the curve. She bucks beneath me, her kisses frenzied, her hands frantic. They're making me insane. It's as though she's trying to erase the day, those hours before I found her at Nadia's. I nudge aside a long, sleek leg and sink inside her, exactly where I've wanted to be all freaking day.

And what a day.

Is it still on her mind? With her head turned to the side and her eyes closed, harsh gasps rising from her lungs with each one of my thrusts, what is she thinking? Who is she thinking about?

She better be thinking about me, her husband.

I move faster, determined to possess every thought of hers, every sensation. I wrap an arm under her shoulders, holding her close. I thread my fingers into her hair and grip hard.

She likes it rough.

She loves it when I lose control and go crazy for her.

"Look at me."

She does. Her blues, a swirling midnight in the dim ribbon of light from the hallway, hook into mine. Her hands grasp my hips, her fingernails dig into my flesh. I increase our pace, moving forcibly above her, in her, until all thoughts of the day leave my head and nothing exists but us.

Until nothing exists but Aimee.

My wife.

CHAPTER 5

IAN

Aimee's gone when I wake up. Sprawled on my stomach, I squeeze the pillow under my head and take in the empty side of the bed. I mull over yesterday's events, picking them apart like a new photo to edit. Memories brighten over my relief of finally having Aimee in my arms when I found her at Nadia's. But that relief dulls with the contrast of why she'd gone there in the first place. James blindsided her, stirring up memories Aimee has worked hard to overcome. At least our night together ended on the high end of the color spectrum. It was filled with vibrancy and fun.

I love having fun with Aimee. We're good together. We're good in bed together.

My body stirs. Groaning, I roll to my back, tempted to haul Aimee back to bed. But her comment last night saturates my drowsy, aroused state.

Do you think we married too soon?

She's never asked that before, nor has it crossed my mind.

What would she do if she believes we did marry too soon? A sick feeling twists in my abdomen. She'd leave me; that's what she'd do.

No, she wouldn't. My inner voice dope-slaps the back of my head.

I rub my face and groan into my cupped palms. *Damn you, James, for putting that thought in her head.*

I get out of bed, yank on a pair of athletic shorts, and drag a loose tank over my head before stopping in the bathroom to relieve myself. I wash my hands, drying them by running them through my unruly hair, and brush my teeth as I inspect my face in the mirror.

Priority number one today: shave.

I rinse my mouth, then go in search of Aimee. I find a sticky note instead.

Maggie called. Family emergency. Aimee xo

Maggie works the café's kitchen, as does Darrell, who's on vacation. Aimee didn't plan to be the one to open the café this morning, but now she's flying solo instead of spending the morning with me, poring over Rapa photos and discussing her meetup with James. That quick, clipped chat in the car wasn't enough. I want to hear the fine print, not the CliffsNotes version.

I glance at the driveway through the window to confirm she took my Explorer. I'd go in and help her if I had a car. Aimee's van is still at Nadia's. I make a mental note to ask Catherine to drop Caty and me off at the café when she brings her home from preschool. By then, Aimee will be exhausted.

I skim a thumb over the *X* and *O* on her note, worrying about her. Between covering for Maggie, meeting with the banks about a loan, scouting property for the new locations, plus overseeing her existing location, Aimee has a lot on her plate today. She's been taking on too much and I hope she's not mixing a recipe for disaster. Something's gotta give. But what?

Yep, it's time for a vacation. I need to get her away from James, and her memories of Phil.

Since I don't have a car and can't go to the gym, I lace up my Adidas and hit the pavement for a fast run. I'll get my circuit training in later today.

Forty minutes later, I return home sweaty and invigorated. I chug a mug of coffee and whip up an omelet that I quickly wolf down. After adding my dirty dishes to Aimee's used cup in the sink, I shower, shave, trim, and 'scape. Content that Aimee will be content with the fine dusting I left on my jaw, I dress and head into my office, the spare room with the slider to the backyard. It's a bluebird day, already warm despite the early hour, and I'm amped to get the trip to Spain booked and our bags packed.

I jiggle the mouse, waking my computer. It hums to life and two thirty-two-inch monitors brighten. The large screens give me enough space to work on multiple images. For now, though, I launch my e-mail app, and, as my editor assured, the contract from *National Geographic* is there.

I grin. This is happening. This is really happening.

I lace my fingers and, flipping my palms outward, stretch my arms until my knuckles crack. I rub my hands, wiggle my fingers, and am about to open the e-mail when my phone rings.

"Ian Collins," I answer.

"Al Foster. Hope I'm not calling too early."

I glance at the clock in the lower corner of the monitor: 7:48. "No, you're good. I'm up and working. What can I do for you?"

"My assistant, Tess, should have sent your contract by now."

"Got it." I click open the DocuSign e-mail.

"Great. Just making sure. Get that signed and I'll sign on my end. When are you flying out?"

I haven't had the chance to check the weather reports. "Sometime next week," I tell him, keeping it open. "I'm thinking Wednesday or Thursday."

"Perfect. There's an inn near Sabucedo—La casa de campo—one of our photographers stayed at for another assignment. I'll have Tess send you the info so you can make the reservation. The contract outlines your expense budget. Keep track of those receipts and we'll get you reimbursed."

"Sounds good. Have you assigned a writer yet?" I want to research the guy before I leave, get a grasp on his style and approach.

"We're working on it. I spoke with the features editor this morning. She's narrowed her selection to two. I think it'll come down to availability. You'll get an e-mail from me as soon as I hear. Either way, he'll meet you there."

We chat for a few more minutes, and after I read through the contract—satisfied with the terms—I sign the document and send it off. Over the next thirty minutes, I check the weather and grimace. It's questionable for the next few weeks. Lots of rain. I then book the inn Al recommended, a rental car, and flights for Aimee and me. Yes, I'm assuming she'll join me because she needs a vacation. And James is in town.

I stab the Enter key, confirming the reservation.

I spend another hour catching up on e-mails before launching the Sonos app and firing up some tunes. Nathaniel Rateliff fills the house and I get to work, fine-tuning images from a short excursion I took to Moab to photograph the arches.

"Daddy!" Caty claps my shoulders and I jolt a foot off my chair.

"Fuhhh . . . fudge." I clamp a hand over my mouth, drowning out my voice. My gaze darts to the time. Where did it go? It's after twelve.

Snatching Caty around the waist, I haul her into my lap. I plant raspberries on her cheek. She squirms, giggling.

"I scared you, didn't I?" she says, out of breath.

"Yes, you did." My rapidly beating heart collapses like an exhausted runner and slips back into my chest.

She frowns at me. "You almost said a naughty word."

I press a finger to my lips. "Don't tell Mommy."

She mimics me with her finger. "Promise."

We hook pinkies in our "secret keeper" handshake. She gives me a look, a slight curve to her mouth, her eyes bright and photo-paper glossy, that strikes me with the force of a SpaceX rocket. It ripples through me like a shock wave. I'd seen that look in my mom a time or two, back when I thought I meant something to her.

"I missed you, Daddy," she whispers like it's a big secret.

"I—" I clear the toad from my throat. "I missed you, too."

Caty slips from my lap and skips to the door. She yawns, arms stretching overhead. "I'm hungry."

"You're supposed to yawn when you're hungry? I thought that meant you're tired."

"Noooo, silly." She laughs.

I wink at her. "Let's eat lunch." I rise stiffly from my chair. "I haven't moved for several hours. "Then it's naptime."

"Can we play princess first? Please?" She clasps her hands together and bats her lashes.

"Sure thing, Caty-cakes. But this time I get to play Rapunzel."

"Deal." She cheers and runs from the room.

I smile to myself, shaking my head, and follow her out. I don't wear a wig and tutu for anyone but her.

In the kitchen, I find Catherine unpacking Caty's backpack. We chat a bit about Caty's day at preschool until Catherine announces she has to leave for a hair appointment.

I walk her to the door. "Do you mind giving Caty and me a lift to the café when you're done? Aimee took my car this morning. We left hers at Nadia's." The least I can do is help Aimee close this afternoon, but right now Caty needs a nap. On cue, she rubs her eyes. Aimee and I aren't the only ones who stayed up late. Someone let Caty stay up past her bedtime and all eyes are on Grandma.

Catherine glances at her watch, a silver number on her thin wrist. "I should be done around two thirty."

Two hours from now, plenty of time for us to eat and Caty to sleep. "That works. Thanks."

Catherine leaves and I make PB&J sandwiches, after which we play princess. Dressed in a light-blue tutu over faded jeans and a long blonde wig that's more knotted than straight, I announce from atop the coffee table to Caty, who's kneeling on the floor, that I'll not let down my hair. Just then, the doorbell rings.

"I'll get it," I say in my princess voice. I leap off the table and float to the foyer. "Hello," I sing, opening the front door. The greeting dies in my throat.

On the porch stands James. At the sight of me, his mouth falls open. Then he grins, albeit hesitantly, like he's fighting not to. He tries to hide his face with a quick glance away.

"You." I should have known James would make an appearance, like at the café, or Wendy's gallery. Not here, at my house, while I'm playing pretend with my daughter. But then James is a Donato. One should expect the unexpected from them.

James holds up a hand. "Sorry, it's just . . ." He slowly shakes his head. "Of all the scenarios I pictured, I didn't see this. You caught me off guard."

I caught him off guard?

Seriously?

"Nice outfit," he remarks.

I scowl. His grin dissolves.

The guy's got nerve knocking on my door.

I would have preferred neutral territory, such as a boxing ring at the gym. I would have made a more positive, lasting impression. Preferably one in the shape of my fist rather than the memory James will have of me wearing a tutu.

James extends his hand. "I'm Ja—"

"I know who you are," I say, cutting him off. Dragging the wig from my head, I scratch my scalp and tame my hair.

"Well, then." James shoves his hand into his pocket when I don't take his proffered greeting.

What does the guy expect? He treated Aimee poorly their last year together only to remind her yesterday of Phil's assault and his own crappy behavior. The dude wouldn't take down the painting of the meadow in their dining room, the site of the incident. Who does that?

Sick bastard.

James made Aimee cry yesterday. He's the reason we've been off-balance all summer, teetering back and forth as we try to find each other again. I still haven't heard the full details about what went down yesterday, and now that Aimee's been distracted with work, I wonder when I will.

"Who's here, Daddy?" Caty tugs the door wider and peers outside. She smiles up at James. "Hello, I'm Sarah Catherine. You can call me Caty. Everyone else does."

James blinks and moves back a step. It isn't a full step, just enough of a reaction to make it obvious Aimee's Mini-Me took him by surprise. Caty has her mom's smile and wild hair. Though Aimee now wears hers shoulder length and does that blow-out thingy to straighten her curls.

"Hi." James's throat bobs with a rough swallow. "Hello, Caty. It's nice to meet you. I'm James a—" He stops, glancing at me, almost daring me to object to what he's about to say. He returns his attention to Caty. "I'm a friend of your mom."

I grimace. So much for our "stranger danger" chats. I yank off the tutu Velcroed at my waist and shove the costume at Caty, nudging her behind the door. "Go get ready for your nap."

Caty clamps the princess outfit to her chest. "I don't wanna nap," she whines.

"Pick out a book, then." I don't care what she does, so long as she's deep inside the house. I pat her head and pivot her around. "I'll be there in a moment."

Caty thrusts out her lower lip, but she obeys.

Gaze narrowed, I study James. Gone is the longer surfer hair. He's still tan, and though he wears a shirt and shorts, his attire is a far cry from the board shorts and old TORNEO DE SURF shirt he wore when I met him on the beach, and again a couple of days later when I ran into him outside Casa del sol's beach bar in Puerto Escondido. Despite the reconstructive surgery to his face, he now looks like a Donato, his posture and attire more aligned with his brother Thomas.

James rubs his forearm, then lets that arm fall by his side, not looking at all at ease under my scrutiny.

"Let me start by saying I'm sorry for—"

"Kissing my wife?" I interject.

His jaw hardens. "For coming here." He motions at the house. "I knew Aimee wouldn't be here and the last time she saw you and me together . . ." He braces his hands on his hips. "I understand it was awkward, back when I was Carlos."

Ah yes, Sunday lunch at the Tierneys' with two surprise guests: Carlos and Natalya. That was fun. Not. I cross my arms. "Go on."

James looks beyond me. "May I come in?"

"No." I step outside, closing the door behind me.

"Fair enough." James nods once and retreats a step. "How is she today?"

"Aimee? Fine," I clip, though truthfully, I don't know. I should have called her this morning.

"Why are you here?" I ask, directing the conversation away from Aimee.

He lifts a shoulder, nonchalant. "Mark me curious. I wanted to meet you."

"You wanted to know if I was worthy enough of Aimee."

He purses his lips, but eventually nods. The man has balls.

"Are you back for good?" I ask.

He shakes his head. "My sons and I are in Hawaii. We live there now."

Thank God for that.

"I'm going to be up front with you." James braces his legs. "I met Aimee yesterday to apologize for some things that happened between us while we were together. I didn't want you to assume anything is going on between us."

"And why would I assume that?"

The corner of James's mouth quirks. "Because I would if I were in your shoes."

Truth, I admit.

I absently scratch my cheek. "Aimee told me she'd forgiven you the last time you saw her. What makes this time different?"

"When we met then, we . . ." James stops as though considering his words. He glances at the pavement. "We left a lot unsaid."

Because his tongue had been down Aimee's throat.

I want to throttle James, but I can respect the man's need for closure. Aimee sought the same thing when she went looking for James in Mexico. Still . . .

"You kissed my *wife*."

I can't let it go.

James's face takes on a red tinge. "At the risk of you planting that fist in my face"—he points at my clenched hand—"Aimee and I will always have history. There's nothing any of us can do to change that. But it's you she's in love with. And me . . . well, I've got someone myself."

"Natalya?"

James flashes a smile. Aimee's right. He's in love.

"But that's not why I'm here." James reaches into his pocket. "A woman found me on the beach last month. She gave me this." He flashes a business card and a chill blasts into my chest, spreading outward. Gooseflesh rises on my arms and the back of my neck.

"I recognized the name from the journals I kept as Carlos. She told me someone I knew was looking for her so I did some checking around. I believe she was talking about you."

I stare at the card pinched in James's fingers, not at all surprised to see the name printed in bold, black lettering. LACY SAUNDERS PSYCHIC COUNSELOR. A "specialist" in finding missing persons and the "answers you seek," as described in neat print underneath her name. Lacy, who I remember telling me her name was Laney, had found me in a ditch when I was nine and had gone missing. She also led Aimee to Mexico to find James, which made me think she could do the same for me and help find my mom.

But Sarah Collins hadn't gone missing. She'd left.

I take the card with the New Mexico phone number, and I'm hurled back to the roadside where an ethereal angel found my dirty and starved nine-year-old self.

James nods at the card. "Random for her of all people to be at the same beach at the same time, like she knew I'd be there. But that's impossible, right?"

Impossible? No.

Improbable? Yes.

But who am I to question Fate? She has no problem being a bitch when she wants to. Everyone ends up somewhere and with someone, hopefully under improved circumstances.

James steps off the porch, catching my attention.

"I hope you find what you're looking for, Ian." He gives me a short, two-fingered abbreviated wave, then turns and walks away. I presume back to his rental car and then on to Hawaii.

CHAPTER 6

IAN, AGE NINE

"What about this shirt?" his mom asked.

Ian scrunched his face at the navy-blue polo. Preppy clothes. No way, Jose. He'd been shopping for school clothes with his mom for thirty minutes, twenty-nine minutes longer than he cared to be at the downtown clothing corral. He gazed longingly out the big, square front window onto Main Street. Three kids he recognized from school pedaled by on their bikes. One rode a skateboard. He popped off the curb. Saturdays were meant for pegging girls with popcorn at the matinee or wrestling his best friend, Marshall, as they balanced on slick rocks in the creek to see who drenched whom first.

Spending the day running errands with his mom was not Ian's idea of a fun Saturday, especially since she'd been shifting a lot.

Last night she flirted with Doug, the cashier at the market. They lived in a small town. Everyone knew everyone, and Doug knew Ian's mom was married. He also knew, as many of the townsfolk did, that she wasn't quite right in the head. But that didn't stop her from asking Doug if he liked her new blouse. Did it look better on her with the bodice buttoned or unbuttoned? Untucked or tucked into the waist of her skirt? Then she demonstrated. Doug wasn't the only one looking uncomfortable as he awkwardly answered her questions and bagged her groceries. Ian was mortified. His face flamed a hundred degrees. He prayed for Doug to bag faster so they could get out of the store before one of his friends saw that his mom was acting like a high school senior looking for a hookup. The last thing Ian wanted was for her to embarrass him again while they shopped for clothes. He silently pleaded that none of his friends would show up at the store.

"What's wrong with this shirt?" His mom admired it and Ian flicked the collar. She made a noise of impatience. "It's the style. All the actors in Hollywood are wearing them."

His mom religiously read her rag mags, as his dad called them, cover to cover.

"I don't like it."

"We're not leaving until you find something."

Ian groaned a complaint and wandered to a rack of graphic Ts. He flipped through the hangers, stopping at a black shirt with an illustrated camera and yellow star for the camera flash. The shirt was ugly. He wouldn't be caught dead wearing it any more than the polo his mom wanted to buy. But the shirt reminded him of an idea he had on the drive home from the market last night.

He showed his mom the shirt. "What if I took pictures of you?"

She returned the polo to the rack. "Me? What for?"

"Remember when you asked me last night why I was upset?"

"Here's a shirt." She showed him a green T.

"Mom," he complained, "you were acting funny at the grocery store and you didn't believe me."

"I still don't."

She never did when he told her. He'd show her the empty vodka bottles and she'd accuse him of pouring them out. Then she'd ground him. Since she couldn't remember drinking the alcohol, it didn't happen.

"Do you remember paying for the groceries?"

Her hand hesitated over the rack.

"Do you remember unbuttoning your shirt in front of Doug?" His neck heated just thinking about it.

She gasped. "Ian Collins, watch your mouth. I'd never do such a thing."

"But I saw you. So did Doug." He muttered the last bit.

She forcibly shoved aside a group of shirts. "I do remember shopping and driving home."

But not those moments in the checkout line.

"What if I take pictures of you when you act differently? You know, those times you make Dad and me call you Jackie."

His mom paused in her shirt hunt. She tugged away a few strands of hair stuck in the corner of her mouth and looked down and away. Ian saw her neck quiver and knew he'd hit a nerve. His mom didn't like hearing that name spoken out loud. Ian first remembered hearing her say the name when he was five, but Jackie had been around since before he was born. His dad always begged her to stop. But how could she when she didn't remember those hours, or days, she insisted her name was Jackie?

His mom fiddled with a hanger hook. "I'm not sure that's a good idea, Ian."

"Maybe the pictures will show you and Dad why Jackie needs money. She's always looking for your wallet and I know you hide it whenever we're home. I can find out why she needs it."

His mom pierced Ian with her gaze over the rack. "How do you know this?"

"I heard you and Dad talking."

"You shouldn't be eavesdropping."

"I know, I'm sorry. But I can show you what Jackie does and where she goes. Don't you want to know what happens?"

"Ian—"

"I can follow Jackie and take pictures."

"It's too dangerous."

Ian put on his brave face. He stood taller. "Jackie's never hurt me. She's just mean and I'm getting stronger." And bigger. He'd be ten soon.

"No."

"But you always ask me what happened even when you say you don't believe me."

His mom yanked the graphic T from him and tossed it over the rack. "I said no." She gripped his wrist. "We're done here."

Ian jerked his arm from his mom's grasp. It was bad enough that she was upset with him in public, but he wouldn't let her drag him from the store like a toddler throwing a temper tantrum. He followed her out the doors, sulking.

"I'll be careful," he insisted when they reached the car, not ready to give up. She might not realize it, but his mom needed him. Baseball season had his dad on the road with the Padres. His long absences made her irritable and anxious.

"You'll do no such thing," his mom said when Ian sank into the station wagon's backseat.

"But I want to help."

"Not in that way. No pictures, Ian. End of discussion." She started the car. "Your dad's due home in a few hours and I have to start dinner. I can't be worrying about you galloping off and playing superhero."

"I don't gallop." Ian pouted. He picked up his camera from the floor and clicked the lens cap on and off. *Click-clack.*

He wasn't trying to play superhero either. But he did see Jackie as the villain.

"Stop that noise. It's annoying."

Ian scowled. He clicked the cap on and off again, faster. *Click-clack. Click-clack.*

His mom braked hard, coming to a full stop. Ian's forehead slammed into the front passenger seat.

"Knock it off."

Ian rubbed his head. His parents barely saw each other during baseball season. Dad had to wonder what his mom was up to when she shifted to Jackie. "I'm going to ask Dad. He might want to see the pictures."

"I don't give a shit what you ask him."

The fine hairs on Ian's neck lifted. His skin prickled as though ants were racing across his shoulders and down his arms.

His mom stomped on the accelerator. The car lurched forward rather than turning toward home. Ian watched the road they were supposed to go on disappear from view. He swung his head around and was about to tell his mom she forgot to turn. But it wasn't his mom in the driver's seat, not anymore. He could tell by her posture, the determined set of her jaw, and the way she gripped the steering wheel. It was all wrong.

Sweat dampened Ian's palms. Suddenly, the idea of documenting Jackie seemed stupid.

"Where are we going?" he dared to ask.

Jackie didn't answer. She popped open the glove compartment and funneled her hand through tire-pressure sticks, paper napkins, and old sunglasses until she found a hair band. Using her knee to steer, she tied her hair into a high ponytail and then rolled down the windows. Pungent air, sour with the odor of fertilizer, clung to the inside of the car like smoke from his mom's burned dinners. It hovered below the ceiling, filling every corner.

"Mom?" Ian asked, not quite stomaching he should be calling her Jackie. Maybe if he kept saying *Mom* she might shift back. "Mom? Mom . . . Mom . . . *Mom!*"

"Mom. Mom. Mom. *Mommeeee!* Stop calling me that. I'm not your mother. I'm Jackie. Say it."

Ian held his mouth closed tight and shook his head.

"Say it," she ordered.

He shook his head harder and Jackie slammed the brakes. His head rolled forward, straining his neck. "Ow."

She gunned the engine and braked again. *"Say it!"*

Ian rubbed the back of his neck and scowled at her.

"I'll keep doing this."

His neck and forehead hurt. "Jackie," he whispered.

"What? I didn't hear you."

"Jackie." *Bitch,* he thought to himself and then felt guilty for thinking it in the first place.

"Much better." She grinned. It wasn't his mom's smile.

Jackie accelerated. The car sped along the two-lane road, taking them farther from town.

Ian took a deep breath and slowly, as quietly as he could, removed the lens cap. He called up his bravery and lifted the camera to his face. He brought Jackie into focus and snapped a photo. The flash went off.

Jackie's head swiveled. She glared at him.

Ian snapped another photo, capturing her twisted expression, her skin blotchy from anger and the wind. She flipped him off.

He pressed the shutter button. The bulb flashed again.

Jackie braked, swerving to the side of the road. Ian swayed violently in the backseat. She thrust the gear stick into Park and dumped the contents of Sarah's purse on the front seat. She opened the wallet and swore. "There's barely any cash." She pocketed a five and flashed Ian the ATM card. "Did you get the PIN?"

He shook his head.

"You promised you'd get the PIN."

He'd also promised himself he'd protect his mom when his dad couldn't. He had no intention of breaking that promise.

"She wouldn't tell me." Because he hadn't asked her.

"Of course she won't tell you, you moron." She cuffed his ear. Ian winced. "You're supposed to watch her withdraw the cash and memorize the numbers."

"You make me wait in the car."

Ian realized his slip as soon as he spoke.

"I don't make you. Sarah does. I'm not Sarah!" she shrieked. "Sarah's weak. She has no guts. That's why I have to do everything for her."

"What do you have to do for her?"

Jackie glowered at him. He squared his shoulders. He had to show her she couldn't intimidate him even though he quaked in his worn Vans.

She looked at him in disgust, then shoveled the contents back into his mom's purse.

"No PIN, no ride. Get out of the car."

"What?" Ian scanned the area around them. They were in the middle of nowhere. Open fields sprawled outward in all directions.

Jackie leaned over the seat and snapped the latch on Ian's door. "I said get the fuck out."

Something about the timbre of her voice kept Ian's rear glued to the vinyl. He didn't move. He couldn't move, his legs were shaking so badly.

Jackie grabbed a pen and pressed the end deep into her neck where it threatened to pierce her skin. "Get out or I stab myself. You'll never see your mom again."

"You wouldn't," Ian dared.

"Don't test me." She pressed harder. A pin drop of blood pooled.

Ian's belief Jackie would never harm him, let alone herself, blew out the car with a gust of wind. He scrambled from the station wagon.

"Close the damn door," Jackie shouted when Ian just stood there.

He slammed the door.

"Walk home, loser," she yelled through the open passenger window. "Don't hitch a ride and don't let anyone see you. You do and I'll make sure you never see your mom again."

The station wagon sped away, engine groaning, tires spitting gravel and dirt.

When he no longer saw the Pontiac, his tears fell freely. Not only had he left his camera in the backseat, but he didn't know his way home.

⌒ꝯ

For five days Ian followed the road in the direction he thought was home. He kept to the edges of cornfields and dairy farms, drinking from the sprinklers and eating ripening corn when he risked being seen. With each approaching car, he ducked behind a tree or into stalks barely tall enough to hide him. He wanted to see his mom again so he followed Jackie's order. He slept days and walked nights so he wouldn't be seen. But after spending the third night wandering alone, he realized he'd taken a wrong turn somewhere.

He was lost.

He wondered if he'd ever find home. He missed his mom. His dad would be worried. Were they looking for him?

On the fifth day, Ian drifted into a fitful sleep on the sloped edge of an irrigation ditch under the shade of a large tree only to wake up when he felt a butterfly touch his head. His eyes snapped open to the blurry image of a woman kneeling beside him.

He shot upright and scooted away, his back pressing into tree bark. His heart beat furiously. He wasn't supposed to be seen. Jackie would find out and take his mom away from him. He tried to stand, to bolt away, but the woman grasped his shoulders and gently urged him down. Bone-weary and weak, he flopped back in the dirt.

"Hello, Ian." The woman smiled.

He squinted against the sun's glare, then blinked at her. Hair fine and fair haloed her head in the late-afternoon light. He stared, transfixed, at the strange blue shade of her eyes. Surely, he must be dreaming.

He heard a car door slam and stiffened. He tried to scoot away. The woman kept her hold on his shoulders.

"It's OK," her voice soothed. She smiled some more, then glanced over her shoulder. "He's over here, Stu."

Dad.

A sob burst from Ian. He croaked like a frog.

"Don't be afraid," the woman reassured. "Your dad's going to take you home."

His mouth quivered. "Who are you?" And how did she know his dad?

"I'm a friend. You can call me Laney."

"How did you find me?" He didn't want Jackie to find out he didn't walk all the way home.

"Magic. And Jackie will never know." She pressed a finger to her lips and stood, retreating.

"Ian. My God, son." Stu sank to his knees and grabbed Ian, holding him firmly to his chest. "I've been looking everywhere for you."

"Mom?" he cried. He started shaking—he didn't know whether from lack of food, relief he'd been found, or fear that Jackie hadn't shifted back to his mom. "Where's Mom?"

"It's time to go." His dad picked him up, cradling him like a baby to his truck.

CHAPTER 7

IAN

She told me her name was Laney. She introduced herself to Aimee at James's fake funeral as Lacy. In Mexico, Imelda Rodriguez, owner of Casa del sol, the hotel where Aimee and I had stayed, knows her as Lucy.

An enigma, I think, recalling the way Imelda described Laney-Lacy-Lucy, or whoever she is, to Aimee.

I watch James drive away, then look at the card in my hand.

LACY SAUNDERS
PSYCHIC COUNSELOR, CONSULTANT & PROFILER
MURDERS, MISSING PERSONS & UNSOLVED MYSTERIES
HELPING YOU FIND THE ANSWERS YOU SEEK.

I had immediately made the connection between the Laney who found me and the Lacy who led Aimee to Mexico in search of James when I saw the photo Kristen Garner had taken at the soft opening of Aimee's Café. You couldn't mistake those lavender-blue eyes.

On a whim, I thought Lacy could help me find my mom. I cajoled Lacy's information in Casa del sol's reservation database from Imelda Rodriguez. But the number Imelda gave me had been disconnected. No shocker there. What did surprise me, though, was my relief. Because if I found my mom, what would I say to her?

What could I say?

Her fractured identity and the ensuing fallout of her life? I'm partially to blame. The words "I'm sorry" will never be enough.

Lacy's card in my hand feels heavy as I wonder why she reached out to me in the oddest of ways: through my wife's ex-fiancé.

Smooth one, Saunders. Please don't tell me this is her way of saying she just wants us all to get along.

So not happening. As for Laney-Lacy . . .

The last time I saw her was on a desolate roadside in BFE, Idaho. She waved good-bye, her ankle-length skirt rippling in the afternoon breeze, as my dad settled me into the front seat of his truck. He drove me to the hospital where I spent the next few days with an IV stuck in my arm, replenishing my fluids.

On my second day there, I woke to my mom whispering my name. She sat on the edge of the bed, leaning over me. She gently brushed aside my bangs and I started to cry. I couldn't help myself. During those hours I drifted through the night, lost and alone, I honestly wondered if I would ever see her again.

"Shush," my mom soothed through cracked lips, the corner of her mouth swollen and bruised. A tear sluiced down her cheek, and when she wiped it away, I noticed the scabs on her knuckles. Rage burned like embers inside me, turning off the tear faucet. That woman living inside my mother had done that to her. Jackie had hurt Sarah. Again.

"I'm sorry, Ian. I'm so, so sorry. I didn't mean to hurt you. Can you forgive me?"

"It's not your fault." Like my mom's fractured mind, my adolescent one disassociated Jackie from Sarah. Through my eyes, Jackie was not my mother but an entirely separate person. They didn't dress alike and they wore their hair differently. Their mannerisms weren't the same.

My mom sobbed. She apologized repeatedly, making me uneasy. I didn't know how to act around this downtrodden and defeated version of her.

"I'm all right," I said, wanting her to feel better, more like herself. I roughly wiped my face and tried smiling.

"No, you're not. Your dad tells me you were missing for days. I . . ." She looked down at the bed. She ran her hand over my chest, flattening the wrinkles in the sheet. Moisture pooled along the bottom rims of her eyes. I watched it collect until tears spilled over and dropped on the sheet. "He told me what happened. I can't believe I did that to you. I can't believe it's taken me this long to get back to you."

"When did you get home?"

"This morning."

"You've been gone this whole time?" That surprised me. Where had she gone?

My mom danced her fingernails across my forehead. She couldn't stop touching me, as though reassuring herself I was safe and alive. She combed my bangs again. "I need your word you won't follow Jackie anymore."

I hadn't followed her. She'd shifted while driving. "But the pictures . . ."

My mom gripped my shoulders. "No more pictures."

My gaze dipped to the tubes stuck in my arm. I would never be a photojournalist if I couldn't get past my fears, no matter how threatening Jackie could be. "I only want to help."

"My goodness, Ian." My mom pulled me in for a hug. "If Laney hadn't helped your dad find you . . ." She sobbed, holding my head to her chest.

But she *had* found me. I never learned how she'd done so other than the explanation she'd given me: magic. My dad wouldn't talk about it.

I flip over the card. The back side is blank, but the front is the same as the card she'd given Aimee more than seven years ago. Same layout, same font, but different phone number.

James has had this card on him for several weeks. That's a long time in Lacy's world.

I tap the card against my hand. She's most likely moved on by now, her phone number ineffective. No point getting my hopes up.

I toss the card into the bowl on the console where I keep my change and tell myself it's not another excuse. I'm not putting off again what I should have done fifteen years ago.

∞

I can't help it. I walk into Aimee's Café with a swagger because I feel like a rock star. I handled myself well around James. So what if I wanted to increase the angle of his bent and obviously once-broken nose? It didn't happen and I won't have to explain to Aimee the bruises on my knuckles because there aren't any. And there never will be, since James is going back to Hawaii.

Good-bye and good riddance.

Aimee and I can finally climb out from under the *what if* of James's return that has been looming over our marriage since . . . oh . . . forever.

"I want a brownie," Caty says, still adorned in princess attire as she prances behind me.

I turn around and give her a look.

"I want a brownie, *please*." She grins big, showing all her teeth. "And chocolate milk."

"Sure thing, Caty-cakes." I lean close to her ear. "But don't tell your mom about the chocolate milk." One afternoon treat is bad enough, but two?

I'm such a sucker.

And Caty knows it. She works me.

We press fingers to our lips, then hook them in our secret shake.

The café is relatively empty, the lunchtime crowd come and gone. A few stragglers linger over coffee and baked goods, their noses in their laptops and phones. I set Caty up at a small table where I can see her from behind the counter, then help myself to the baked goods, plating a brownie. The biggest one left, of course. I mix a cup of chocolate milk using Aimee's custom blend of cocoa, powdered sugar, and vanilla.

Trish wipes down the countertop. "Hi, Ian."

I smile over at her. "Hey, Trish. How was it today?"

"Busy. We were slammed this morning. It always happens when we're short staffed."

"Murphy's Law."

"Never fails. Aimee kept her cool, though." Trish folds the dish towel. "It's been a long time since I've seen her work the kitchen. She seemed to love it. I think she misses being back there."

"I bet you're right. Is she here?" I glance toward the kitchen.

"She just got back from running errands. She's in her office." Trish moves to the sink to rinse mugs.

"Thanks."

I bring Caty her brownie and chocolate milk. She's spread her crayons across the table and has her notebook open to a blank page. "Stay here where Trish can see you. I'm going to go talk with your mom."

"OK, Daddy."

I kiss the top of her crowned head and make my way down the back hall to Aimee's office. She sits behind her desk, head in her hand, flipping through a stack of paperwork. They look like lease agreements or loan documents, lots of black print from what I can see.

I lean against the door frame, not wanting to interrupt. My fingers tingle, the desire to go to her almost pushing me into the tiny office space. But I don't move, I just watch. I could watch her all day.

Five years married and I still get a rush when I set eyes on her. That rubber band of emotion connecting us hasn't snapped. It grows taut in her absence and draws me back when I'm in her presence. I felt it the day we met at Wendy's gallery, and for the first time since I'd moved back to the States from France, I didn't feel the need to keep on moving. Because of Aimee, I wanted to stay.

Aimee yawns, covering her mouth with the back of her hand. Her face looks drawn, her hair twisted up in a bun stabbed with two pencils.

She must have sensed me, for she looks up and smiles, a weary curve of her lips. Circles darken the pits under her eyes like night shades. "Hi." Her voice is soft, tired.

"Hey," I murmur, pushing away from the doorway. I go around her desk and settle on the edge. Wisps of hair have escaped the latticework of pencils, lending her face a soft, endearing appearance despite the exhaustion weighing down her expression. I trace a thumb along her cheekbone. "Long day?"

Her eyes drift closed. She leans into my hand. "I'm tired." She laughs lightly at stating the obvious and lifts her chin. I take her invitation and kiss her, lingering on her lips. I taste coffee and cocoa, a hint of mint. And I taste Aimee, luscious and divine.

"I missed you this morning. I was hoping for a repeat of last night." I trail the back of my fingers down the column of her throat.

She hums. "Last night was good. I would have loved spending the morning in bed with you, but duty called." She wiggles a pen in the direction of the kitchen, then taps the stack of documents on her desk. "And these are due. I've read the same paragraph five times in this lease agreement. My eyes keep crossing." She pushes away from the desk and stands. She stretches, arms high and hands linked as she leans left then right.

I glance at her paperwork. "Which retail space did you decide on?"

"I haven't. I'm feeling overwhelmed."

"Are you sure this is what you want to do?"

Aimee looks at me. "Open another location? Of course. We've discussed this. Why would you ask?"

I shrug. "You don't bake anymore." And I'm not saying that because I'm addicted to her snickerdoodle cookies. She used to be passionate about baking. A genuine artisan.

A slight smile touches her lips like a brief kiss. "I did like working the kitchen this morning."

"Then, why aren't you? You don't need another location, let alone two. We don't need the extra money." But I do need my wife. She's been distracted all summer, barely taking the time to tuck Caty into bed, let alone sparing me a few moments before she dives into her plans. Until La Fondue last night, we hadn't had a date in weeks. Make that months.

Aimee motions at the agreements. "It's a little late to change my mind."

I fan through the paper stack. "I don't see any signatures. Look, I'm not trying to change your mind. Just think about it."

I stand and plant my hands on her shoulders. "You're pushing toward a deadline you created, Aims. You steer the ship. Slow it down. There's no rush to get this done." I knead the knots and she moans, letting her head fall forward.

"That feels amazing."

"It's supposed to." I breathe in her scent. A flurry of images shuffles behind my eyes, each of them involving Aimee and me. Naked. In the office. Door shut and locked, obviously.

And with that thought . . .

I completely lose track of what I want to say. Something about us, but without the stress and that constant feeling there's something unsaid between us. I miss her. I miss *us*.

I skim my mouth along the line of her exposed neck and kiss the base. My hands slip down the side of her ribs and skirt around to her abs. "What were we talking about?"

"Ah . . . um . . ." Aimee tilts her head to the side, giving me access to the curve of her shoulder. "Something about reconsidering leases and loans."

"That's right." I smile against her skin. "You've been wound up since June and—"

Aimee moves out from under my hands so fast I feel a breeze. My balance wobbles. She crosses her office and whirls around, the desk between us. "There you go again, bringing up James."

"Hey now." I wave both hands in front of me. "I didn't say anything about him."

"You didn't have to." She tosses up her hands. "I give up."

Everything inside me tightens, and not in a good way. "What do you mean you give up?"

"I told you what happened with him, every single detail. You know how I needed to say good-bye to him as the man he is now, not the guy he was in Mexico. Yes, we kissed, and yes, he groped me. He was desperate and lost and had been through hell. How many times do I have to tell you that you're the one I've chosen to spend my life with? What do I need to do to prove to you that it's you I love? Apologize? I think I've apologized enough. But if you need to hear it again, I am sorry. I am so, so sorry I hurt you."

"I'm not looking for an apology."

"Then, what do you want from me?"

I grind my teeth and glance away.

"What do you want?" she repeats, sounding desperate herself.

I want James to never contact her again, and I want his paintings off the walls. I want her to drop the pile of agreements on her desk and focus on what she loves—baking—not what she thinks she needs to accomplish: conquer the coffee-serving world. I want to be the best damn husband possible and a dad who sticks around. I want to kick ass on the *National Geographic* assignment so that subscribers remember my work for years to come. For my images to be burned in their memories like those on photograph paper.

There's so much I want, but when my eyes hold hers, I can't vocalize any of it except . . .

"I want to find my mom."

CHAPTER 8

IAN

"Your mom?" Aimee's stiff demeanor deflates like a sail that's lost its wind as the fight in her leaves. "Really?"

"Yep." Now that I said it out loud, I realize this is something I need to do that I can no longer put off.

"What brought this on?"

I shrug, rolling my lips over my teeth and biting down. I'm not going to mention Lacy's card, because if I do, I'll have to mention James. I'll prove to Aimee I don't always bring him up.

"You haven't talked about looking for her since Mexico. Why now?"

"I've been thinking about her a lot lately. I see a lot of her in Caty."

"She's beautiful."

"So was my mom."

Aimee rolls her eyes. "I know. I was talking about your mom. You've shown me pictures. There *is* a lot of her in Caty," she says as she wanders around the desk. She reaches for my hand. "There's a lot of her in you, too. So, will you hire a PI? A legitimate one?" she quips.

The corner of my mouth pulls up. We can laugh about it now, but it wasn't funny six years ago when Aimee hired an investigator to search for James. The PI fed her lies and absconded with her money.

"I haven't thought this through yet."

"When are you going to start looking?" she asks. I don't immediately reply, finding fascination in the tiny scars on her fingers. Battle wounds from years of working in a commercial kitchen. I turn her hand over and trace her life line with my thumb. She groans my name, tugging her hand from mine. "You're still going to Spain, right?"

"I'm not sure." Once I get an idea, like for one of my next photo expeditions, I'll exhaustively research it, and that worries me. I won't be able to focus on my assignment until I make progress with my mom.

Aimee gives me a hard look, then gathers her purse, keys, and phone. "Let's get my car. I'll have Trish close up."

Her tone gives my heart a shove. It beats faster. I've made her angry. "You're mad."

She stops at the door, hand on knob. "No, I'm not. I'm confused."

I cross my arms. "You don't think I should look for her."

"I didn't say that. I support your decision one hundred percent. I'll even help you. What I'm thinking, though, is that we need to discuss this tonight." She zigzags a finger between us. "Because I want to understand why you need to do this now. Why it can't wait until after Spain. Why are you willing to give up your dream of working with *National Geographic* to go after a woman who abused and neglected you?"

Sarah didn't abuse me, not intentionally. Jackie, the monster inside my mom, was a different story. Aimee knows I spent my childhood caring for my mom more often than the other way around. How she'd shower me with love one moment and shout her hatred of me the next. I grew accustomed to having her read me a bedtime story in the evenings and throw her books at me in the morning when she couldn't find the car keys she'd hidden from herself. Bedlam was the norm in the

Collins household. I adjusted to the shifts in temperament as smoothly as she switched personas.

What is difficult for outsiders to understand, as I think is the case with Aimee, and I sometimes wonder myself, is why I still love my mom. It's my belief that had she not had such a traumatic childhood and had I not played a role in exacerbating her mental illness, she would still love me. She would not have left me. Given the chance to apologize, I could change things with her. Not her illness, unfortunately. I cannot fix that. But maybe she can find a place for me in her heart again. She can forgive me.

I drive us to Nadia's garage to drop off Aimee and Caty. After I agree to be home by dinner and they're in Aimee's van, I head to the gym. We're talking tonight, which means I need to figure out the answer to Aimee's question. Why must I search for my mom now?

I do my usual routine of dead lifts, squats, and burpees, then run a fast 5K on the treadmill. When I finish and my body is still a tightly coiled roll of film, I slip on a pair of gloves and work over a punching bag. I deliver several solid blows, wind up for a fourth, and nearly hit Erik's grinning jaw.

He swings his head aside at the last second. "Whoa, watch the aim." He grabs the swinging bag.

I point a gloved hand at him. "Good thing you've got quick reflexes. I would have sent you back to the orthodontist."

"Not a chance." He runs his tongue along his gleaming piano-key set of teeth.

"Warn me before you spot." I huff the words. I drag my forearm across my damp forehead.

Erik stabilizes the bag. "You're on a roll and look like you want to murder someone. Have at it. I've got you covered." He braces his legs.

For the next ten minutes, I take the last three months out on the bag. The Rapa in Spain. James's arrival while I was there and his repeat return. My overwhelmed and overworked wife who's done much better than I have with James's revival. I think of our daughter, who every day looks more like a blend of my wife and mom, which makes me think of the business card I'd left at home. What's Lacy's role in all this? Of course, thoughts of her bring me full circle to James and the Rapa, reminding me of the photos I took and who I thought I saw through my camera lens sitting in the stands. That's when I know why I've been on edge since June, and it has nothing to do with James and Aimee, not directly. That one slightly out-of-focus image among thousands of photos I took at the Rapa has been quietly at work in the back of my mind, stealthily fueling my frustration and disappointment in myself. And I've been taking it out on Aimee, using her history with James as an excuse for my inaction.

I deliver one last punishing blow, the impact of which vibrates up my arm and rattles my teeth, and back off from the bag. I owe my wife a serious apology.

Hands clasped behind my head, chest heaving, I walk a tight circle.

"Who's the victim?" Erik asks.

"Me." I choke out a laugh and rip open the Velcro closure on my left glove.

Erik slaps the bag. "I guess that's one way to beat yourself up. What's got you worked up?"

I shake my head. That's a conversation between Aimee and me. I foresee groveling in my future.

Erik waves his fingers for me to give up the goods. "I just spent the last ten minutes praying I didn't leave the gym today with a shiner. The least you can do is let me leave knowing why I risked my gorgeous face." He crosses his arms over his chest.

"Can you get any more full of yourself?"

He shrugs a shoulder. "Probably."

I shake my head, tugging off the glove and tucking it under my arm. "I'm not turning this into a pity party."

"Suit yourself." He dusts my shoulder.

"What's that about?"

"Whatever's got the squeeze on you"—he holds up a fist and grips air—"shake it off." He breaks into a falsetto rendition of Taylor Swift.

"Thank you for reminding me how much older I am than you."

"Seven years my senior."

"Enjoy thirty while it lasts." I yank off the second glove and drop both on the floor. I shake out a towel and wipe down my face and neck. The acrid odor of old sweat that never washes out from gym towels burns the back of my nose. "Did you submit your Big Sur photos?"

"Yep. The article ran this morning. Which you obviously missed."

I shoot him a guilty-as-charged glance and chug my water. The paper I brought inside after this morning's run was last seen folded and unread on the kitchen counter.

"What about you?" Erik knocks his knuckles into my shoulder. "*National Geographic*, eh?"

Elation shoots up me only to nose-dive at my feet. "Al called with the assignment. He's sending me back to Spain."

"Fantastic. Your Rapa photos are brilliant. I knew they'd select you. When are you going?"

"I'm not sure I am." I collect my gloves and phone and gesture for Erik to follow me to the locker room.

He gawks. "What do you mean you're not going?"

"I might have a conflict." As in an I-can't-put-off-the-search-any-longer conflict. "I'll explain later." I have to get home and call Al.

"That better be a life-or-death conflict. You'll never get another opportunity like this."

My phone pings with a message from Aimee and I jump at the distraction. I read the text. Kristen has gone into labor, and as with her two previous pregnancies, she wants her friends at the hospital for moral support. Aimee's worried about me. Another text pings.

Join me. We can talk there while we wait for Kristen.

Guess we're chatting in the hospital cafeteria. I hope they're serving humble pie.

"Gotta run," I tell Erik. "The wife's hailing."

"My reputation is on the line, man. They'll never let me refer you again. You better go to Spain."

∽

"I'm pregnant."

As I drive to the hospital, I recall Aimee's declaration from five years ago. Two words that packed a punch.

She'd whispered the announcement, the pregnancy stick shaking in her hand.

She was worried. We both were. Given my own childhood, I had serious doubts how I'd handle myself as a father. Would I be like my dad and make myself scarce when life at home became difficult? Did I even want to be a father? Aimee and I had only been dating a few months. We had yet to discuss marriage, let alone the future. But within a heartbeat of her announcement, I realized two things. I wanted to be the father of Aimee's child and I wanted to spend my life with her. I'd do anything to make her happy. I'd give up photography, I loved her that much. Still do.

In a whirlwind of activity, she moved in with me, and by early June we were married. Six months after we'd officially started dating.

Six months after she'd left James behind in Mexico.

Did I rush her into marriage? I mull over Aimee's question while waiting at a light. I'd been crazy sick in love with her for more months than I care to admit and to finally have her want me just as much? It meant everything. Because up to that point in my life, I had no one except me, myself, and my photography, which I didn't want to give up—*ever*—I realized back at the house while I showered after the gym. I want it all: my family, to make peace with my mom, and that *National*

Geographic assignment I've been pining for since I first picked up a camera.

The light changes and I acknowledge that the plan I worked out at home, the one I convinced Al Foster to agree to, is the right one.

Turning into the hospital parking lot, I find an empty space near the main entrance—lucky me—and head upstairs to the maternity ward. I find Nadia flipping through a rag magazine in the waiting room, which smells of hand sanitizer and floral bouquets. Plastic plants fill the corners. Over the intercom, an Evelyn Wright is requested to come to the nursing station.

Nadia puts aside the magazine and stands up when she sees me. "Hi, Ian." She gives me a hug.

"Hey, how's Kristen?" I remember to ask as I look around for Aimee.

"She's good. Aimee and I were just in there with her until the doctor arrived." Nadia glances at her phone. "Baby Theo should arrive any moment. Nick's over the moon."

His first son. "That's great." I nod, somewhat distracted. "Where's Aimee? I tried to reach her to let her know I was on my way."

"She probably didn't get your call. The reception in here is spotty. She's over at the nursery."

I give Nadia's arm a squeeze. "Thanks."

Going on memory from when we were here for Caty's birth, I make my way to Aimee. She stands in front of the nursery window, arms crossed, hands clasped over her elbows. I come up beside her and wrap my arm around her, letting my hand rest on her lower back.

"Can you believe Caty was that tiny?" Aimee asks, awe in her voice.

"Her head used to fit in the palm of my hand."

"And her scent." She inhales deeply, lost in her memories.

"Which end? Because the smell I remember—"

"Ian. Gross." Aimee laughs, a low vibration, and I can't help grinning. She ribs me with her elbow. "Her scalp, not her rear. And her skin, her special baby scent." She sighs, wistful. "I miss that."

"Me, too," I say, looking down at Aimee, remembering the way she held Caty as she nursed, the way that special mother-daughter bond evolved before my eyes.

Aimee's gaze roams over the babies aligned like cars in a sales lot. We both grew up as only children and neither of us has broached the subject of giving Caty a sibling. We've been too busy, but I see the longing in Aimee.

"Ian." She turns to me. "Do you—"

I rest a finger on her lips, halting the question I know she'll ask. *Do you want another baby?* I do. With Aimee, I'll have a dozen. But there is something I must tell her, the apology I realized I owe her. And there's something I need to do before we consider bringing another child into the world. I need to resolve my own issues and put my past to rest.

Aimee frowns, her expression asking me what's wrong.

"I had a really good workout. I cleared my head and figured out why I've been such a dick toward you lately."

"You haven't been a—"

"Yes, I have," I interrupt. "I haven't been fair with you about James. It's not your history with him that bothers me. We both have past relationships, some more meaningful and intense than others." I quirk a brow in reference to her ex. "We can't change our past, but we can do something about how we move forward together."

I grasp her shoulders and dip my face so that my eyes are level with hers. "I trust you, Aimee. I believe you when you say you love me and want to spend your life with me. I know James is in your past and that you've moved on. You've had closure on that chapter of your life, where with my mom, I"—my arms fall limp at my sides and I take a step back—"I haven't."

Her eyes dart left and right, searching my face. "What are you saying, Ian? Your tone sounds funny."

"There's been a change of plans. I leave for Spain tonight."

"Tonight?"

"My flight's in a few hours. I'm packed and ready to go."

"But I thought you wanted me to go with you."

"Next time."

Her frown deepens. Worry clouds her eyes. "You're not making sense, Ian. What does Spain have to do with your mom?"

"Everything."

CHAPTER 9

IAN, AGE ELEVEN

"Did you have a nice sleep?" Ian's mom asked when he entered the kitchen. She was sitting at the table, sipping tea.

"Yes." Ian yawned, scratching his head through sleep-tousled hair, and fixed himself a bowl of Wheaties. He joined his mom at the table and shoveled a spoonful into his mouth. With an empty expression, she watched him chew. She might be looking at him, but she wasn't seeing him.

Ian hated when she stared at him like that. His chest twinged and his chewing slowed as he watched her, waiting. Who knew who his mom would come back as when she retreated into her head? He noticed her uncombed hair and the shadows under her eyes, the misaligned buttons on her robe. She picked at her ragged nails.

Ian pushed the cereal flakes around in his bowl. "I heard the phone ringing. Was it Dad?"

She nodded and sipped her tea. "Yes."

Ian exhaled with relief when it was his mom who answered. "What time will he be home?"

Kerry Lonsdale

"He wants to stay for the press conference. He'll be home late tomorrow morning."

Ian slumped in his chair. He'd been hoping they could go fishing at the lake this afternoon like they used to. They'd wait for the fish to bite and his dad would teach him new tricks with his camera. Ian had read an article about time-lapse photography and wanted to give it a try. He didn't have the skill or the equipment. His dad did, though. But now with the trip extension, they wouldn't have time together before his dad left for his next assignment.

He missed his dad.

He missed spending time with him.

For almost a year after Jackie had abandoned Ian on the roadside, his dad had stayed home and worked for the local paper. Ian's mom agreed to be admitted to the hospital, where they kept her under observation, as his dad referred to it, then released her with an order to see a psychiatrist. A woman had also shown up at Ian's house soon after he arrived home from the hospital himself. She asked Ian all sorts of questions about living with his parents. That's when his dad decided he needed to be home more. He didn't want to be the negligent father and risk Ian being placed into foster care.

When Ian had listened to the woman with the beige wool suit and thick file tell his father he could end up in foster care, he swore to himself he'd watch his mother more closely. He'd make sure no one outside the house knew how often his parents used to leave him alone. He didn't want to be taken from home. And for a year, life in the Collins house was almost normal. He and his dad went on adventures together almost every weekend. They'd go exploring after school, quick photo expeditions around their property.

But his mom started resisting her therapy and wouldn't take her medication. His dad grew weary of arguing with her. They'd always argue until his mom started crying and his dad pulled her into his arms and just held her. A couple of times Ian swore his dad cried, too.

Then there were the overdue medical bills. Ian once overheard his dad explain to his mom that there was much their insurance wouldn't cover and his job at the paper barely paid to put food on their table. He needed to start taking on more assignments or they could lose their home. Soon Ian and his mom saw less of his dad. And eventually, their routine reverted to the way it was before Ian had been lost.

Appetite gone, Ian took his bowl to the sink, overflowing with dishes. His mom often let the dishes collect throughout the day and washed them after dinner. Ian hadn't seen them pile to this extent before. Pots and plates cluttered the sink and counter. The meat loaf from two nights ago and last night's spaghetti had been left out to spoil.

His lip lifted at the milk curdling in yesterday's cereal bowl and glanced over at his mom. She sat unmoving, staring beyond the kitchen window. A layer of dust from the plowed fields clouded the glass. Dried cornstalks had been cleared for the next planting cycle. The sloping landscape stretched toward the mountainous rise on the horizon.

"Do you want me to do the dishes?"

She didn't answer, which worried Ian. She'd been detached since his dad had left earlier this week. She napped each day and had stopped reading. Ian came home with an A on his science test yesterday. She'd taken the test from him and uttered a simple "That's nice, honey" before setting it aside without a further glance.

"I'll wash them," he muttered to himself. He doubted she was listening.

He cleared out the basin and turned on the faucet. Twenty minutes later, counters cleared and dishwasher loaded, Ian skimmed through his mom's planner.

"Did you finish the shirts for Mr. Hester's Boy Scout troop?" He glanced at her and she nodded once. Ian flipped the page. "Have you started Mrs. Layton's costumes for the"—he squinted at the note—"*Oklahoma!* musical?"

The teacup clattered on the table. "Yes, Ian." His mom's voice took on a perturbed tone.

"I'm just trying to help."

"Thanks, but that's not necessary." She buried her face in her hands, took a couple of deep breaths, and folded her hands under her chin. Her mouth pulled into a little smile. "What are you doing today?"

Ian looked out the window. Cotton-white clouds mottled the blue sky. "I'm going on a photo expedition."

"You are?" she replied with exaggerated interest.

"Wanna come with me?" She could use a day in the sun. She'd been hiding in the house all week, burrowed under blankets like a rabbit in the brush.

His mom stood and took her teacup to the sink. "Invite Marshall. He'll go with you."

"Nah." Ian didn't want to invite his neighbor. He didn't want any friends over.

"Why not? You haven't had him over in a long time."

Ian didn't want to risk the chance his mom went Wacky-Jackie in front of his friends.

He could go to Marshall's house instead, but then he'd worry about his mom. His dad wanted him to stay at Marshall's when he was out of town. He even asked Mrs. Killion to keep an eye on him. But if Ian left home, there wouldn't be anyone to watch his mom until his dad returned.

"Marshall's busy today."

His mom frowned. "Are you two getting along?"

"Yeah, we're fine. I don't want him to come over here, that's all."

"Oh." She studied her hands, then crossed her arms, hiding her unkempt nails.

"I didn't mean . . . What I meant was . . ." Ian rubbed his hand through his mop of hair, looking at his bare feet. "I want you to come with me," he said in a small voice.

Ian could feel his mom watching him so he lifted his head.

She smiled. "All right. I'll come."

Fifteen minutes later they were dressed and walking in the direction of the duck pond near the western property line. The air smelled of fertilized dirt and dry grass. A field mouse scurried past.

Ian stopped and motioned for his mom to be quiet. "He'll be back." He lay in the dirt, leaning on his elbows with the camera poised near his face, and waited.

His mom eased to the ground beside him. Within moments, the brownish-gray mouse peered from under a bush and raced by, disappearing into the tall grass. Blades shimmied in the sunlight, tracking his path. They watched the mouse circle around until he shot past them, grass blades and needle-size twigs in his mouth. He scurried under the bush.

"What's he doing?" she whispered.

"Fixing his nest, I think."

The mouse returned, pausing in his trek to scrub his nose. The camera shutter snapped. His mom flinched and the mouse ran off.

"Got him." Ian jumped to his feet and dusted off the dirt on his shirt and shorts.

They continued walking, past the white ash tree. His mom snapped off a twig. She twirled it in her fingers. "Do you still want to be a photographer when you grow up?"

Ian had wanted to be a photographer since the day his dad bought him his first real camera on his fifth birthday and showed him how to use it. He also taught him how to develop film. Ian treasured those hours they stood side by side in the darkroom.

"Yes, but I don't want to do football games like Dad. I want to travel the world and take pictures of everyone I meet." Aside from accompanying his dad on a few trips, Ian hadn't journeyed outside Idaho. "If you could go anywhere in the world, where would you go?" he asked his mom.

"That's easy. Paris."

Ian grinned. "Me, too."

"I'm sure you will one day."

"What about you? Won't you go?"

"I love being here." She glanced back at the house. "It's safe and peaceful. Besides"—she turned back to him—"I travel every day."

"No, you don't."

"It's a special kind of travel."

Ian gave her a sidelong glance. "Really?"

She leaned over and whispered in his ear. "Armchair travel."

"*Pfft,*" Ian scoffed. "That's not traveling."

"It is for me. I go where my characters go in the books I read."

"But that's not *real* traveling."

She just smiled. "Promise me something, Ian."

"What?" He snapped a photo of a red leaf.

"Promise that when you fall in love you're as good to your wife as you are to me."

Ian's face screwed up at the mention of a wife. He liked a girl at school. Lisa was quiet and cute, but he hadn't had the nerve to say anything other than "Hi." He was eleven. He hadn't yet kissed a girl so why was his mom talking about marriage? Yuck.

Unless . . .

"Is Dad good to you?"

His mom broke the twig in two. "I remember the first time I saw your dad. I was working in the concession stands at the Padres ballpark. The line for drinks was huge, and we were filling sodas as fast as we could during the seventh-inning stretch. The Padres were losing and some of the fans were getting unruly. They were loud and rude and impatient.

"There was this guy and he was big, much bigger than your father. He ordered two sodas and started barking at me to hurry before I could grab the cups to fill them. It was pandemonium behind the counter. We constantly ran into one another, which is exactly what happened. I carried the sodas back to the order counter and someone bumped my arm. The drinks flew out of my hands and drenched the man who ordered them. He got so mad at me." She whistled at the memory. "Then there was your dad. He appeared from nowhere. He calmed the man down by sweet-talking him or something. Your dad even paid for his drinks."

"What did you do?"

"Nothing. I froze. I couldn't move. Your dad had to ask for the drinks several times before I realized he was talking to me. He must have noticed how shaken up I was because he came back after the game to check on me. He walked me to my car and asked for my phone number."

"Did you give it to him?"

"I sure did. Your dad was the first man who was nice to me. He assured me he'd always love me and would take care of me. He wanted to keep me safe."

Just as Ian wanted to do for his mom. He liked how he and his dad were the same in that way. "Did Dad—" He stopped abruptly and looked at his hands. He rolled the lens cap between his fingers.

His mom crooked her finger and lifted his chin. She smiled gently. "Did Dad what?"

"Did Dad know about you . . . I mean . . . did he know about Jackie before you got married?"

A crow cawed loudly as it flew over them. His mom glanced up and looked around. They'd arrived at the pond. "We're here."

Ian's mom sat on a tree stump and Ian cased the edge of the pond, seeking his next Kodak moment. Spotting a toad, he sank on his heels and positioned the camera.

His mom crashed through the brush and landed on her knees beside him. "Whoa! Look at the toad. He's huge."

The toad splashed into the water before Ian could take a picture.

"Oops." She laughed. "I think I scared him off."

No kidding. Ian groaned in irritation. "Be quiet. He might come back."

"OK," she whispered loudly. She sat cross-legged and pulled a reed. She chewed on the end, then twirled it in her fingers. She stuck the reed in her hair and repeatedly poked her head. She tossed the reed in the pond and sighed dramatically. "This is boring. Let's go to the creek."

Ian lowered the camera to his lap and looked at his mom, who was no longer his mom. Sarah wouldn't chew reeds and stick them in her hair. But Billy would.

Ian guessed Billy was a perpetual eight-year-old because he acted the way Ian imagined an annoying younger brother would act. Billy showed up after Jackie abandoned Ian on the roadside two years ago. Ian once overheard his parents talking about his mom's appointment with a psychiatrist. The doctor reasoned Billy was his mom's way of coping with her guilt over the roadside incident. Her mind fractured further and along came Billy. Ian noticed the less he had his friends over, the more frequently Billy appeared, as though his mom knew on some level that Ian needed a companion.

He liked hanging out with Billy, except those times he wanted to tag along when Ian and his friends went to the skate park. That would be weird.

Billy lunged to his feet and ran off. The toad returned. Awesome. Ian snapped a photo, then heard a large splash. He lifted his head in the direction of the noise and gawked. "Billy! What are you doing?"

His mom stood in the center of the shallow pond, water up to her hips. She skimmed her fingers along the water's surface, humming. A lilting tune Ian didn't recognize, the beauty of the melody at odds with the water's filth.

Ian made a disgusted face. He could see the pond scum on his mom's forearms. Ducks swam, ate, and defecated in the pond. Even he didn't venture into the water except that one time when Marshall tripped him. Ian had stumbled back, arms flailing like windmills, and fallen on his rear. He'd been soaked. The smell alone had him hightailing it back to the house for the hose.

But despite the water thick with moss, mud, and who knew what else, his mom appeared serene. Beautiful. Billy had left and Sarah returned. Sunlight danced across the ripples she caused as she swayed. It glittered along the glossy strands of her hair. She continued to hum, head tilted toward the sky and eyes closed, the touch of a smile highlighting her face.

Ian raised the camera to his face. He wanted to remember his mom like this. Peaceful, not splintered. This was the way he was beginning to understand how her mind functioned. He pressed the shutter button. The camera clicked and his mom jerked. She stretched her hands skyward, flared her fingers, and screamed, fuming.

"Gross!" She swiveled around looking at the water, then at Ian. Her expression mirrored the disgust he felt a moment ago. Then she saw the camera. She gritted her teeth, her lips pulled back, and trudged through the thick water and up the bank, coming to stand in front of Ian. Water dripped from her drenched skirt. Her chest rose and fell, the breath coming from her sounding like an engine in the back of her throat.

Jackie.

Ian didn't know what propelled him to take a picture at that moment. The difference between Jackie and Sarah a moment ago was startling. He wanted to document the shift. But he knew he was tempting fate. The shutter snapped and the camera flew out of his hands. Fire blistered across his cheek. Ian clapped a hand over the burn, his gaze darting from his camera in the dirt to Jackie.

"You hit my camera."

"I hope I broke it." Jackie stomped her feet and shrieked. "I feel disgusting." She wrung out her skirt. "What day is it?"

Stunned from the smack she'd delivered, Ian stared at her, mute.

She gripped his upper arm and Ian hissed.

"What's the date?" she asked.

"Fuck you," he spat, finding his voice. He'd learned that word from her. Sarah would wash his mouth with soap should she learn how he back-talked Jackie.

Jackie shoved him away and ran to the house.

Ian stumbled over to his camera. He blew dust off the lens, inspected the film casing, and looked through the viewfinder. He pressed the shutter button, and the camera clicked. He heaved a sigh of relief. Everything was intact.

He turned to the house the same moment Jackie swung open the rear screen door. His parents didn't want him photographing Jackie. Dogging her was too dangerous. She was unpredictable. She either spent hours prowling the house like a caged animal or left to get to God knows where. Jackie would never tell him. She treated Ian more like a brother than a son. And Ian was beginning to see her as a malicious sibling who wouldn't think twice about harming him.

But if he wanted to be a photojournalist he couldn't let fear keep him from going after his subject.

A shadow moved behind the lace curtains in his parents' room. Jackie was up there. Ian bolted to the house, and the second he stepped inside, glass shattered. He glanced up at the ceiling. Drawers slammed and something heavy dropped on the floor. He ran up the stairs, taking two at a time, and skidded to a stop at the room Jackie was ransacking. Clothes spilled from his mom's dresser like a bubbled-over pot of oatmeal. His dad's underwear and T-shirts pooled on the floor, puddles of clothes. Drawers had been upended and tossed aside. His mom's soiled clothes were in a heap by the door. Jackie had changed into a blouse and jeans.

She opened the closet door and shoved aside his dad's shirts and his mom's dresses. She felt through pockets.

"What're you doing?" Ian stepped into the room. He tightly gripped his camera as though an anchor.

She tossed her hair over her shoulder. "Where're the car keys?"

"I don't know." Ian took in the room. In less than five minutes, Jackie had created more of a mess than a passing tornado. He snapped a photo.

"I swear, kid, you take one more and I'm gonna strangle you with the camera strap." Jackie reached for a shoe box on the top shelf.

Ian moved farther into the room. "You shouldn't be in there."

Jackie smiled at him over her shoulder. It wasn't a nice smile and it took everything in Ian not to cower. Jackie raked her arm across the shelf, clearing its contents. Shoe boxes and purses landed with a thud, their contents spilling out.

"Stop making a mess." Ian grabbed a shoe box. Jackie yanked it from him. She peered inside and laughed. "You're such an idiot." She held up a set of keys and shook them in Ian's face.

Ian's stomach turned over. It looked like they were going for a ride.

Jackie pocketed the keys. "Where does your dad keep his guns?"

Ian made a strangled noise in the back of his throat. He lurched back. Jackie grabbed his wrist.

"Speak up." She gave his arm a sharp tug.

"He—he doesn't have any guns," he said, trying not to piss his pants.

"Seriously?" she scoffed. "I know he has them, so you don't have to lie. Where are they?"

Ian clenched his jaw and locked his knees. He still shook like a high-strung mutt and hoped Jackie didn't notice.

She bitch-slapped his temple. "Don't be a shit, Ian. Tell me."

Ian clutched his head. "No."

"God, you're a pain. Fine, whatever." She pushed him away from her. "Where'd you put my money?"

"It's not your money." Ian rubbed his wrist. "Where're you going?"

"None of your business." Jackie searched the purses, coming up empty. "What's the date?" she asked again.

"Why do you care?"

She snatched a metal nail file from the vanity table and held it against her wrist. "Tell me the date or I'll make your precious mommy bleed all over the carpet."

"July tenth," Ian divulged, too scared not to answer.

"Shit." She tossed the file and lapped the room, her hand in her pocket jangling the keys. "He's moved again. Shit, shit, shit." She roughly gripped her hair, stretching the skin on her forehead. "Is there still time?" She peered through the window curtains. "It's still light. OK, OK, OK. There's time. He'll come."

Ian frowned, not sure of what he heard. "Time for what? Who'll come? Dad?"

"Screw your dad." She pivoted from the window and sneered. "He's out of town again, isn't he?" She crossed the room and got into his face. "Do you miss your daddy?" she asked in a baby voice.

His dad was photographing the Padres game against the Cardinals. Yeah, he missed him, but he wasn't going to let Jackie in on that secret. Hoping to distract her from asking about his dad, he moved the camera between them and snapped a photo. The lightbulb flashed, temporarily blinding her.

Jackie lunged for him. Ian dodged under her arm. He leaped on the bed and slid across, landing on the other side. But Jackie didn't go after him. She ran from the room, slamming the door behind her.

Jackie was taking his mom away from him.

Ian raced after her, skidding to a halt on the front porch. The station wagon arrowed down the driveway, kicking up a cloud of dust.

He'd been left alone again.

Slowly, feet dragging, he returned inside the house.

It looked like he'd be eating cereal for dinner. Again.

CHAPTER 10

AIMEE

Ian and I have been married for more than five years. I'm used to the way he carefully selects the next destination for one of his photo expeditions. I've watched him meticulously research the area, its culture and weather patterns, the natives' customs. By the time he arrives, he knows exactly the types of photos he wants to capture. But this suddenness to get to Spain when he wasn't planning to leave until next week is completely out of character for him. He's talking about James one second, his mom the next, and then tells me he's leaving for Spain within three hours. And somehow the three of these things—my relationship with James, Ian seeking closure with Sarah, and his *National Geographic* assignment—are all connected.

To say I'm baffled is an understatement.

"You're not making sense, Ian. Can't you postpone Spain until next week like you originally planned? Can we talk about this first?" But his facial muscles are tight and there's a determined set to his jaw. His eyes are far away and I know he's already on the plane headed for Spain. "I'm worried about you."

"Don't. Everything will be fine. Just know that I can't apologize enough for how I've been treating you. I'm going to fix this."

"Fix what?"

"Me. Us. I know this is crazy and sudden, but I've got a plan to make everything right. To make me right. I just need you to trust me. I'll call when I land. I love you."

He kisses me and gives me a rib-cracking hug. He then has the audacity to walk away.

I'm frozen. I can't get my words out. *We need fixing?* He's almost reached the stairwell before I snap out of it. He wasn't kidding. He really is leaving tonight. And I don't want him to go, not like this.

"Ian, wait!"

I run after him, forgetting how fast he moves. I dodge nurses and visitors carrying corridor-width-size bouquets. I shout his name again only to have the heavy, metal stairwell door slam in my face. I flinch, yank open the door, and look down. Ian's already two flights below. A door slams. He's gone.

I leave the stairwell. The elevator beside me dings and doors open, expelling a set of grandparents carrying balloons and a stuffed Eeyore. I look at the empty cab and debate what to do.

Whatever Ian's going through, I don't want him to feel like he must do it alone.

"I saw Ian take off. What's his rush?" Nadia asks, coming to stand beside me, phone in hand.

Distracted, I blink at Nadia. "What?" The elevator doors close without me inside.

I should be with him.

I repeatedly jab the down button. Numbers light above the door. The elevator continues its climb up.

"Where's he going?"

I pound the button. Ugh. "He's flying to Spain."

Nadia finishes a text and sends it off. She looks at me with a tilt to her head. "Tonight? I thought he didn't leave for another week."

"He changed his flight." The elevator begins its crawl down.

"Right now? No way. He won't find an international flight tonight." She checks the time on her phone. "It's six o'clock." An incoming text pings. She reads it and smiles.

"He told me he was able to book it." I tug at my lower lip. The elevator doors slide open and I let them close. There's no chance of stopping him. He's probably on the road by now. I guess we'll talk when he lands.

I send Ian a text to that effect and add a kissy-face emoji. My phone shows one bar fading in and out, depending on which way I face. I hope he gets my message, and I'm going to worry about him until I know he did.

The desire to be with him, to join him in Spain, grows stronger. But I won't find a flight at this late hour.

Suddenly, the café's expansion doesn't seem important. In fact, my interest started waning long before Ian confronted me this afternoon. *Is this really what you want to do?*

No, it's not. A smile appears on my face as I think about how I felt while gazing upon the newborns.

Nadia's fingers fly over her phone. She sends off another text. My brows push up in the middle. "You're getting reception in here?"

"It comes and goes."

"Who are you texting?"

"A friend."

I grin at the flirtatious note in her tone. "You're texting a guy. Who is it? Are you dating?" She hasn't gone out with anyone since she broke up with Mark last year. Talk about a dead-end relationship. He's successful and very committed to his career, which would have been admirable if he'd shown that same level of commitment with Nadia.

But she didn't like coming in second place. What woman does in a serious relationship?

"Yes, it's a guy. No, we're not dating. It's work related."

"Aimee! Nadia!" Nick Garner runs up to us, grinning. His hair stands on end and his dress shirt from his day job as an attorney is unbuttoned at the collar, with the sleeves rolled up. One shirttail has escaped the waist of his suit pants. "I'm a dad! Again! I have a son! Oh my God, I have a son." He grasps his face with both hands and laughs.

"Congratulations," Nadia and I say in unison. Nick hugs each of us, picking me off my feet when it's my turn. I feel myself grinning as stupidly as he is. The man is on cloud nine.

He waves for us to follow. "Kristen's asking for you. Come meet baby Theo."

After cooing over Theodore Michael for a couple of hours and watching Kristen's daughters meet their baby brother—I *so* want to give Caty a sibling—Nadia and I leave the Garner family to enjoy their new addition in privacy. As soon as we exit the hospital both our phones ping with notifications. Nadia immediately dives into hers.

"I'm thinking of pulling the plug on my expansion plans," I tell Nadia when we stop on the walkway before going our separate ways. She'd asked about the project's progress in the elevator on the way down since I hired her to design the new locations.

"That's because you're in the not-so-fun stage of paperwork and financing," she says, multitasking on her phone. She taps out another text. "Every project seems dull at this point."

"It's more than that." I look across the parking lot. Evening traffic, the steady hum of passing cars, and the occasional horn and siren, noise polluting the evening. The first hint of fall permeates the air, wood smoke and the after-scent of brush fires. Drying leaves and apples. My stomach growls. It's past dinner. I need to pick up Caty and find something to eat. It's going to be a late night and I've been up since before dawn.

"I worked the kitchen this morning. I had my hands wrist deep in dough and I loved it. I thought up three new drink mixes while waiting for the coffee to brew. I chatted with my regulars and . . . and who are you texting?" I ask, wondering if she's even listening to me. I try to peer at her phone. She tilts it away.

"I told you. A client." She sends the text and tucks her mobile under her arm. "You were saying?"

I jut a shoulder, thinking of my day. "I miss all that."

"Miss what?"

"Did you hear anything I said?"

"Umm . . . dough?"

"Yes, that!" I hold up my hands, curling my fingers in frustration. I want to give Nadia a good shake. I want her to understand my desire to get back to basics. "I miss kneading dough and brewing coffee. The simple things. Does that sound lame?"

Nadia's phone pings. "Sorry."

I feel my brows push into my hairline. "Really?"

"One second." She shoots me an apologetic smile. "This project is on deadline." She reads the text. So do I. I can't help it. She's standing right beside me and her phone is right there and she isn't hiding the screen.

Meet me for a late dinner.

"Who are you meeting for dinner?" I hear myself asking as my gaze glides to the contact name at the top of the screen. Thomas Donato.

It takes three seconds of dead silence for Thomas's name and who Nadia has been texting to register because I can't process what this means. Nadia and Thomas. Together.

She senses the instant I see his name. Her arm falls to her side and her expression clouds with guilt.

I gape, pointing at her phone. "You're working with Thomas?" I sound incredulous. Heartbroken. Betrayed by my best friend.

"I was thinking about mentioning it to you last night but—"

"But what? James came to town? You thought I was too emotional after seeing him to handle the news you're working with his brother?"

"Something like that," Nadia admits in a small voice, which is very unlike her. She understands how much she's hurt me.

"What I don't get is why you'd agree to work with him in the first place. After everything he did to me."

"It's only a small job. It'll be done in two weeks," she defends.

"You thought I'd never find out."

Nadia looks at the ground. "I'm not even supposed to mention the project. I signed an NDA."

"How could you?"

Nadia opens her mouth only to close it and slowly shake her head. She looks past me and my heart sinks.

"You like him," I say. She once had a crush on Thomas, but that was in high school.

"No. It's nothing like that."

"Then, what is it?"

Her lips press paper-thin flat. She puts away her phone. "I can't discuss the specifics, or why I took on the project. Besides, I doubt anything I say right now will make you understand."

"Try me." My phone pings and I hold a flat palm in front of her face to stop her from talking. "Forget it. I don't want to hear. I can't even . . ." My words fall away. I need a moment to collect myself. I need Ian.

I look at my phone and read through a series of messages from him.

I'm on the red-eye to JFK out of SFO. Flying to Spain tomorrow AM. Here's my flight info.

I'm at the airport waiting to board.

Boarding the plane now.

Are you getting these?

Are you angry?

You're angry.

I'm sorry, Aimee, baby. The timing sucks, but I've got to do this.
I'm sick of it hanging over my head. Can you forgive me?

I'll call when I land. I love you. Sweet dreams, darling.

My heart breaks. I shouldn't have listened to Nadia. I should have
gotten into that elevator. I should have called him. Ian's left and I didn't
even get the chance to say good-bye.

"I can't deal with you right now," I say to her and walk off.

"Where're you going?"

"Spain," I yell over my shoulder. Then I flip her the bird.

CHAPTER 11

AIMEE

It's past midnight when I arrive home with Caty. My mother offered dinner when I told her I hadn't eaten, and while I ate, my father remarked that Ian had swung by on his way to the airport to say good-bye to Caty.

"Daddy's going to see the ponies again," Caty said, scooting into the chair beside me with a bowl of ice cream. It was after nine p.m. and a school night. I tossed my mother an accusatory look. She shrugged a shoulder and returned the carton to the freezer.

"He's going to take some pictures for me." Caty dipped her spoon into her chocolate chip cookie dough.

"I can't wait to see them," I told her, wishing I'd made a point to have Ian show me the ones he'd taken this past summer.

By the time I'd finished eating, Caty had fallen asleep on the couch. I couldn't call Ian as he wasn't due to land for several more hours, and by then I'd be off in la-la land. We won't have a chance to talk until the morning before the second leg of his flight, so I stayed and chatted with my parents about the pros and cons of the café's expansion. They'd spent decades working in the restaurant industry and I valued their advice, even though it wasn't anything I hadn't already heard. What were my priorities?

Family, obviously. But more important, they told me to do what I love, not what I thought I needed to do.

Hmm. Sounds familiar.

Caty stirs in my arms when I close and lock the front door. I let her slide to her feet where she sways from weariness. Hands on her shoulders, I steer her through the house to her room. She changes into her pajamas in autopilot mode and crawls up her bed, flopping on top of the pillows. I kiss her forehead and return to the entryway where I left my purse. I need to charge my phone. I also want to respond to Ian's messages with one of my own.

> Worried about you. Miss you. Call me when you land. OK to wake me.

I collect the receipts Ian had left scattered on the table, drop some coins that hadn't made it into the change dish, and swipe the business card that didn't belong there, adding it to the receipts I'd leave on Ian's desk. The name on the card catches my eye and I almost drop it.

LACY SAUNDERS

Memories scramble all over the place. They bombard me all at once. Lacy finding me at James's funeral to tell me he's alive. Her appearance on my doorstep with the wallet I hadn't been aware I dropped. Her showing up unannounced at the café's opening only to disappear before talking to me. James's painting she'd shipped from Mexico along with the handwritten note that changed everything.

Here's your proof . . . Come to Oaxaca.

I might have flown to Mexico to find James, but it was Ian's arms I landed in.

Ian.

Where did he get this?

Dropping everything but my phone and Lacy's card, I go into the other room and sink onto the leather sectional. Only one name crosses my mind.

James.

I need to talk with your husband. Do you mind if I contact him?

I roll my phone end over end, thinking about yesterday. James had called me on the café's main line. I didn't expect to hear from him again, let alone see him. I didn't want to see him. But his voice carried an edge of desperation I found hard to ignore. He had a few things that needed to be said. Long, overdue, important things I deserved to hear from him. He wanted to meet face-to-face, assuming I was OK with this.

Not really, but call me curious. I met with him, anyway, at a coffee shop in Palo Alto. He was visiting with college friends from his Stanford years—friends who'd thought he was dead, he added with a short laugh—and he was staying at a hotel nearby.

"The coffee shop is neutral territory," James said with a note of vulnerability I'd never heard in him before. It was a place we hadn't been to together. No risk of stirring up old memories.

But stir up they did.

Being in James's presence alone, even from across the café, was enough to slice open the old wound. I stopped just inside the entrance and waited for the familiar pain to engulf me that arose whenever I thought of James. The sensation came, but it felt duller, weaker, and it didn't arise from a longing that things might have turned out differently between us. It never had. The pain clenching my chest and holding on to my breath stemmed from the old hurt over the way we ended. The secrets, the lies, the betrayal. And finally, my forgiveness.

I took a meditative breath and the sensation faded almost as quickly as it had appeared. Unlike when I saw James earlier in the summer, I was determined to remain in control.

I made my way over to him. He stood when I approached, even pulled out my chair. I noticed that when he did so, he kept his distance. He also didn't attempt to hug me before I sat down.

"Can I get you something? I ordered when I got here." He pointed at his coffee when he returned to his seat.

I eyed the murky liquid. "It's not black with no cream."

"No, it's not." One side of his mouth lifted into a half smile. "I now take it with cream and a shot of coconut."

"Kauai's rubbing off on you."

He tapped his chest. "This old dog can learn new tricks."

"Yeah, well, we've all changed."

James frowned slightly. I looked away. I hadn't meant to sound sarcastic. It just came out that way. Inhaling deeply, I took a moment to collect myself. *Stay in control of your emotions, Aimee.*

I wasn't in love with James, but sitting across from him reminded me of what it felt like to be in love with him. It reminded me of the person I used to be with him. Naive, timid, and immature.

We had so much history together. He was my childhood.

But he wasn't my future, and it had taken me months and plenty of counseling to come to terms with my own ineptitude during my relationship with him. I'd been so down on myself.

At my invitation, Ian had attended some of my therapy sessions with me. He'd held my hand and listened attentively as I explained how I didn't want to be that woman again—one with her ears covered and blinders on—while I was in a relationship with him. Ian had held me and fallen more deeply in love with me as I learned to love myself again.

I apologized to James. "What I was trying to say is—"

He held up his hand. "Don't worry about it. I get it." He pointed at his cup. "Can I order you a coffee?"

I regarded the menu on the wall. The selections were bland and ordinary compared with Aimee's Café. "No, thanks. I've had my share today."

"That's right. You've got an unlimited supply at your fingertips." James leaned on his forearms and peered at the contents of his cup. "I never had the chance to tell you, but I'm proud of you." He lifted his gaze to mine. "For opening your own restaurant."

I nodded, absorbing the compliment. James had been the one who'd encouraged me, but at the time, I'd been afraid of venturing out on my own.

"Thank you," I said. "That means a lot to me. Did you notice my logo?"

"I did. That was a rush sketch. I didn't mean—" He abruptly stopped and took a long drink of coffee. He set down his cup, his expression turning sad and regretful. James had been in a hurry to leave for Mexico.

"I can draw you a better logo."

"I like the one I have." I didn't want to change it. The logo with the coffee cup and swirl of steam represented everything I'd been through to get where I was today. From making the decision to go out on my own to opening the additional locations. If I opened them.

But there was something I should change about the Los Gatos location.

"I'm thinking about taking down your paintings. Do you want them?"

He shook his head. "Keep them. They're yours."

"I can't."

His brows lifted. "Can't or won't?"

"Both." I had to do more than tell Ian I'd moved on from James.

He smirked. "Send them to my mother."

"Your mother? She hated your paintings."

"Why do you think I told you to send them to her?"

I laughed, shaking my head. "You're terrible."

"Would you believe she used to be an artist?"

"No way."

"She was. *Is.*"

"She paints?"

James nodded.

"I can't picture that." But his talent had to have come from someone.

"I couldn't either at first." His gaze turned inward, but he didn't elaborate. I knew there was a story somewhere in there, but it wasn't mine to hear. Not today.

"Do you really want me to send them to her?" I asked, double-checking.

"No, I'm kidding. Box them up and ship them COD to me." He took out his phone. "What's your number? I'll text you my address."

I hesitated. Did I want James to have direct access to me? Did I want that with him?

Grow up, Aimee, I silently admonished. I'd block his number should he text me about anything other than shipping his art.

"Let me see your phone." He gave me his device and I added my cell number to my contact. James had the café's number. I gave him back the phone and he immediately sent a text. My phone pinged.

"Give me a heads-up when you ship them." He placed his phone facedown on the table. "You look good. You cut your hair."

I absently touched the wave on the side of my head. "Do you really want to do this? Small talk?"

He shook his head once. "No."

"Why did you ask me here?"

"This isn't easy for me to say." He rubbed the bridge of his nose, then let his arm fall back on the table. "I want to apologize for the way I acted that last year after . . . after . . ."

"After Phil assaulted me?" I supplied in an even tone.

"Yes. That."

I swallowed the knot that formed in my throat and momentarily looked out the window. We were in a crowded shopping mall across the road from the Stanford campus. The high school next door had just let out. A line at the order counter was steadily growing as we talked.

Phil had attacked me moments after James proposed. His way of getting back at James for the Donato family's ousting of Phil from the family business. Stunned, scared, and demoralized, I'd agreed with James's plea not to speak a word of what happened with Phil. According to James, something big was going down at Donato Enterprises that involved Phil and, as I later learned, the DEA.

I thought of last June. "You've apologized, and I've forgiven you."

"I want to explain why I did what I did."

"You don't have to."

"Please. Let me say this," he said, his voice a dry husk.

I didn't owe him anything, but if he wanted closure, the least I could do was give him that.

I nodded slowly.

James cleared his throat behind his fist and steeled himself. "Phil had been using Donato Enterprises as a cover for trade laundering. I didn't know Thomas was working with the DEA, or that the feds were going after Phil's broker, not just Phil. I hadn't been privy to that information," he added, derisively. "I believed if you had filed charges against Phil, he would have run. And if the feds couldn't have Phil, they would have gone after Donato Enterprises. The company would have had to forfeit its assets and most likely fold.

"Had that happened, I wouldn't have the funds to open my gallery, or to help you launch Aimee's Café, which I really wanted to do. I wouldn't have had any money left to provide you the life I wanted to give you. I thought I would have lost everything. I thought I would have lost you."

"James." My heart ached for him and everything he had lost. For in the end, his mistake had cost him everything. He'd lost the life he had. He'd lost me.

James leaned back in his chair and his hands fell into his lap. "I sometimes think you should file charges against me."

"Why would I do that?"

"Because I insisted you pretend it never happened."

I had pretended, for more than two years, until I found James as Carlos and I acknowledged how much I'd been hurt. We'd both been hurt. And James had suffered enough.

"James, no. I won't do that to you. We need to move on. And your sons need you."

I caught the glimmer of moisture in the corners of his eyes. "Yes, they do. Thank you for understanding."

I rested my hand over his and took on a serious expression so that he understood I meant every word. "I'm not going to press charges. I forgive you. Now, forgive yourself. It's OK to go forward."

"I'm trying. But Aimee, about Phil."

My blood ran cold. "I don't want to talk about him."

"Neither do I. But if you want to press charges, I'll help you. Use me as a witness."

I shook my head hard. "I'm not filing charges. I don't want to invite your family back into my life. I don't want anything to do with them."

"Including me."

"James . . ."

He held up both hands. "No, you're right. It's best this way." Then he smiled, the first genuine smile I'd seen on him since he left for Mexico before our wedding. My throat tightened with emotion.

"I met someone. I knew her from when I was Carlos, but I got to know her as me. Her name's Natalya. I'm falling in love with her."

I'd be lying if I said his words didn't hurt. But the happiness I felt on his behalf was stronger. I congratulated him; then we talked about his sons and how Carlos came to be in Mexico. He explained that Thomas had hidden him by having him placed in that country's witness protection program. Then the time came to say good-bye, and in this instance, James did hug me. He told me to take care of myself and I said the same to him. I turned to leave, but then he called my name.

"I need to talk with your husband. Do you mind if I contact him?"

I hadn't given him an answer because the weight of our conversation was starting to hit me. But he obviously had spoken to Ian this afternoon, I think, holding Lacy's card. And Ian hadn't mentioned it.

I'd deal with my husband about that later.

I text James.

> You met with Ian. Where did you get Lacy's card?

It's late, almost twelve thirty. I have no idea if he's back in Hawaii or still in California. I don't care. I send the text, not expecting a response until morning. I toss the phone aside and start to rise when it pings.

> He didn't tell you?

No, he didn't. But I'm not going to tell James that.

Another text pings.

> Lacy gave it to me.

He met Lacy? My thumbs tap-dance across the keyboard.

> When? Where? What did she want?

> Last month. She found me on a beach in Kauai.

My body feels freezer-box cold. I shiver. OK, that's creepy.

She said I knew someone who'd need her card. That he'd been looking for her. I didn't tell you because I didn't want to make you more uncomfortable than our conversation yesterday had.

I have no idea how James deduced Lacy wanted him to pass along her card to Ian, but here we are. Lacy's back and there's a good chance she has information about Sarah, which explains Ian's renewed interest in finding his mother.

Dammit, Ian, why didn't you tell me?

Another text comes through.

Aimee?

Yes?

Good night.

I let him have the last word. Despite the hour, I call Lacy's number. It rings once before a recording answers. "The number you have reached—"

I end the call, not at all surprised. Ian wouldn't have reached her either. The number on the card is more than a month old. We'll never learn what she knows about Sarah or how she can help Ian find his mom.

But I do know of one person who might be able to. Lord, help me.

CHAPTER 12

IAN, AGE ELEVEN

Ian might have eaten cereal for dinner, but he hadn't spent the entire night alone. His mom returned around two in the morning. He knew the time because he'd been lying awake, ever watchful of the numbers on his digital clock until he heard the crunch of gravel. Headlights brightened his room as the station wagon came to a stop in front of the detached garage. The engine cut and his room returned to black. Keys rattled and the front door opened. A few seconds later the bottom step on the stairs creaked and that was it. He heard nothing further. Ian loosened his grip on the sheets he'd been clutching. Lungs filled to the max expelled.

Sarah had come home, not Jackie.

His mom was considerate. She took off her shoes and walked quietly through the house while others slept. Jackie couldn't care less. She'd bang doors and slam cabinets. Clomp like a horse up the stairs while singing John Cougar Mellencamp's "Jack & Diane" at the top of her lungs. She sang horribly. A screechy chicken.

Ian curled onto his side, facing the wall. Clothing rustled just outside his room. Skin tightened across his back. He could feel his mom watching him, checking to make sure he was there. Jackie would have kept walking, past his door and straight to his parents' room. She'd flop on the bed, facedown in a starfish position, an arm and a leg dangling over the edge. She wouldn't dare let his dad share the bed if he happened to be home. Ian's dad slept on the beat-up leather couch in his office when Jackie was around.

Ian feigned sleep. While relieved his mom had come home, he was still shaken. Jackie had wanted his dad's gun. Ian had called his dad as soon as Jackie bailed. His dad ordered him to leave the house. But what if his mom returned and didn't find him there? Ian didn't want to worry her, so he stayed. His dad would be angry and Ian expected he'd be grounded this weekend. He'd called Marshall earlier and canceled their movie plans. He'd catch *Jurassic Park* next week.

Ian heard his mom leave. His body grew heavy and he started to drift. He was exhausted. He had spent most of the day and a better part of the night cleaning the mess Jackie had made. Sarah would be sad if she saw the state of her room and Ian didn't want her to feel that way. She'd spend the rest of the day in bed. She'd miss her embroidery deadlines and lose clients. If she lost business, his dad would have to take on more assignments. He'd be away more often than he was already, and Ian was tired of doing everything alone. He was always alone.

"Ian," his mom called from her room late the next morning. "Would you come help me?"

Ian tossed aside his dad's *Popular Photography* magazine and stared at the ceiling above his bed. His heart raced like a jackrabbit in his chest. Yesterday had been rough.

"Ian, come here. I need help."

He swallowed the lump in his throat and swung his legs over the side. Pushing off the bed, he walked slowly down the hallway.

"Ian," his mom said with more impatience.

He stopped in the doorway and gripped the jamb. His parents' room smelled like a department store. Jackie had shattered a perfume bottle and soaked the braided area rug during her rabid search for the car keys and cash yesterday. He had picked up the glass but couldn't get out the smell.

His mom sat at the vanity table, her back to him and dress partially zipped. She capped a pen and folded a slip of paper, which she put in the vanity's top middle drawer.

"What do you want?" Ian asked in a reluctant tone.

She looked over her shoulder and smiled a little. "There you are. My hair is stuck." She gestured at the back zipper.

Ian came into the room and stood behind his mom. Cosmetics, makeup brushes, and hairpins cluttered the tabletop. Another mess Jackie had left. He'd forgotten to straighten it up, he'd been so tired.

His mom draped her long sandy-brown hair over a shoulder and pointed at the snarl clutched in the zipper. "Can you free my hair?"

He glanced at his mom in the mirror and did his best to differentiate her features from Jackie's. Sarah smiled more. Jackie scowled. His gaze met his mom's. Her mouth curved into a crescent moon. She whispered a thank-you. He nodded and started working the tangled hair from the zipper's teeth.

"Your fingers are cold," she said with a low laugh and shivered.

"Sorry." He frowned. The zipper wouldn't budge so he broke the strands, one by one, trying not to let it bother him. He liked his mother's hair, a lighter shade of his. She brushed it every night before bed until it shone. Jackie liked to tease the hair, as she once explained to him when he found the nerve to ask. It gave it lift. *Volume.* Ian recalled the word Jackie had used. Jackie hated Sarah's hair. She called it limp and boring. Poor-girl hair.

Outside the open window, he heard his dad talking to Mr. Lansbury about his land lease and the season's crop. Production was low and Mr. Lansbury needed an extra two weeks to make his payment. Ian's dad wasn't pleased.

Ian felt his mom watching him.

"Did I do that to you?" she whispered in a way that told him she already knew the answer.

Ian looked in the mirror. The shiner on his cheekbone from when Jackie knocked the camera from his grasp bloomed red, angrier than it had been yesterday.

"It wasn't you," Ian replied. His eyes dipped to the faint oval shadows on her wrist. He gently touched one.

She jerked her arm away. "They'll fade," she murmured, organizing her cosmetics. Nervous, busy work. She crumpled a piece of paper, dropping it into the waste can where it landed beside the pills her psychiatrist had prescribed. Ian reached for the small plastic container.

"Leave them," his mother said. "They make my stomach upset."

"But won't they help?"

His mom shook her head.

Ian slowly straightened, wishing there was medication that would make Jackie go away, and went back to work on the zipper.

"What happened yesterday?" Sarah asked.

He knew his mother didn't like hearing the answers, but she forced herself to ask the questions. And Ian would always tell her, no matter how uncomfortable the events had made him.

"Jackie knocked the camera from my hands."

"Looks to me like I . . . *she* . . . missed."

Ian popped up a shoulder. He struggled with the zipper.

"Ian," his mom said after a moment, "I'm sorry."

"It's not your fault. It's all right."

"No, it's not." She shook her head, pulling against the imprisoned hair.

"Don't move." Ian finally freed the snarl and unjammed the zipper. He asked for the comb and as he worked out the tangle, his mom silently cried. Tears glistened on her cheek like snail trails on concrete. Seeing them made the back of Ian's eyes burn. He kept his focus on his mom's hair so he wouldn't have to see her in the mirror. His hand followed the comb down the length of her back with each stroke until her hair glistened.

Ian returned the comb. "All done."

She tugged free a tissue. She wiped her eyes and blew her nose. "Did you photograph Jackie?"

Ian rolled his lips inward and nodded.

"Ian," she bemoaned, "that's why she hurt you. I've told you, she's dangerous. Why do you continue to put yourself in harm's way?"

He picked up his mom's blush compact. He opened and closed the case before returning it.

"Very well," she said, resigned. She dropped a brow pencil into a glass jar of lip liners and mascara tubes. "Have you developed the photos yet?"

Ian nodded.

She swiveled in her chair and smoothed the skirt over her lap. "Show me."

She wasn't going to like them. She never liked them.

Ian retrieved from his room the photos he'd developed in his dad's darkroom yesterday after Jackie left. He gave them to his mom.

She closed her eyes and took a deep breath. Then she dipped her chin and studied the top image, Jackie ransacking the master bedroom. Ian's mom had learned to keep her ID, credit cards, and ATM cards hidden. Jackie had drained their bank account once before.

"She's looking for cash again," she surmised.

"Yes, and . . ." Ian gripped his shoulder and shifted feet.

She lifted her head. "And what?"

He tugged the hem of his shirt.

"Ian. Tell me."

"She wanted . . . she wanted a gun."

Her face paled. "Jesus." The photos trembled in her hands. She flipped to the next picture, a close-up of Jackie's face and her screeching at him, *I'll strangle you with the camera strap!*

She flipped through the next two. Jackie getting into the car and then driving away.

"I wish I got more pictures."

"I'm glad you didn't." She wiped her nose. "I would give anything to keep you safe from me," she murmured.

"I am safe from you. It's Jackie. She's the mean one, not you, Mom."

"I know, darling." She cupped Ian's cheek. "What did I do to deserve you? You're too good for me."

"I love you." He tugged his shirt some more, stretching the fabric. "I wish Dad was home more often." He always knew what to do when Jackie came out. What he didn't know was how often Jackie made an appearance, and lately those appearances had become more frequent.

Ian once heard his dad suggest to his mom that they check her in to a hospital, should her transitions become more violent. But Ian didn't want to lose her, and he believed his mom didn't want to leave either because she didn't like his dad's idea about the hospital. Besides, Ian would be alone since Stu couldn't stop working. So Ian took it upon himself to care for his mom. It wasn't as though his dad was doing a great job at it, anyhow.

His mom returned the photos to him. "Put those with the others in your special place." A place he'd sworn never to show her or Jackie. Because one day those pictures might come in handy.

CHAPTER 13

IAN

I was twenty-two and had just graduated with a BA in photojournalism when my mom was released from the Florence McClure Women's Correctional Center in Las Vegas, Nevada. She'd served her term without incident. She was a free woman. She immediately went off the grid.

Hoping to see my mom for the first time in nine years before my parents drove back to Idaho, and before I knew she'd disappeared, I met up with my dad at his hotel room at the Mirage in Vegas, where he told me she was gone.

"I waited for over an hour for her to show up. I'd been hoping to see her in the floral print dress and blue leather flats I'd picked out and shipped to her," he explained in a rough and raw voice. "They told me to pick her up at two. Two p.m., I swear to God that's what they told me. But no." He dragged out the word, his face hardening. "She'd left at one. She was gone when I got there."

Panicked, he peppered the security officer with questions. Had she taken a cab? Did she walk? Did she leave with someone else, another man? Please don't tell him she'd fallen for someone else.

She hadn't, but the officer suggested that my dad go to the bus terminal. It wasn't uncommon for an officer to drop off a newly released inmate if the inmate requested a means of transportation. He might get lucky and find her there if she hadn't yet left for wherever she intended to go.

My dad hadn't been lucky. And, in my opinion, he hadn't looked thoroughly enough. Call the cab companies. Check the airports. Buzz every hotel reservation line in the city. "Do something!" I had yelled at him. She could have gone anywhere. She could be anywhere.

"Your mother's message is crystal clear. She doesn't want to be with us," my dad said into his glass of watered-down whiskey, the single ice cube long melted. He tipped back his head and swallowed a mouthful.

"That's it, then?" I argued in utter disbelief. "You're giving up?" Not just on looking for her. He was giving up on *her*.

I wasn't ready to do that.

"I'm giving her what she wants!" My dad slammed his hand down on the tabletop. The glass rattled. Cigarette butts jumped in the dirty ashtray. A ghostly line of smoke rose from the end of his burning cigarette, hovering between us like a wraith in the night. He reached for the cigarette and took a long, deep draw.

"I have done nothing but give her what she wants," he said on the exhale. Smoke circled his head. It filled the room. "And what she wants is not us."

"Bullshit." I swatted his whiskey glass. It bounced off the wall, leaving a dent. Whiskey sprayed the TV and bureau, soiled the carpet. The alcohol's peaty smell of disinfectant and sharp ink expanded around us.

"If you're not going to look for her, then I will. I'll find her."

My dad held my gaze for several ticks of my watch. He dipped his chin and stared unfocused at the table where he sat. He tapped off the ash. "She doesn't love you. I wouldn't waste my time on her."

I would for the single reason she was my mother. I needed to know she was all right. That she was healthy and mentally stable. Was that even possible?

My dad raked a hand through his hair, greasy from the natural oils on his skin. He tilted up his face to look at me with eyes red-rimmed from weariness and I would imagine his own failure as a husband. Gray stubble peppered his jaw. "You're setting yourself up to get hurt, Ian."

"That's my problem." I left the room. Other than when I called to let him know I was getting married, it was the last time I spoke with him.

Six months after Vegas, I'd worked enough freelance jobs to hire Harry Sykes, a private investigator I found in the Las Vegas yellow pages. I was moving to France in a month and wanted to find my mom before I left. I hadn't had any luck on my own. Harry volleyed questions about Sarah's personal information and background, her known acquaintances, and places of residence. I returned each with a definitive answer. I'd once known her best. We then discussed the events leading up to her arrest and sentencing.

"Court transcripts are public record. Have you read hers?" Harry asked.

"No," I admitted. I'd only been fourteen at the time of her trial. Other than when I testified, my dad hadn't allowed me to attend.

"I'll request to look at them. There might be something in there that pinpoints where she could have gone. You should read them, too." He pointed his dull no. 2 pencil at me across his 1970s-era metal office desk. "She's your mother. Something in there might ring a bell." He tapped the pencil on his head. "It might help me find her for you."

I followed up on his suggestion, read the transcript, and discovered a whole lot of something. I'd contributed to the cause of her illness. I'd exacerbated her condition. No wonder she didn't love me.

Harry Sykes left a message several weeks later. He'd located Sarah Collins. I never returned his call, or the others that followed. I figured one day I'd make the effort to go to her. I owe her the apology of my life. I only needed to find the courage to do so and that time is now. I made a promise to my wife. I'd confront my issues about my past so that we could move forward together. I would fix my relationship with my mom.

I land in New York at dawn and scope out a relatively quiet corner away from the morning rush. It has a lounge chair, an outlet, and a USB port. These and a Venti-size coffee are all I need as I settle in for the three-hour layover.

I launch my laptop, charge my dead phone, and guzzle the coffee. Fingers poised over the keyboard, I catch my breath and stop to think. *What have I done?* The past twenty-four hours sink in like photo paper absorbing printer ink and the picture isn't pretty. I left Aimee high and dry. She's consumed with work and parenting our daughter and I packed and left.

Smooth move, Collins.

Granted, I planned to leave next week anyhow. But my spontaneous rush to split town earlier has left her with additional days of adjusting her work schedule and planning Caty's care since I'm not there to watch her in the afternoons. To make matters worse, I don't know how long I'll be gone. I have five days to cover the assignment before I have to be in Idaho. And once I get there? I could be stuck there for twenty-four hours or a couple of weeks. I can't help but compare myself to my dad.

He repeatedly left my mom. A last-minute press conference would yank him out of town. A scandal would arise about some multimillion-dollar contract player tampering with equipment. A star rookie safety would be arrested for soliciting a hooker. My dad would leave us at a moment's notice so he wouldn't miss any candid photo opportunities he could sell to the news outlets. We needed the money, he'd say as an excuse, leaving me to wonder if that was the only reason he left. He never admitted outright, but I think as much as he loved my mom and wanted to keep her safe, he was also scared of her. He knew how to handle her shifts, by giving her space and letting her be, but I was sure her alters made him uncomfortable. Their personalities and mannerisms were entirely different from the woman he married.

It was during my teen years that my relationship with my dad didn't become problematic. It became the problem. I didn't care where he was or when he'd be home. I picked fights, neglected homework, and became a downright belligerent pain in the ass. By the end of sophomore year, I had enough tardy and detention slips to cover my bedroom walls the way bars wallpaper theirs with paper bills. Staying in trouble kept my mind off the very public fact that my mother was in prison and that I was in therapy because of her.

PTSD. That was my psych's diagnosis. To the outside world, living with a mother diagnosed with dissociative identity disorder and an absent father was hell. I always saw it as a warped version of purgatory. I'd pay my dues and one day I'd receive my get-out-of-jail-free card. When that happened, I'd leave Idaho and never look back.

It wasn't until midway through my junior year and after a couple of suspensions with the threat of expulsion—the black cloud looming over my immediate future—that I got my act together. Mrs. Killion, Marshall's mom, took me under her wing when my dad asked her to watch over me while he was on contract and traveling with his sports teams. Good thing Mrs. K stepped in when she did, else college would have been out of the picture for one aspiring photographer. She ordered me to sit at her kitchen table until I finished my homework. She then insisted I remain for dinner. It was like this five days a week.

Sure, I could have left at any time. Go home and drink my dad's beer and play video games. It wasn't like Mrs. K tied me to the chair and held a gun to my head. I wanted to be there. For the first time since my mom had left, someone cared.

Therapy helped me process the years I lived with Mom. But it was Mrs. K, God rest her soul, who restored my confidence in myself.

My phone vibrates, charged enough to power on. Notifications blow up my screen. I open the last message from Aimee and read through the ones she sent during my flight. She isn't mad about my leaving. I sag into the deep curve of the chair back, thankful she hasn't banished me to the old sofa in the garage. Damn, I love that woman.

It's predawn in California. She's still asleep and Caty's most likely with her, sprawled on my side of the bed where I've known her to sleep when I'm out of town on extended trips. I text Aimee rather than calling like she asked, else I'll wake them both. I let her know that I've safely landed. We'll have plenty of time to talk later. Next, I e-mail Al Foster asking about the assigned writer and when he's expected to arrive.

I power through the rest of my e-mails, then launch my browser, ready to rock 'n' roll with the hunt, my determination to locate my mom renewed. My hands hover over the keyboard, fingers twitch, and I do . . .

Nothing.

Nada. Zero. Zilch.

Once again, I croak.

I slam closed my laptop.

Outside the large window beside me, planes take off and land. Baggage trams loop the tarmac like Disney World's PeopleMover. Inside, over the speakers, flights are announced and passengers are called to the gates.

During high school, I despised my mom for the embarrassment she caused me. While my friends' mothers cheered them on at our track meets and football games, my mother sat in prison.

Anger and resentment fueled my hate. But in college, I fell for a woman who reminded me in appearance and temperament of the Sarah side of my mother.

Eventually, my rage reduced to a simmer and resentment moved aside, making room for regret. I should have tried harder to understand her illness. I should have insisted more often and despite my mom's objections that my dad force her to get the help we all knew she needed. My therapist often reassured me that what happened with my mom was not my fault. Yeah, well, she didn't read the court transcript from her trial.

Come on, Collins. Man up.

There's a reason I left early for Spain. I might as well make use of my time while waiting for my next flight.

I scratch at the scruff on the underside of my jaw and transfer the laptop perched on my knees to the low table at my feet. I Google for the search engine Erik told me about, the one programmed to search only for people. Erik's ex-girlfriend had moved out of state and in with a man she'd met on a business flight to New York. He was about to go into obsessed-ex-boyfriend stalker mode until I knocked some sense into him, a literal thwack on the back of his head. I plug *Sarah Collins* into the search field and select "entire USA" from the drop-down menu. I hit Enter and wait. A list of more than twenty-five Sarahs displays. Way too many. I edit my search parameters to include Sarah's middle name: Elizabeth. The engine drops three Sarah Elizabeth Collinses residing in the United States on my screen. One in Virginia, another in Utah. The third? She's in Las Vegas, Nevada.

Viva Las Vegas.

That's her. It's got to be.

And it kills me she never traveled that far.

A knot forms inside my stomach, hard and sour at the base of my sternum. Has she been living in Vegas the entire time? Lower cost of living. No state taxes. Plenty of questionable employment opportunities for a woman to fall into with a record and mental illness. It makes sense, assuming that's her.

Doubt creeps in, a burglar lurking along the recesses of my mind, thieving what inkling of hope I have left. It could be another Sarah Elizabeth Collins, for all I know. My mother could be anywhere, phone and address unlisted.

But this Sarah has a number.

I reach for my phone. My hand shakes so badly I almost drop it. I tap out the number and the phone rings once, twice. On the third ring, a recording picks up. The greeting is garbled, a woman's voice, and I can't tell if it's my mother's. I haven't heard her voice since I was fourteen and memories aren't always honest.

I'm about to leave a message—*Is this you?*—when I remember what I'd committed to before I left for Spain.

I disconnect the call. I've waited half a lifetime of days. I can wait five more.

It's late in the evening when I arrive at the inn, a converted farmhouse made from stonework. A yellow Lab runs over to me as I pop the trunk and remove my bags. He barks a greeting, his tail thumping the rental car's bumper. He nudges at my legs and sniffs my hand.

"Hey, boy." I scratch under his chin. He follows me to the entrance until he catches a whiff of a chicken clucking in the grass. He lets out a loud bark. Valet responsibilities forgotten, he chases the hen around the building.

Set among a picturesque countryside in Galicia, a region in north-western Spain, I notice right away the inn, La casa de campo, is an ideal vacation spot for honeymooners. A young couple lounges on the front patio admiring the dusky sky darkening above forests of pine and eucalyptus. While sampling cheeses and drinking white wine, they wave at me. *"Buenas noches,"* they greet in unison.

"Evening," I reply.

The man briefly smiles and turns back to his wife. He leans toward her and nuzzles her neck. She giggles, then moans softly, languidly, tilting her head aside to give him more room. His eyes lift to mine over her shoulder when he notices I'm still standing there, watching them.

Shaking my head, I sling a bag over my shoulder and enter the front office, longing for my own wife.

In the dining room off to the side, guests eat dinner. Scents of roasted chicken and warmed bread make me think of home and Aimee. I miss her. We played phone tag during my layover, and other than texting her when I landed in Santiago de Compostela, at a small airport an hour from here, I haven't spoken with her since I'd left her at the hospital. I owed her a call and an explanation. It wasn't solely her closure with James that prompted my own need for closure.

A fire blazes in the lobby lounge and a woman seated with her back to the room chats on her cell in French. I make my way to the registration counter and drop my bags at my feet. I'm hungry and exhausted. I want to check in, order in, and crash.

A short man with round wire-rim glasses smiles from behind the counter. He introduces himself as Oliver Perez, the owner. "*Buenas noches*. Do you have a reservation?"

"*Sí*. Ian Collins."

Oliver brings up my information on his computer. "There you are. You're with us for three nights." He takes my credit card and dives into a spiel about how he and his wife of thirty years own the inn and that dinner is now being served in the dining room. An oven-baked chicken roasted in Spanish sherry and red wine vinegar. "The chicken was raised here on the property."

"And butchered by your dog?"

Oliver's eyes go wide behind his glasses. "Excuse me?"

"The yellow Lab out front I saw chasing the chicken."

He presses his lips into a flat line and mumbles something in Spanish. "He's not supposed to be chasing the chickens," he says, switching back to English.

My mouth twitches. "Sorry. Bad joke." Awful joke. God, I'm tired. I rake back my hair. "You were saying?"

He slaps my card on the counter. "We don't have room service. I suggest you eat now if you're hungry and before we run out of food." He gestures toward the dining room. "My dog won't slaughter any more chickens until tomorrow."

"What?" I look up from where I was slipping my credit card back into my wallet. Oliver holds my gaze, his expression serious. Then he grins, showing me a full set of cigarette-stained teeth.

I wag a finger at him. "Touché, Oliver."

He gives me a real key—no plastic cards at this place. "I trust you'll find your room comfortable with all the necessities."

Except a complimentary fridge. *"Gracias."* I pocket the key and bend to pick up my bags.

"Ian. Collins."

My name comes from behind me, spoken as two distinct sentences. That voice.

An onslaught of memories from my late teens and early twenties download. Corona-soaked spring breaks in Ensenada. Adrenaline-fueled winter weekends shredding snow-packed Colorado mountainsides. Sleep-deprived finals weeks punctuated with heated interludes among the book stacks at the university library. Long coffee-filled afternoons working side by side at a sidewalk café in the South of France. Her cold bed and chilled shoulder when she left. She'd had her fun. She'd had her fill of me.

Everything in me tenses as I straighten to my full height, bags left on the floor. I don't have to turn around to know who's behind me, but turn around I do. The woman yammering on the phone a moment ago stands before me, one arm crossed as she taps her phone against her chin. Her eyes hold mine, looking left and right as if she can't believe she's seeing me either. With her long dusty-blonde hair, hollowed-out cheeks, almond eyes, and rail-thin physique, she hasn't changed in thirteen years yet looks older all the same. A shot of disgust dives straight into my gut. Clear as a high-resolution image, I plainly see what I denied back then, what she'd thrown in my face. She has the look of my mother.

I'm speechless even though I shouldn't be surprised she's here. It was bound to happen at some point. We've been running in the same circles since my work has taken a more human, journalistic approach.

She cocks her head. "It's good to see you."

Too bad I can't say the same about her.

At least now I don't have to follow up with Al Foster. One less call to make tonight, as it's evident *National Geographic* scrambled with my request for the schedule change and got their writer here on time.

I take a breath and upload my patience. I'll need it over the next few days because I know how she works. I can already anticipate the angle she'll take on this story, and it won't be favorable. I've got three days to convince her otherwise if I want to attach my name to this feature.

I force a smile. "Hi, Reese."

CHAPTER 14

IAN

The Rapa das bestas happens annually the first weekend of July. During my visit earlier this summer, I had just been granted access to the curro floor packed with wild Galician horses when I first saw her. This was my second of three ten-minute slots that allow a photographer who signed a disclaimer into the center of the Rapa's commotion. I was stressed, worried, and exhausted, my head on Aimee, a long distance from the mind-set I should have been in while surrounded by thousands of pounds of horseflesh.

I'd been up since dawn trying not to read into—but doing so anyhow—my call with Aimee the previous night, along with the several conversations we'd had since I arrived in Spain nine days prior. She said she was fine whenever I asked, but her voice implied that she was anything but OK. We'd been married long enough. I knew when my wife was out of sorts. She couldn't hide the tears in her voice. I offered to come home. She insisted I stay. I'd been talking about the Rapa for years. I'd been planning this excursion for months. We'd talk when I got home. She disconnected the call and I tossed and turned through the night only to drag myself to mass the following morning with the villagers, many of them knights, local men on horseback who'd be rounding up the horses, and aloitadores, the horse handlers, who'd been up most of the night themselves, celebrating. The church smelled of incense and booze, a nauseating combination that left me feeling faint. They prayed to San Lorenzo that those participating in the Rapa survived injury-free. I should have taken that as my warning.

After the service, I hiked with the villagers and tourists into the hills, following the paths the knights had taken to round up the herds. What surprised me the most about the event was how calmly and methodically the entire process unfolded. It wasn't rowdy. The horses weren't agitated. They obediently moved down the hill and into the village where they were penned in a large, open field until their time to be herded into the curro.

The second surprise was not how many horses they crammed into the small arena, which was about two hundred at a time, but why. Without room to move, the risk of injury to the horses drastically diminished. That wasn't the case with the aloitadores. They suffered broken noses, toes, and cracked ribs from wrestling the beasts to stillness. One by one they worked in teams of three to trim manes and tails, deworm, and inject a microchip should the horse not have one. They sacrificed their own safety for their love of the beasts that roamed the green hills surrounding Sabucedo. It's how they managed the herd, how they kept them healthy and wild. An ancient ritual that has evolved with the times and is nothing short of spectacular. I couldn't believe I stood in the middle of it all.

The packed curro smelled of manure and horse sweat. Barbecue smoke thick with the scent of burning meat filled the arena. I snapped picture after picture, following the aloitadores around the floor. I kept one eye on them and the other on the horses near me, ready to jump out of the way should they rear up or kick. The back of my neck dripped with sweat from the blistering sun and my clammy hands rapidly worked the controls on my camera. While the horses were relatively calm, their panic was all too evident in their eyes. And it was getting to me. Flashes of my mom's own panic that I'd captured in my photos kept clouding my vision.

Chest tight, I took a momentary breather, looking away so as not to get further sucked into the emotional turmoil my lens captured shot after shot. I knew all too well the types of shadows that lurked in a subject's eyes and shooting the Rapa was affecting me in a way I hadn't anticipated, reminding me of why I'd initially taken the path of landscape photography.

I wiped the sweat from my brow, lifted my gaze to the stands, and saw my mom. Dizziness washed over me and time stalled. She turned her face toward me, unseeing, and the anguish tightening her expression, the tears that drenched her cheeks, smacked me hard in the chest. I stumbled back only to realize it wasn't my mom, but Reese. What was she doing there?

I lifted my camera, zoomed in, pressed the shutter button, and an aloitador shouted in my face. *"¡Cuidado!"*

A stallion reared up beside me, his flank knocking my shoulder hard. I fell back into another horse, my camera swinging around my neck. Regaining my balance, my heart pounding wildly, I looked back up into the stands. Reese was gone.

Later, in my hotel room as I iced my shoulder, I reasoned she'd never been there in the first place. That I'd imagined her because I'd been caught up in the energy of the arena and my mom had been on my mind. The image was too blurry on the camera's viewer screen to confirm if the woman was, in fact, Reese.

Guess I hadn't imagined her, after all.

My eyes narrow on Reese. She smiles. "How've you been, Ian?"

"Why are you here?"

Her gaze shifts away and returns. "Same reason as you. *National Geographic* sent me."

"You don't like covering wildlife."

"I'd hardly call semiferal horses wildlife. They aren't lions, tigers, or bears."

"Oh my," I sarcastically add.

She mocks a laugh. "You're funny. I don't like animals penned. Surely you remember."

"That's right. You let the cat I adopted for you go free. Same day, while I was at work so I couldn't talk you out of it, as you told me."

"I was allergic."

"I didn't know."

"You didn't ask," she huffed.

"It got hit by a car."

"That was an accident. I'd never had a cat. I didn't know he'd run straight for the road. You know how bad I felt." Remorse flashes across her face.

"It was going to be euthanized. I was trying to save it."

"Well, you should have asked me before you brought it home. Not everyone needs saving. Or fixing," she adds.

"What's that supposed to mean?"

"Are we really doing this?" She spins her index finger in the air. Around and around we'd always go, when we stopped, we'd never know.

"No, we're not."

Not this time. I could point out she should have asked me to return the cat to the shelter or find him another home, but that's an old ride of an argument, and it's not a vehicle I'm getting back on.

I squint at my phone. Still no e-mail from Al. "I haven't heard from my editor yet that we've been assigned to work together."

"What? You won't talk to me about the story until then?"

I slip the phone back into my pocket. "Aren't you supposed to be in Yosemite?"

She looks taken aback. "How do you know about that?"

"Mutual acquaintance." She stares at me, waiting for me to share who, and I resolve to act more pleasant, to be more amicable. We're stuck with each other for the next few days. I might as well do my part to not make it a living hell. "Erik Ridley. He's a friend of mine. Good guy. Go easy on him." The corner of my mouth lifts.

"I'm not that much of a bitch in the field." Her tone is teasing. "I've heard great things about his work. That assignment's been pushed back two weeks so I can do this one with you."

Something about the way she said that has me pausing as I pick up my bags. I don't know what to make of it and I decide not to read into it. I'm too exhausted.

"Have dinner with me. We have a lot of catching up to do."

I shoulder my camera bag. "I need to shower and call my editor." And my wife.

"You heard Oliver. There's no room service. The only dinner around is in the dining room. And since I remember that you research your photo assignments until your eyes bleed, I bet you already know there isn't another restaurant for miles. I feel like we got off on the wrong foot. Please"—she presses her hands together as though in prayer—"let's have a nice meal, catch up, and hash out our plan of attack for the next few days. I'll be on my best behavior."

She smiles, brilliantly big, and I feel the punch of it in my gut. At one time that smile got her anything from me. French perfume, a beach cruiser bike she rode everywhere. Deliriously long, sweaty nights of incredible sex. A ginger cat. But not anymore. Right now that grin makes my stomach cramp. Or maybe I'm just hungry.

I glance at my watch. "Get us a table. I'll meet you in twenty."

I leave through the front entrance and walk across the lawn. Rooms are scattered about the property in two-story cottages, each housing four suites. My room is on the ground floor with a patio facing the forest. It's decorated in drab colors and the linens appear worn and tired, but the bed is comfortable. For the next few days that's all I need.

I sit on the edge of the bed and call Aimee, unlacing my sneakers while the phone rings. Her voice mail answers, and trying not to feel disappointed I'm not talking with her directly, I leave a message. I'm at the inn. I miss her. *God, I miss you, baby.* More than I can remember feeling on my other trips. It's probably because of the way I left. I tell her I love her and ask her to call when she's free.

I strip, shower, and shave, then check my phone. That blasted e-mail from Al finally arrived. He apologized for the delay. He'd been waiting to hear back from the features editor. Reese Thorne has been assigned. She was on assignment in London and should be able to join me in Spain immediately. Al included links to her three most recently published articles. One of them appeared in last month's *National Geographic Traveler,* a piece about the world's best hikes for the regular person.

After dressing quickly in jeans and a navy-blue henley, I meet Reese in the dining room. She's ordered a bottle of wine and appetizers, a plate of local cheeses and meats. A waitress appears as I sit and starts pouring me a glass. I hold up my hand to stop her. With the room's low lighting, the candlelit table, and the googly-eyed couple at the table next to us, sharing a bottle with my ex doesn't sit right.

"I'll have a beer, Alex," I say, spotting her name tag. I crane my neck to look at what's on tap at the bar. "A San Miguel."

"*Sí, señor.*"

Reese points at her glass for Alex to top off her wine. Alex complies, launching into her pitch about dinner. They have no menu, serving only what the chef elects to cook. Tonight is *caldo gallego,* a Galician bean and vegetable soup, and oven-roasted chicken. She'll get my beer and give us time to finish up the appetizer before she brings out the soup.

Reese waves her fingers at me when Alex leaves. "Give it up. How do you know Erik?"

"We met several years back at a conference. He's trying his hand at landscape photography while giving me tips in photojournalism. We've been mentoring each other."

Alex arrives with my beer. I thank her and take a deep drink.

Reese sips her wine, watching me over the glass rim. "I have to admit, when you mentioned Yosemite, I thought you'd been keeping tabs on me."

"Your name has come up a time or two over the years." But I never went out of my way to look her up. I usually heard about her work from another photographer or when I came across her byline in a magazine. Otherwise, I had no idea what she's been up to personally.

"I've been following you. I mean, your career."

This is surprising considering the way she left. No warning, no explanation, no let's try working on us. I'd come home early from an assignment in the Loire Valley. A winery wanted professional photographs of their vineyard for their marketing campaign. I arrived at our flat to find her friend Braden waiting outside in his convertible Fiat. "Sorry, man," he said when I asked why he was there.

"For what?"

Braden held up his hands. "Go talk to Reese."

I craned my neck, looking at our windows two floors above. The panes were open to let in the evening breeze. A shadow passed behind the gauze curtain.

Reese.

I took the stairs to our flat two at a time with my heart racing and stopped in the doorway of our shoe box–size bedroom. "What are you doing?"

Her back to me, Reese shrieked, spinning around. The pile of clothes she held flew from her arms. I'd spooked her.

She pressed a hand to her chest and gasped. "Ian, what are you doing here?"

I saw the open suitcases on the bed behind her. She followed my gaze. "I wanted to be gone before you came home."

My bags dropped on the floor with a loud thump. "Gone? Where?"

"I haven't figured that out yet. I'll stay with Braden for a while. You can send my stuff there in case I forgot something."

I moved into the room, thoughts jumbling in my head until they lined up and the picture cleared. She wasn't leaving for a weekend get-away, or an assignment out of town. She was leaving me.

I gripped the wrought-iron bedpost. We'd found the bed frame in a secondhand store. Reese immediately fell in love with the scrolled design. We purchased it on the spot.

All the hours we spent cleaning the iron of rust and dirt. All the hours we spent entwined on the mattress. Those hours meant nothing without Reese lying beside me. Those hours meant nothing without her here.

"Why?" I rasped.

"I can't be with you anymore," she said, her voice shaking.

"I love you."

"I don't. Not anymore."

I reached for her and she dodged my hand, going to the other side of the bed. "You don't just fall out of love, Reese. What happened? Where did I go wrong?"

"You . . ."

"I what?"

She shook her head. "Never mind. I need space. That's all."

She needed space. My grip tightened on the footboard, my knuckles white. I swallowed, fighting the painful memories those words induced. "For how long?"

She looked down at the bed. "Permanently." She zipped her bag.

For the longest time, I hadn't forgotten that sound, the way the zipper pierced my ears. A sound of finality. Nor did I forget the silence in our flat after she closed the door behind her, or how lonely I'd felt.

136

That feeling of being unloved and unwanted? I'd been around that block before and it didn't hurt any less.

"Your work is phenomenal." Reese's voice breaks through the play-back of memories. "I can't tell you how pleased I was to hear we'd be collaborating. After all these years."

Something about what she said earlier in the lobby has me frowning. I rest my forearms on the table. "How did you get this assignment?"

Alex brings over our soup. I lean back, out of her way.

"Smells delicious." Reese grabs her spoon. "The assignment came down to me and another writer, Martin Nieves. He's a seasoned contributor to the magazine."

I nod my thanks to Alex and pick up my own spoon. "I've heard of him," I say to Reese. "I only know of one article you published with *National Geographic*. Why did they select you?"

Her spoon hovers above her bowl. "You don't think I'm qualified."

"I didn't say that. You're more than qualified. Al sent me links to a couple of your articles, including a recent one on hiking. I read them while I was back in my room."

"You *just* read them?"

I blink, frowning. "Yeah, is that a problem?"

Reese finishes her wine and watches the couple next to us. Her index finger listlessly traces the base of her wineglass.

"Is something the matter?" I ask.

She aims a dejected smile in my direction. "I know it sounds stupid, but I guess I'd hoped you were lying."

"About what?"

"That you weren't following my career."

I park my elbows on the table and clasp my hands. "They're good. The ones I read."

"Thanks. Two reasons I'm here." She holds up her index finger. "I was already in London so it was easier for me to get here at a moment's notice. And two." She adds her middle finger to the count. "I was at the Rapa this summer. Nieves wasn't."

"You *were* in the stands." The words are out of my mouth before I can stop them.

She slowly lowers her fingers and looks at me in shock. "You saw me? Why didn't you come talk to me?"

I press my mouth into a flat line.

She looks down at the table and wipes a spot of soup from the edge of her bowl. "I think I understand why you didn't. For what it's worth—"

"I wasn't sure it was you," I interrupt before she takes us back fourteen years. "I was on the curro floor surrounded by horses when I saw you. You were gone by the time I returned to the stands."

"I had to leave." She doesn't elaborate and I don't prod her further. Alex removes our bowls and returns with the main course. We start eating, Reese seeming lost in her own thoughts. I'm about to ask her what time she'd like to get started tomorrow—I understand the herds aren't always easy to find so we may need the entire day—when she asks, "How long have you been married?"

I look up from my plate. "You've been following more than my career."

"You're wearing a wedding ring." I glance at the tarnished gold band and she admits, "But yes, I have. What's she like?"

My body warms, thinking about Aimee. "She's the most exceptional woman I know," I say, cutting off a bite of chicken.

"She's a lucky woman." Reese watches me while I chew. The chicken is succulent and spicy, but it doesn't compare to Aimee's cooking.

Reese purses her lips and I sense she wants to ask me a question. I raise a brow.

She leans forward. "The journalist in me needs to know. Your mother. Did you ever find her?"

I shake my head. "No." But I would soon, as early as next week.

"Are you still looking for her?"

I take another bite of chicken and chew, meeting her eyes.

"You are." She whispers the answer for me. I look at my plate and pick at the vegetables. "Does she look like her?"

"Who?"

"Your wife. Does she look like Sarah?"

I put down my utensils. They clatter on the plate. "We need to get an early start tomorrow. I'll meet you in the lobby at eight." I push back my chair.

Reese reaches across the table. "I didn't mean . . . My stupid mouth. Some things don't change. I still have that bad habit of blurting out questions without thinking. I didn't mean to upset you."

I flag the waitress. Alex rushes over.

"Please charge the meals to my room."

"Ian . . . wait."

I stand. "Get some sleep, Reese. We have a long day tomorrow."

CHAPTER 15

IAN, AGE TWELVE

Ian sat on the porch steps, cleaning his camera lens. Early May sunlight bathed the driveway, warming the gravel. Inside, Jackie nursed a glass of his dad's bourbon. He was out of vodka. Jackie had been calling some guy named Clancy all morning. Clancy wasn't answering his phone, making Jackie furious.

Ian folded the cleaning cloth and held the lens up to the light, checking for streaks and spots. The lens passed inspection. He reattached it to the camera and, elbows on knees, chin propped in hand, blew the hair off his forehead. He glanced around, waiting. His mom's potted columbine swayed. Leaves on the sawtooth oak shimmered. The limbs and trunk creaked, expanding in the direct sunlight.

Ian should be doing his chores but he preferred to be outside when Jackie was in one of her moods. It was the best he could do to stay out of her way like his dad expected. But Jackie had the car keys. His mom hadn't had the chance to put them in their new hiding spot, a lockbox in his dad's desk, before she shifted. Ian knew Jackie planned to leave soon and he was ready. So what if his dad would ground him, or worse, take away his camera, when he found out Ian hadn't gone to Marshall's like he'd been instructed to do when Jackie was the dominant. It wasn't like his dad was there to watch over Sarah. Someone had to make sure she didn't harm herself.

Jackie's voice carried through the screen door. An electric buzz of anxious excitement. Ian strained to hear the conversation, catching snippets about a man Jackie had been looking for whom Clancy had finally found. She had to meet with Clancy to get the man's location from him.

"Two hours. I'll be there." She slammed down the receiver.

Ian slung the camera over his shoulder and rose to his feet. He kept his back to the station wagon and his front to the door. He was ready.

Ten minutes later, Jackie came outside and stopped abruptly. Ian widened his stance. She sneered. "Move."

Ian straightened. He pushed his shoulders back and crossed his arms over his chest. He'd had a recent growth spurt and now stood an inch or so taller than his mom. The platform slides Jackie wore brought her to eye level. Still, Ian did not back down. He didn't budge. "You're drunk." He held out his hand. It shook. "Give me the keys."

Jackie wore low-slung jeans and a white blouse that his friend from school, Delia, called a peasant shirt, clothes that didn't belong to his mom. She wouldn't dress like that, especially the makeup. Jackie had applied it thickly to her face. Ian could see cracks in the foundation, exaggerating the laugh lines bracketing her mouth. Black mascara weighed down her eyes.

A smile suddenly split her face, exposing bright-pink lipstick smeared on her upper front teeth. "Are you talking about these keys?" She shook the keys in his face, making as if she planned to throw them at him. He startled. Jackie shoved his shoulder, knocking him off-balance. His gangly frame stumbled into the porch post behind him.

Jackie sauntered down the steps, swinging the keys around her index finger, mocking him. She'd curled her hair. The tight waves bounced on her shoulders. She stumbled in the gravel, her ankle twisting in the platform slide. Her arms flew out, a goose spreading its wings, as she righted herself. She giggled. "Whew, that was a close one."

Ian eyed the clothes he'd never seen his mom wear. The lipstick shade he'd never seen her wear. He thought of the lockbox where his mom kept her credit cards and cash. Jackie must have her own stash, unless she figured how to access his parents' when Ian wasn't watching.

He wondered what else she'd hidden and he inhaled sharply. Nervous sweat slicked his skin as a memory from the previous year crystallized, bright and startling. Jackie had wanted one of his dad's guns. Fear for his mom's safety had his heart beating in his throat, forcing him to make one of the dumbest decisions of his life, his dad would later tell him. As Jackie sank into the driver's seat, Ian slid into the backseat. They shut their doors at the same time. The car rocked.

Jackie started the engine and flipped through radio stations, stopping at Eric Clapton's "Lay Down, Sally." She shifted the car into reverse, meeting Ian's gaze in the rearview mirror. Ian's hands shook in his lap but he didn't look away, meeting her challenge. He wasn't going anywhere. He intended to tag along.

Jackie pushed her pursed lips to the side. Her eyebrows lifted. "Suit yourself, moron." She floored the accelerator. Wheels spun, spitting gravel, and the Pontiac fishtailed before the tires caught. The car sped to the end of the driveway.

They drove for almost two hours, heading toward Boise National Forest. He'd been near there before, deer hunting with his dad. Stu likened hunting to photography. Look through the scope. Study your subject, or prey, however you want to look at it. Don't breathe. Point and shoot.

Ian hated everything about hunting, from stalking the animal to his dad posing by his kill, gripping the antlers to lift the head like a trophy. Ian couldn't stomach it. He was a disappointment, his dad had told him more than once that day after Ian had a deer lined up in his scope and failed to take the shot. He didn't care what his dad thought of him. Ian refused to pull the trigger. Shooting a living animal was nothing like pushing the shutter button.

Ian pressed his forehead against the glass window. Seventies tunes blared from the speakers. Jackie didn't speak to him. She barely acknowledged him. Fine by Ian. He'd learned not to ask questions or say anything that distracted her from driving. He also kept his camera out of sight. He wouldn't risk her ordering him from the car again, especially this time. They'd driven the farthest yet from home. Ian kept a mental note of landmarks and highway signs. His mom would be confused and disoriented after this trip. She'd need him to help her find their way home.

Jackie sang along with the tunes. Her fingers drummed to the beat on the steering wheel. Her singing voice royally sucked, but he kept that to himself. Instead, Ian took interest in the passing scenery. He wished he'd brought along food or something to drink. He had to pee.

A ballad came on, the Bee Gees' "How Deep Is Your Love." Ian had started to doze when the car slowed. He sat upright, rubbing his eyes, and looked around. The highway stretched long behind them and curved around a bend in front. Jackie turned into the parking lot of a rundown motor lodge and cut the engine. Tall pines fringed the lot. Across the street a neon mini-mart sign flashed high above a gas station. Ian's stomach grumbled. His bladder burned. He squirmed on the seat.

"Stay here," Jackie ordered, getting out of the car.

"Where are you—" The door slammed. "Going?" he finished meekly.

Ian watched her cross the parking lot to a pay phone. She made a call, then paced in a tight circle. Every so often she glanced down the highway. Who was she waiting for? Clancy? Aside from their car, the lot was empty. The place looked like a dump. Windows on several rooms had missing screens. One door had a hole near the base in the shape of a booted foot. Definitely not good signs of a safe place to hang out.

A half hour went by, which seemed like forever to Ian, and nothing happened. Jackie had moved toward the highway, her back to him, and that was about it. Hopefully she wasn't planning to hitchhike out of here. Ian wouldn't have a way home.

His bladder burned. He scooted toward the door, thinking he could make a run for the gas station, when a big guy on a Harley cruised into the parking lot. His full beard, dark brown threaded with gray, reached his chest. His gut peeked from under his faded black shirt. He lifted off the motorcycle and ambled across the lot toward Jackie. He must be Clancy.

Finally, something was happening. Ian scrambled for his camera.

Jackie waited for Clancy, arms crossed and hip popped out. He walked right up to her, gave her rear a rough squeeze, and yanked her against his fat stomach. He kissed her, his tongue thrusting out of his mouth before it reached hers.

Ian gasped, dropping the camera. It thudded on the vinyl seat. Clancy eventually came up for air. Jackie's chest heaved. Saliva drenched her lips. He went into the lodge office and Jackie wiped her mouth with the back of her hand. She glanced at the Pontiac. Ian sank low, peeking over the seat back. He felt physically ill. His damp palms slid against the seat.

Jackie smoothed her blouse and rubbed her hands back and forth on her hips the way Ian did when he was nervous. The lodge office door slammed, drawing Ian's attention. Clancy showed Jackie a key and pointed to one of the rooms.

Who was Clancy and what did he want with Jackie?

Ian picked up the camera. He didn't trust this guy, not one bit. Hands shaking, he took a picture of Jackie standing beside Clancy, who stood more than a head taller than she did. She shuffled her feet, waiting as he unlocked the door. He stood aside and, hand on her ass, nudged her into the room. Ian snapped another picture and the motel room door closed.

Now what was he supposed to do?

His stomach growled, and worse, he had to piss before he burst. For a split second he thought about getting a candy bar at the gas station mini-mart and using the bathroom, but he quickly discarded the idea. He couldn't leave. What if his mom surfaced and Jackie receded while alone with Clancy? Ian needed to be there for her. He might have to help her get away from Clancy.

Ian shouldered the camera strap and opened the door. He stood there, legs shivering with nerves and fear, for a good five minutes. For something to happen. For one of them to come out of the room. An occasional car passed on the highway. Crows pecked at trash. A breeze wafted through the lot carrying the scent of pine and wood smoke, nudging his back. It was the push he needed.

Ian unzipped his fly and relieved himself right there in the parking lot in the V between the car and the open door. He groaned with relief and then, bouncing on his toes, gave himself a shake and zipped up his pants. He looked around to make sure no one had seen him.

All clear. He quietly shut the door and went to the motel room. He raised a fist to knock and hesitated when he heard a noise. He pressed his ear to the door. Muffled groans and gasps, the repeated slap of flesh, penetrated the hollow door. A deep, guttural voice cursed. More grunts followed.

Ian fell back, almost tripping over the concrete parking bumper. He'd heard sounds like those before. They came in the dark of night from his parents' room.

Ian felt like he'd swallowed a toad. A foul, sickly lump kicked around his stomach, rose up and thickened in his throat. He almost dry-heaved.

Hunger pangs forgotten, Ian ran across the parking lot, stumbling in his haste to get to the pay phone. Gravel scraped his hands and chin. He barely registered the cuts, the burn of raw flesh. He stood and shoved open the phone booth's glass door. He collect-called his dad's hotel, asking to be transferred to his room. The phone rang and rang until the operator came on the line and confirmed what Ian suspected. His dad was out. Ian was alone.

He hung up.

He wanted to cry.

He wanted to run away.

He didn't want to ride home with Jackie. He didn't want to be anywhere near Jackie. She'd betrayed Sarah in the vilest way possible. Sleeping with a stranger was a thousand times worse than the purple blemishes that marred his mom's skin whenever Jackie took off on one of her mysterious outings.

Outings that probably led her to Clancy. Someone had to have given her those bruises.

The phone rang, a shrill cry, and Ian jumped. He grabbed the receiver and said a croaky "Hello?"

"Ian, is that you?"

"Dad!" Relief floored him. He sagged against the scratched glass wall covered with Sharpie-inked phone numbers and *Call me* messages.

"What the hell are you doing in Donnelly?"

Ian rubbed the heel of his hand in his eyes to stem his tears. "Jackie brought us here." Ian explained what he'd seen and heard.

His dad didn't say anything for a long time. Ian thought he had hung up when he heard a dull thud. It sounded like a fist punching the wall. His dad cursed.

"Dad?" he asked, his voice unsure.

"For God's sake, Ian, I told you to never ride along with Jackie. I also ordered you to get yourself to Marshall's house and call me the moment your mom shifted."

"What's the point?" Ian yelled back. "She'll be Mom again by the time you get home."

"Dammit. Do as you're told for once. Get back in the car so she doesn't leave you there. She'll come home, she always does. But don't you dare tell your mother what happened. Let me talk to her when I get home. This'll be too much for her to handle."

"But, Dad, she—"

"Do it! That's an order," his dad bellowed loud enough for Ian to pull the phone from his ear. "You damn well better go to Marshall's when you get home. You wait there until I get you. I don't want anything to happen to you."

"I don't want anything to happen to Mom. Jackie will get her hurt."

A door slammed, snagging Ian's attention. He turned back to the lodge and his chest caved. "Gotta go." The receiver slid from his ear.

"Ian? Don't you hang up. Ian! *Ian!*"

His dad kept yelling until Ian hung up, cutting him off.

Across the parking lot, Jackie stood outside the motel room. Their eyes met. Ian could see the sheen of tears illuminated on her cheeks despite the distance between them. Her mascara smeared, hair knotted, and shirt hanging off one shoulder reminded him of the deer his dad instructed him to shoot. Just as he'd raised the rifle all those months ago, Ian slowly, carefully, lifted the camera to his face, else she spook. This time, he took the shot. He pressed the button. The shutter clicked. Then Ian cried. Because it wasn't Jackie he'd caught in his lens.

CHAPTER 16

AIMEE

What in the world am I doing?

I should be at the café for the morning rush, or calling the banks to pull my loan application. I should be on a plane to Spain. The last place I should ever be is the lobby of Donato Enterprises, waiting for a meeting with the company's owner, Thomas Donato.

But here I am.

Seeking Thomas's assistance seemed the perfect solution last night, and again this morning when I woke with the same resolve. Thomas is the shortest means to the end I need: locating Lacy Saunders.

Now that I'm here, sitting alone in the waiting area of an office I never imagined I'd set foot in again? My resolve is dissolving.

My knees won't stop bouncing. The coffee I drank this morning has soured into a hard knot below my ribs. I flip my phone over and over between my hands.

I can't do this.

I can't face Thomas again.

I start to rise when I remind myself why I'm here.

Ian. I'm doing this for Ian. I'm looking for Lacy for him.

How different my life would be had I listened to her at James's funeral when she told me he was still alive. I had lost James, and the future I believed I wanted with him, because I failed to act. But . . .

I wouldn't have met Ian.

We wouldn't have Caty.

The thought of not having either of them in my life induces an unexpected wave of sadness. Grief momentarily immobilizes me. It wrenches at my soul.

That's why I intend to listen to Lacy now, to find out what she wants with Ian. I can't lose anyone else in my life.

Closing my eyes, I breathe through the pain. Then I reread the text message Ian sent while I slept. He landed safely in New York. He wanted me to call when I woke.

I didn't, fearing he'd somehow suspect what I'm up to today. I didn't want to distract him from his assignment and we'd been arguing too much lately. We'd argue if he knew whom I'm planning to meet.

By now Ian's on the second leg of his flight, soaring to Spain, where I'll join him tomorrow night. I hope to have news of Lacy by then.

Why didn't Ian tell me about Lacy's card? He didn't mention meeting with James either. Only that he intends to start looking for his mom again. I understand why he must. He's kept his past locked away far too long, and he's worked hard to keep it that way. As much as he likes to think he hides it, I know he's hurting. He needs closure.

I glance at the time on my phone. Thomas's teleconference has already gone over by fifteen minutes. I slide my phone into the front pocket of my purse, feeling antsy. How much longer am I willing to wait?

Long enough to get what I want from him.

I imagine Thomas's surprise at finding me on his schedule. I called the receptionist first thing this morning, insisting she reserve ten minutes of Thomas's precious time.

I only need five.

Colorful magazines are stacked on the side table. I select a furniture catalog and flip through the glossy pages of exotic imports from Chile and Brazil, quickly reaching the end. I return it to the table.

"How much longer, do you think?" I ask the receptionist.

Marion Temple glances at her monitor. She clicks her mouse. "I'm showing he's still on the phone. He should be off shortly."

That's what she said eight minutes ago. "Thanks." I politely smile.

"I hope you don't mind waiting until he's done. Thomas had me clear an hour from his calendar. He's very interested in seeing you."

I bet he is, considering I did everything within my legal rights to keep him away from me. After we met in Puerto Escondido and he admitted what he'd done, how he manipulated both my life and James's, the mere sight of Thomas brought on severe physical reactions. Heart palpitations. Shortness of breath. Nausea.

Thomas tried approaching me on multiple occasions those initial months following Mexico since I'd blocked his calls and e-mails. Ian always escorted him from the café before Thomas had the opportunity to reach me. Thank goodness for Ian and my therapist. They kept me sane until the day I snapped.

I came home one evening after a long shift to find Thomas waiting for me on the porch.

"Who have you told about James?"

His demanding question startled me. I hadn't seen him lurking behind the overgrown hydrangea plant. I screamed. Then I got mad. Madder than I'd ever been in my life. I picked up a potted fern and threw it at his head. My aim was off and the clay pot shattered on the porch. Dirt sprayed the front of Thomas's pristine white dress shirt.

"Christ." He lowered his arms where they'd been shielding his head. "What's wrong with you?"

"Are you kidding me? Are you *fucking* kidding me?" I wanted to gouge out his eyes. I wanted to make him bleed. To think this man was the same guy I once thought of as a big brother, who *was* the kind and considerate older brother of the boy I had loved. Thomas would pick us up from school before James had his license and drive us to the pizza parlor downtown. Then he'd wait in his car so that James and I had time alone together. Time their parents wouldn't know was spent with me.

I picked up another pot. Thomas's arms immediately shielded his head as he leaped off the porch. "Just answer the question, Aimee. That's all I want."

I didn't care what he wanted. He didn't deserve an answer. I shook the potted tulips at him, beautiful bulbs my mother had gifted me the previous winter. Getting Thomas off my property and out of my life was worth their sacrifice. I took a threatening step toward him. "If you ever set foot—"

"I'm leaving. *I'm leaving!*" he yelled again, backing away, when I lifted the pot above my head. He pointed at it clutched in my hands. "My head's not worth it. They're too pretty."

His remark caught me off guard. I lowered my arms, holding the pot against my hip. I had to look away from the sadness he tried to hide and I didn't want him to see my own tears. He'd been a good friend. How did we get to this point? I wanted to murder him.

"Just leave," I said, trying not to cry.

He did, albeit reluctantly, his arm reaching out as he backed away, his expression pleading for an answer. My stance firm, my gaze hard, he didn't get one from me. The following morning, I contacted an attorney and started the process of filing a restraining order against Thomas.

James told me yesterday a little about why Thomas had kept him hidden, how he'd pulled some strings and put James in Mexico's witness protection program. I could understand Thomas's reasons, barely, but I don't think he needed to go to those extremes. I'm sure there had been other options.

But if Thomas had taken them, I never would have met Ian. I'm waiting here, in the lion's den, because of Ian. And that lion is preying upon my best friend, Nadia.

Anger spikes. My hands fist. I grab my purse and approach the reception desk on the brink of barging into Thomas's office. Marion hangs up the phone from the call she'd been on and pleasantly smiles at me. "That was Thomas. He'll see you now, Mrs. Collins. Follow me." She rises and walks around the semicircle-shaped desk.

Finally.

I follow Marion down a wide hallway, past cubicles and offices. She stops at the end and opens a wide set of double doors stained a dark mahogany. "Mr. Donato, Mrs. Collins is here to see you." She steps aside.

Before I lose my nerve, I swiftly cross the gray carpeted floor. Thomas starts to rise from his chair behind his desk. I lay into him before he's on his feet. "There are hundreds of architects in the Bay Area and you chose Nadia. Why?"

Thomas's mouth parts and his brows rise, crinkling his forehead. I inwardly cringe. That's not how I planned to open our conversation.

His gaze slides from me to behind me. He nods and I hear the doors shut. It's just the two of us, alone. My heart pounds but I won't let Thomas see me sweat. I straighten my posture, crossing my arms so he doesn't see how badly my hands shake, and meet his eyes.

He tosses his pen on the glass surface of his desk. "I admire her work."

"I don't believe you."

The corner of his mouth quirks. He shrugs his shoulders. "Of course you don't."

I shake a finger at him. "You'll screw her over like everyone else. Find another architect."

Thomas's face darkens. He spreads his fingers on the desk and leans forward, his fingertips supporting his weight. "I can work with anyone

I please. You have no authority to come in here and decide who I work with and how I run my affairs."

"This is Nadia we're talking about. You know she's my best friend."

"You think I'm working with her to get to you? News flash, Aimee. My devious plans don't revolve around you."

His sarcasm rankles. "Don't mock me."

He slides his hands into his side pant pockets. His expression softens. "I'm not a monster."

"Just a man with a plan who could care less about ruining lives. As long as you get what you want."

Thomas purses his lips and roughly exhales through his nose. "Can I offer you a drink?" He moves from behind his desk to a dry bar off to the side.

"It's ten in the morning." I toss my purse on the leather chair beside me.

"It's turning out to be a rough morning." He pours himself a finger of scotch and tosses it back.

As he refills his drink, I take the opportunity to collect my thoughts since they veered off track the second I crossed his office threshold. Thomas works in a large space done in muted tones, glass, and steel. Darker and colder than the warm textures of the furniture he imports and exports. The office is a perfect reflection of the man he's become.

Thomas sits in the center of the couch and gestures for me to join him.

"I'll stand, thanks."

He lifts a shoulder. "Suit yourself."

I do, walking a circle around the office, restless, unsure how to begin. I feel Thomas watching me. His gaze tracks my progress. I catch a photo on the shelf behind Thomas's desk. A picture of him and James. They're younger than when I first met them. I'd been eight, James eleven, and Thomas thirteen. Long before life for James became difficult at home. Rather, it had already been difficult. It just got worse.

I don't know the full story of what happened between Thomas and James, or entirely what life was like for them living with their parents since he apparently kept much of their dynamic hidden from me. It's James's story to tell should he be inclined to share.

I return to the center of the room and stand behind a leather chair, across from Thomas. "What's Nadia working on for you?"

"She didn't tell you? Good."

"She knew it would upset me, the two of you working together."

"And here you are," Thomas murmurs in his glass before taking a drink. "She didn't tell you because she signed an NDA. It's also not your concern."

"It's not, but you'll tell me, anyway." I sense Thomas wants to talk. He cleared an hour for me. I'm not wasting this opportunity.

"I bought a house in Carmel."

"You're moving?" I come around and sink into the chair. I'll never have to see Thomas walk by my café again, wondering if this time, this morning, he'll come inside. The restraining order expired a few years ago and I didn't have a cause to renew it. True to his word, Thomas left me alone, except the one instance he'd asked through Nadia for James's photos and contacts to download to a new iPhone. He planned to ship it to Carlos, the man James had been while in his fugue state.

"In a year or two," Thomas answers, glancing at the door. He leans forward, elbows on knees, glass balanced between his hands. "I'm tired of this city. I'm tired of running this company. I'm just"—he rubs the inner corners of his eyes with his thumb and index finger—"tired."

He's more than tired. He seems defeated.

Interesting.

"Are you selling Donato?"

"Getting ready to, yes." He arches a brow. "Do I need you to sign an NDA before you leave or can I trust you not to speak a word of this outside those doors?" He tilts his head in that direction. "My employees don't know."

"Nadia does, though."

"She signed an NDA. I trust her." His tone implies it's more than trust.

"You have feelings for her."

Thomas's gaze narrows. He pushes against his knees to stand, I assume to buzz his assistant to print an NDA. I roll my eyes. "Fine, you have my word. Your secret's safe with me." No way will I sign any of Thomas's contracts.

Thomas settles back onto the couch and downs the remainder of his scotch. "The house I bought was recently remodeled. I'm only expanding the master bed and bath, and redoing the kitchen. Nadia's drawing up the plans for my contractor. She's not managing the project. That's it. I'm not interested in anything from her beyond that."

His last statement is spoken in a low tone, his gaze fixed inside his empty glass.

"Your text messages to her say otherwise," I quietly point out.

Thomas sets down the glass with a hard plunk and looks at his watch.

"Why are you here?"

I get my purse where I left it on the chair by Thomas's desk and take out a folded sheet of paper. I'd made a copy of Lacy's business card. I give it to Thomas, watching as his brow arches, holding my gaze while he unfolds the paper. He glances down and reads it, his eyes slightly widening. He looks up at me.

"What is this about?"

"Lacy met up with James on a beach in Kauai and gave him her card."

His face and neck lighten a shade. "Have you ever met this woman? She looks through you rather than at you. It's the weirdest feeling." He shivers, giving me pause. Thomas truly looks uncomfortable.

"You've met her?"

"Once, briefly. She was an acquaintance of Imelda Rodriguez. They were having lunch during one of my trips to Puerto Escondido."

A memory tickles the recesses of my mind like a cat's whiskers poking at my face. "You recognized her at my café on opening day." Thomas came to congratulate me, considering he funded me the money, and as I later learned, convinced Joe Russo, the building's owner, to lease the space rent-free during build-out. Thomas had noticed someone that day and left in a hurry. It wasn't until afterward when Kristen forwarded pictures from the opening that I saw Lacy had been there, too. Most likely looking for a chance to reach out to me.

"I did notice her," Thomas admits. "What does she want with James?"

"Not James. Ian, my husband." I point at the paper I gave him. "The number on that card is out of service. James told me how and why you kept him hidden in Mexico. I believe you have the resources to find her."

"You spoke with James. He's in town?"

"Yes. About Lacy—" I stop. Thomas isn't listening to me. He stands, going to the window, and gazes out at the city below. He slides one hand into his pocket, the other waves the paper he holds against his leg. After a moment, he turns back to me. "What do you want with Lacy?"

"None of your business."

"I told you about Nadia and my house. You know about my plans for Donato. I'm also letting you walk out of here without signing an NDA. Although"—he digs his fingers into his collar and scratches his neck—"I'm reconsidering that. You owe me an explanation if I'm taking up my time to search for a woman who gives the appearance she can't keep her feet planted in one place for more than a couple of months at a time."

He knows about Lacy.

"Tell me and we'll call it even."

"I've got three answers for you." I stand up. "I don't owe you a thing. You and I will never be even." I count down on my fingers.

Thomas quirks a brow. "And the third?"

"Lacy went through my ex-fiancé to get that card to my husband. I want to know why."

"The plot thickens." Thomas casually walks over to me, folding the paper. He slips it into his breast pocket. "That is curious." He crosses his arms and breathes deeply. "All right. I'll find her."

"Really?" I can't hide my surprise. I expected a fight. My mouth parts and I immediately close it. I don't want to thank him.

His mouth twitches. "You're welcome," he says with the sincerity I refused to show him and returns to his desk. "Give me a few days." His tone is dismissive.

I tuck my purse under my arm. "Make that one day. I'm on a plane headed for Spain this afternoon. I'd like to have her info by the time I land."

CHAPTER 17

I A N

"Sorry I'm late." Reese drops a small backpack in the chair across from me and yawns, covering her mouth with the back of her hand. "I'm on deadline for another project and was up late writing."

I glance at my watch. Ten minutes after eight. I've been up since four—thank you, jet lag—and chugging coffee in the dining room since six.

"Do you need to be back at a specific time? We can take separate cars." Who knows how long it'll take to find the herds. I'm limited on time and can't extend my stay. I don't want to cut off the search earlier than necessary.

She shakes her head. "I sent the draft to my editor this morning."

That's a relief. Standing, I polish off my coffee. There's no guarantee we'll see the herds today. We have to find them first and I'm anxious to get on the road. We could be traversing the hills past sunset.

I snap my fingers. Flashlights, we may need them.

Opening my bag, I double-check I packed them, which I did, along with extra batteries. Satisfied, I zip closed the pocket.

Reese points to the breakfast buffet. "Let me get some food to take with us."

I shoulder my pack and check my messages. Still no word from Aimee. She hasn't returned my calls either.

"Ian?"

I look up from my phone at Reese, a frown plastered on my forehead. "What?"

She quirks a brow. "What's up with you? You look worried."

"Nah, I'm good." I put away my phone. "Ready?"

She shows me her *magdalena*, a Spanish breakfast pastry, and apple. "Yep. Let's go."

"I'll drive," I say when we reach the parking lot. She turns a full circle, looking at the cars. "That one." I aim the key fob at my rental, a compact sedan, and disarm the alarm. We settle into the car and I reverse out of the parking lot.

"About last night," Reese begins after she clips on her seatbelt. "My comment about your wife looking like your mom, it was uncalled for."

"Forget it." I brush it off, wanting to focus on the assignment, not Sarah. Or my wife, who's not answering my calls. There will be plenty of time to think about them later.

"For what it's worth, I don't want things to be weird between us, so again, I'm sorry."

I tightly nod and shift the car into gear. She bites into her apple. The interior cab quickly smells like juice and pie. It reminds me of fall and Halloween and Caty. I miss her giggles and want to FaceTime with her this evening, assuming Aimee answers her phone. Briefly, I think about calling Catherine, but decide not to. I don't want to worry her, or give her reason to think there's friction between Aimee and me. Because there won't be, not anymore. Turning onto the road, we head for Sabucedo, a fifteen-minute drive from where we're staying.

"Have you thought about your angle for the feature?" I ask when Reese finishes her apple.

She wraps the core in a napkin and puts it in the cup holder. "I have some ideas."

"Care to elaborate?" I ask when she doesn't, glancing her way. She watches the passing roadside scenery, hillsides of dry grass and rock, groupings of pine trees.

She adjusts the backpack on her lap. "Are you going to talk me out of it?"

I shake my head, cracking a smile. Good ole Reese, always quick on the defense. Following the road signs to Sabucedo, I downshift, taking a right. "I found the men managing the herds almost as interesting as the horses."

"How so?" Reese asks. She rips off a piece of the pastry that looks like pound cake.

"Before the event, the aloitadores vibrated with anticipation. You could feel the energy. They'd been waiting all year for this event. They're tense and focused, almost as if they're preparing for battle. But afterward, they're exhausted and dirty and sweaty. Some of them have contusions and broken bones. You can see the pain etched in their expressions. But they're smiling because they're relieved. They survived. And they can't wait to do it all over again next year."

Reese slowly nods, chewing. "Makes you wonder why they would after the way you described it."

"It's a rite of passage. I took a lot of pictures of them. I just thought you could touch upon that emotion in the article. That way Al can use the photos."

"Maybe," she says, popping another bite of spongy cake into her mouth.

"You don't seem that interested."

"Oh no, I am. It's a good idea," she agrees. "I just didn't get the same impression as you. I left before the first session finished. It was hard for me to watch."

Her grief-stricken face and tear-drenched cheeks come to mind. So does her quick exit. She was gone before my ten-minute access to the floor was up. That's when I make the connection. She doesn't like animals leashed, tied up, or penned. The neighbor two doors down from the house where she grew up kept his rottweiler penned in his chain-link-fenced front yard with nothing to keep him company but a plastic doghouse and the twenty-five-foot rope that kept him leashed to the yard's solitary myrtle tree. Other than feeding his dog once a day, the owner neglected the animal. The only stimulation the dog received was watching kids bike past and neighbors walking by with their own dogs.

Reese walked by the dog every day on her way home from school, until the one afternoon he wasn't there. She had no idea if the dog died or the owner gave him up. Animal services might have taken him away. But two weeks later, a shepherd-mix puppy appeared in the yard, and over the next couple of months, he lived the same neglected, solitary life until animal services picked him up. It didn't matter how much love she had to give. Reese resolved to never own a pet.

Of course, she tells me this after I'd adopted the cat for her.

This makes me wonder why she was at the Rapa in the first place, so I ask her.

"Michael wanted to go. He loves horses. He grew up around them."

"Who's Michael? Your boyfriend?"

"Ex-husband, as of three weeks ago." Reese pinches a crumb from her magdalena, looks at it, then absently wipes her hand on her pack.

"I'm sorry." I don't know what else to say.

"Don't be. It was an amicable separation. We went to the Rapa in July as friends. It's been on his bucket list for years. He asked me to go with him, and I did."

I ease to a stop at an intersection and wait for several cars to pass. "If you didn't like watching it, why'd you submit a proposal to write the article?" It doesn't make sense to me.

"I didn't submit anything. Jane Moreland, she's the features editor, she called me. Do you remember Simon Dougherty?"

"The guy we worked with at ASU's paper?" An image of a man of medium build with dark hair and black-rimmed glasses downloads. "Didn't he grease his hair and wear a plastic pocket protector?" I grin at Reese and she shares a smile.

"That's him."

I'd worked as the paper's photographer for two years and hadn't kept in touch with any of the staff from my time there. "I remember Simon. I could always rely on him for a BIC."

"That's because you never carried your own pen."

"What's the need to when there was Simon?"

She shakes her half-eaten pastry at me. "You used to call him Clark Kent, remember that?"

"That's right." I lightly bounce my fist on the gearshift, softly chuckling. "He obsessed over Superman comic books and he dyed his hair."

"He did not!"

"Did, too." A Volkswagen passes and I shift into first, turning onto the highway. "I bought him Clairol hair dye as a gag gift for his birthday. You know what he said? 'Thanks, dude, but it's the wrong shade. I use *darkest* brown.'" I pitch my voice to sound like how I remembered Simon, rumbling and serious. "I'd bought him *dark* brown. As if there's a difference."

"I'll be damned." Reese looks out the front window. "I never knew." She finishes her pastry and crumples the napkin.

"Is his hair still darkest brown?"

Her face scrunches up. "I have no idea. It's brown. Plain old brown."

I rest an arm on the center console and lean toward her. "So, what's up with Clark Kent? You still keep in touch with him?"

"Yes, and *Simon*"—she emphasizes his name—"is a close friend."

I look at her doubtfully. "You aren't that close if you can't tell he colors his hair," I challenge.

"Stop!" Reese playfully slaps my forearm, then jerks her hand away. She folds her arm over her pack and fiddles with the zipper tab, keeping her hand occupied. Her face sobers.

I grip the steering wheel at ten and two, not at all comfortable with how easy it is to banter with Reese. She can still be as fun as she is aggravating.

Forking my hand through my hair, I keep my gaze forward. I tell myself it's because I don't want to miss our turnoff.

"What's Simon got to do with you and the Rapa?" I ask.

"He's on staff at the magazine. He mentioned to Jane I attended and she reached out to me."

A thought occurs to me and it doesn't sit well. "Did you know I'd been assigned to this story?"

The air changes in the car and Reese shifts in her seat. My stomach rolls, sloshing the pot-size amount of coffee I ingested this morning.

"I'm moving back to the States. Michael's British. Now that we're divorced, there's no reason for me to stay."

"Reese," I push. "Did you know?"

"Not at first, no," she says, irritated. She pushes the pack off her thighs. It slides to the floor. She folds her arms over her chest. "I initially declined the assignment."

"But you agreed when you found out you'd be working with me."

"Yes, all right?" she says, angling her face toward me without looking at me. "I wanted to see you."

She's got to be kidding me. I jam the gearshift hard into fourth. "I'm married, Reese. Happily."

Her mouth falls open. She gapes at me. I meet her with a steely gaze. She slams her mouth closed and her face hardens. "You are so full of yourself."

I'm about to lay into her because what else am I supposed to think, but a sign blows by outside. SABUCEDO. I quickly downshift and turn, barely making our exit.

I coast along the narrow street.

"Do you know where you're going?"

"Yes." I think. I glance around. There are two main trailheads that could lead us to the herds. The question is which one is the better option.

"Stop the car. Pull over. Let's ask him." She points at a man resting on a bench outside the village's lone café. I recognize him as an aloitador from my photos.

"Good idea."

After a round of introductions, Manuel directs us to a trailhead on the opposite side of the village. The herds have been grazing those hills for the past week and we should come upon them just over an hour into our hike. Reese exchanges phone numbers with Manuel and they agree to meet at the café later in the afternoon. She wants to interview him about his experience with the Rapa.

"Thanks," I say when we get back into the car.

"For what?"

"For wanting to talk with him. He's one of the guys I photographed that I was telling you about earlier."

Reese nods once and checks the time on her phone. "Let's hurry. I have to be back here by four."

Five minutes later we are parked at the trailhead. Reese adjusts her pack on her back. "What's the plan, Collins?"

I squint at the overcast sky. The air is ripe with precipitation and the sharp scent of eucalyptus and damp dirt. "Find the horses before we get rained on. I also want to get some panoramic shots of the area."

We hit the trail, falling into step. We hike in relative silence for the next twenty minutes, following the well-worn path uphill. My thoughts drift to the years Reese and I were together and how things ended abruptly between us, like a favorite television show that's canceled between seasons. You're left with nothing but a cliff-hanger of an ending. Your brain works out various scenarios, but none of the conclusions are as satisfying as you imagine the real deal would have been had you just been allowed to watch the first episode of the next season.

I always wondered if Reese and I would have stayed together. It wasn't until I met Aimee at Wendy's gallery that I finally had my answer. Reese and I would have never worked out because I was meant to be with Aimee.

I always believed things happen for a reason. They can't always be explained, like Reese leaving me, or my life intersecting with Aimee's through Lacy. But the answers eventually reveal themselves, sometime in the strangest of ways. Some are obvious and others you have to look for.

"Do you have kids?" Reese asks as we make our way around a bend. Pines line the trail, our elevation increasing.

I look askance at her, trying to not let the question bother me. "You already know that answer."

She raises a hand. "Guilty." I frown, wondering how much she does know about me and why. She's the one who left.

"Reese." I grip my pack's straps, lifting the weight off my shoulders. "We're ancient history. Nothing's happening between us."

She scowls. "That's quite presumptuous of you. Forget I asked." She quickens her pace, moving ahead of me.

The clouds hang low, the sky gloomy. So is my mood. A single drop lands on my forehead and slides into my eye. I wipe my face. A few drops hit Reese's pack and more splatter on my shoulders. Soon we're ensconced in a steady drizzle. I flip up my hood.

Reese's remark rankled, but she's right. I'm being presumptuous. Any credible journalist is going to do her research before she goes on assignment, including who she'd be working alongside. I would have done the same had I known she'd been assigned.

I fully zip up my jacket. "I have a daughter. Her name's Sarah Catherine and she's four."

Reese slows, but she doesn't turn toward me. I lengthen my stride. Her hair is damp, stringy. She looks up at me and I meet her gaze. "We named her after my mother, and Aimee's. We call her Caty, and she's incredible. Smart, daring, tenacious, caring, and I can keep going." I laugh. My chest warms from thinking of her.

"She's a lucky little girl to have you for a dad."

"Thanks," I say simply. She knows about my dad and how, even in my early twenties, I strived to be nothing like him.

We reach a crest in the trail and Reese turns to me. "We've been hiking for over an hour and no horses."

"You're welcome to turn back. I'll give you the keys. You can wait in the car."

She tosses me a disgruntled look. "I'll hike all day if I have to, but how do you know we're going in the right direction? Manuel could have been wrong. The horses could have moved elsewhere."

"It's possible, but not likely. I've been seeing horse manure for the last quarter mile. Can't you smell it?" I dramatically inhale. Damp hay, wood rot, and mushrooms. I grin.

She screws up her lips. Her nose wrinkles. "No, thanks, I'll pass. Keep walking."

She steps off the trail so I can lead. At that moment, the clouds split and the mist we'd been walking in turns into a torrential downpour. Within seconds, my clothes are soaked to my briefs.

I point at a pine, its branches wide enough to provide some cover. "Over there!" I yell. We run, skidding in the mud, our packs bouncing on our shoulders. I slick back my hair and scan the horizon. There isn't much to see. Thick clouds and the heavy rain obscure the hills. Fat drops steadily fall around us from the limbs. "We can wait out the rain here. It shouldn't last long." My weather app showed sunshine in the afternoon. But it also showed the morning would only be partly cloudy. We could be in for a long wait.

I slip the pack off my shoulders to check my gear and grab a protein bar. Behind me, Reese screams. The skin on the back of my neck tightens and my heart pulses in my throat. I bolt upright. "What? Where?"

She points at the ground. About ten feet from us is the carcass of a foal. It's been picked over by other animals. There's nothing left but skin, bone, and rotting organs. Dried blood stains the ground.

"What happened?" Reese asks. She backs away to the edge of the branch cover. Her head is soaked, her eyes huge.

"Wolves. They roam these hills," I explain, taking out my camera. She scans the perimeter and I shake my head at her dismay. "It's been dead for several days. We're fine." I adjust the camera settings and snap a photo.

"We don't need pictures of this for the article. Have some respect, Ian. It's dead."

"It's life. And my editor wants me to document what it's like up here for the herds." I lower my camera and arc my arm to encompass the surrounding landscape. "The Galician horses have roamed these hills for centuries. They're shorter and hardier than the horses we're used to, with shaggy coats and thick hair on their muzzles. They've adapted to life up here, and like any group of wild animals, the herd moves on, leaving the sick and injured behind." I indicate the dead foal. "I want to see what that life is like for them, don't you?"

Reese hugs her body and reluctantly nods.

I look back toward the trail. "It's a good guess our herd has moved elsewhere. And I don't think this rain is going to let up anytime soon." I squint overhead, feeling discouraged. One more day, then I have no choice but to leave. "We should head back. We can ask Manuel where else to look."

"Tell me, Ian," Reese begins when we start walking downhill. She finally flips her hood onto her head. Rivulets of water rain over her shoulders, down the front of her jacket. "What is it about these horses and the Rapa that fascinates you so much? Why did you apply for this assignment?"

"Easy. The symbiotic relationship between the herds and the villagers. One can't survive without the other."

She hums.

I shoot a side-eye. "What're you thinking?"

"That there has to be another way aside from cramming two hundred horses into a small arena to manage the herds. Whoops!"

Reese's boot skids across the mud and her arms fly out. I grip her elbow so she doesn't fall.

"Thanks." She rights her balance and I let go.

"That was close."

"Yeah, it was."

I don't share her laugh when she does.

The rain wants us to run—we're seriously drenched. Water sloshes inside my shoes—but we keep our pace steady. Neither of us wants to end up hobbling back to the car with a broken leg or sprained ankle.

It is just after noon when we enter the café, waterlogged and starving. We're early, but fortunately, Manuel is there, eating lunch with friends. Reese orders a coffee and I drink a beer, feeling unsettled, but I can't pinpoint why. The café's owner brings us plates of *pulpo*, boiled octopus doused in hot paprika on a bed of potatoes, a Galician-style dish. Reese is delighted. The smell turns my stomach.

We eat while Manuel and his buddies Paolo and Andre enlighten Reese with tales of the Rapa das bestas. They count their broken bones and show off their scars in a show of one-upmanship as they passionately describe their love for the horses that wander their hills. But the longer they talk, the more upset I get—both my stomach and my frame of mind. *What is wrong with me?* I think, irritated. Reese is smiling. She's laughing at their tales. She's asking about the necessity of the festival and a sudden realization comes to light. I know the angle Reese intends to approach in this story, or, at least, her opinions she'll weasel into it. She doesn't think the festival is a necessity to manage the herd.

But that's not the point, I want to argue. It's about tradition and our dependence on others. It's about two species supporting one another.

After years of working toward this goal, I'm finally on assignment for *National Geographic*. For an article I'm not sure I want my name associated with.

It's after six when we arrive back at La casa de campo. We're damp as opposed to drenched, and I want a drink, something stronger than a beer. I jerk open the front door, stepping aside at the last minute to let Reese enter ahead.

"What's with you?" she asks when the door shuts behind me. "You hardly said anything this afternoon. Did I do something to upset you?"

I point a finger at her. "Be careful what you say in that article. Your words can decimate that village's main source of income. Funds they use to care for the horses."

She laughs, brushing me off. "As if I'm going to let you tell me what to write. Last I checked, I'm the writer on this assignment. You're just the photographer."

"But it's my name, too, in the byline." And I didn't want to be the cause of any negative press. I sent my photos to the magazine because I wanted to share an unusual event steeped in history. Traditions are fading every day, and one day we won't have this connection to history. As a photographer, it's my role to document them, to help keep them alive.

Reese removes her jacket. "You better decide what you want to do, Ian. I'm still submitting my article by the deadline, whether or not you're on the assignment."

She looks at me, brow cocked and ready for a challenge, and I meet her gaze with a steely one.

"Ian."

Reese and I both turn. I blink. "Aimee?"

She rushes over to me and I sweep her up in my arms. Warmth ripples through my rain-cold chest. "Oh my God, you're here." I squeeze her hard, dropping kisses all over her face. "What are you doing here?" I press my mouth to hers and kiss her deeply.

A throat clears beside us and I surface from the haze.

That's riiiiight. Reese. She's still here.

I lift my head, grin at Aimee, and wrap an arm around her waist. I pull her into my side.

"Aimee, this is—"

Aimee extends her hand at the same time. "Hi, I'm Aimee. Ian's wife."

Reese grasps her hand. "Reese Thorne. His ex-wife."

CHAPTER 18

IAN, AGE TWELVE

Ian hovered outside his parents' room. He felt no shame eavesdropping on their conversation. After what happened at the motor lodge yesterday, Ian had a list of questions longer than the roll of film he'd developed early that morning.

Inside their room, he could hear his dad cautiously asking his mom questions. She cried, choking on words that didn't make sense to Ian. Words like *bounty hunter* and *payment*. He knew what a bounty hunter was. He and Marshall had watched the movie *Unforgiven* about a bounty hunter in the Old West. They carried guns and hunted down robbers and murderers.

Who did Jackie want to find?

"Stop hiding your wallet," Ian's dad pleaded.

"No." His mom hiccupped. "I'll drain the accounts . . . max the cards . . . ruin us."

"Then we'll leave out the money. We'll make it easy to find."

"No." She cried out the objection. "You work enough hours because of me. I need you home. Ian . . . Ian needs you more than me. He feels responsible for me. I hate that he thinks he has to take care of me. We're not being fair to him. You're not being fair to us."

Ian peeked around the doorjamb. His mom sat on the bed, her legs folded underneath her skirt, head bowed. His dad faced her, one leg bent, the other on the floor as he leaned toward her. Their bodies silhouetted against the bright window behind them, the space between them the outline of a heart. His mom was breaking his.

Sarah showed Stu the pictures Ian had taken. She'd removed them from the darkroom in the basement before Ian could hide them. He'd kept his word with his dad not to tell his mom anything about what had happened at the motel. His dad worried how she would react should she learn what Jackie had done in the motel room. Ian suspected his mom already knew. Her clothes had been askew and her makeup smeared. She had a different scent on her, musk and sweat. His stomach had coiled whenever he smelled it. He would have kept the car window rolled down as they drove home had his mom not complained of being cold. She couldn't stop shivering.

They'd left immediately after Ian got off the phone with his dad. Ian's mom drove several miles until she had to pull over, she was shaking that bad. She washed her face in the dirty bathroom of an old gas station while Ian purchased Skittles and Milky Ways with the change he found between the car seats and in the ashtray. His mom ate half her Milky Way, murmured her thanks, and whispered the words, "I wish you hadn't come." She could barely look at him. They both cried.

They drove the rest of the way home in silence. When they reached the town limits, the car idling at a stop sign, his mom looked over at him in the front passenger seat. "You're a good son, Ian. I hope you grow up to be a good man."

Ian nodded and looked away. He discreetly wiped his eyes. Good men didn't cry. They were strong. But Ian wasn't feeling very strong at the moment. He didn't have the strength or nerve to tell her thanks. Because she wouldn't stop chanting, *He'll be a good man. He'll be a good man.* She repeated it as though she had to convince herself. And it creeped him out.

Sarah handed the photos to Stu one at a time. As they studied the images, her complexion took on a greenish hue, reminding Ian of the murky pond on their property. She gave Stu the last picture, the one Ian guessed was the photo he'd taken right after she'd left the hotel room. His doe caught in the light. His mom burst into tears.

Stu put aside the photos on the floral quilt and tried to soothe her. When she'd quieted, he showed her a handful of folded notepapers. "I found these in your drawer." He gestured at the vanity table. "Are you communicating with Jackie?"

Sarah shrank away.

"Has she written you back?"

She shook her head.

"Do you know what you want with a bounty hunter? Who are you looking for?"

"I can't say." A fresh wave of tears flowed. Her body quaked. She buried her face in her hands.

Stu reached for her. His hand hovered alongside her head, hesitant, before gently resting on her greasy hair. Sarah lowered her hands in her lap. Stu's thumb drifted over her cheekbone and she flinched.

"Sarah," he said in a tone one would use for an injured animal.

She turned her head away from his touch, tucking her chin into her shoulder.

"I love you. Let me help you."

Ian couldn't watch them anymore. His parents' exchange gouged a hole in his chest. He pressed his back against the wall and stared at the ceiling, blinking back the burn.

His parents' mattress creaked and the floorboards groaned. A drawer slid open, then closed. Booted footfalls approached the door, and whispered instructions reached him. Ian flew to his room, landing on his back on the bed. He opened a book, pretending to read when he heard his dad coming down the hallway.

Stu stopped in Ian's doorway, his shirt wrinkled and untucked, face unshaven. The blazer he wore faded at the elbows. His aftershave smelled stale. He'd arrived home after midnight and hadn't slept.

He raked a hand through his unkempt hair, a mannerism Ian had picked up from him.

"I'm taking your mother to the hospital."

Ian sat up, dropped his feet to the floor. "Will she be all right?"

"I'm not sure. I hope so."

"When's she gonna get better?" Ian so wanted her to be normal like Marshall's mom. He had to believe she wouldn't be like this for the rest of his life. He grew weary and timid from wondering who he'd come home to after school or from hanging with his friends. He hated feeling that way.

Stu tucked his fingers into his front pockets and came into the room. "I don't know if she can get better. But, let's talk about yesterday—"

"Why did Jackie go see that man? What does he want with her? What did he do to my mom?" The questions tumbled from Ian. He stood up, his stance rigid. He wanted answers.

"I'm trying to figure that out."

"You never know what's going on," Ian yelled. "You would if you were home more often. I bet if you were here, Jackie wouldn't have gone to see that man and Mom would be OK."

"No one can tell your mom what to do when she's Jackie," Stu firmly replied. "I've tried. Lord knows, I've tried."

"No, you haven't!"

"Enough!" Stu bellowed. To Ian's mortification, sobs volleyed from his chest. Why, oh why, did he have to cry in front of his dad? Stu pointed a finger at Ian. "What you did yesterday—"

"I was trying to help her," Ian defended before his dad could reprimand him. After yesterday's pay-phone call, he knew it was coming.

He'd been expecting it. Ian roughly dragged his sleeves across his eyes. He smacked his chest. "I make sure she's safe and doesn't get hurt." And he'd done a horrible job in that department. He and his mom were both hurting today because Ian had failed to get the keys from Jackie. "It's my fault she went to see him," Ian sobbed. "I'll try harder next time. I know I'm stronger than Jackie so I should be able to stop her next time."

"That's not your job."

"Then do yours!" Ian's guilt shifted to anger faster than his mom shifted personas, flaming his disappointment in his dad. Stu had failed them.

Stu raised a fist. Ian flinched, but he stood his ground, his muscles so tense he felt the beginnings of a headache.

Stu swore loudly, then lowered his arm. "Do not take that tone with me. That's your warning." He showed Ian his fist.

"Or what?" Ian challenged. "You'll hit me? You'll ground me? I'm stuck here already. You're never home. I take care of her because you don't." He took a step forward. He might be only twelve, but he was taller than his mom. Stronger and faster, too. He'd been exercising a lot lately, running on the school's track team. He could do one hundred sit-ups and almost fifty push-ups. In another couple of years, he might be as tall as his dad. Maybe taller. "I know she won't admit it, but Mom wants me to take pictures. She asks to see them all the time. I know she wants me to help because she can't rely on you. You don't care about her."

His dad saw red. His cheeks turned purple and he raised his fist again. Ian braced for the blow. He deserved it. He'd been pushing his dad's temper, testing them both. He couldn't help it. Yesterday had scared him. He'd been fighting that fear all night. What if Clancy had physically hurt his mom? Or worse, murdered her?

Stu shook out his hand and put some distance between him and Ian. He locked his hands behind his neck and circled the room before coming to a stop in front of the closet on the opposite side of the room from Ian.

"I care about your mother. More than you can imagine," he said quietly, his tone carrying a note of anguish.

"No, you don't." Ian shook his head as he spoke the words. "You're always leaving us, and when you're home, you spend the whole time in the basement. You don't want to be with us. You hide now when Jackie's around."

"Because she doesn't want me around." He swore. "Ian, just—"

"My pictures will help Mom keep Jackie away." He hiccupped. Tears dampened his face, dropped off his chin. "Then, maybe . . . maybe you'll stay home with us."

Ian roughly wiped his face. He hated crying. He gritted his teeth and tightened his fists, focusing on his anger to staunch the flow. Movement in the doorway yanked his attention. "Mom?"

"Hi, Ian." She smiled and went straight to the corner where Ian kept the plastic bin of LEGOs. She dragged the bin to the center of the room. It scraped across the wood floor. She sank to her knees and removed the lid. "Do you want to build a starship with me?"

"What are you doing, Sarah?" Stu looked down in horror at his wife. "We have to go to the hospital."

Sarah scooped a handful of bricks and spread them out on the floor. "Maybe you can build a space station and I'll do the starship. Is that something you want to do, Ian?"

Stu's face turned white. He gripped Sarah under her shoulder and lifted her off the floor. "Sarah, we have to go."

"No." She twisted from his grasp and scooted out of reach. "I want to play with Ian."

"Sarah." Stu reached for her again. She smacked away his hand.

"That's not Mom. It's Billy." Ian had told his dad about Billy, but Stu hadn't met Sarah's newest alternate personality, or what the doctors referred to as *alters*, yet.

Stu visibly swallowed. He dragged a hand down his mouth and chin, unsure of what to do. Ian hadn't seen his dad look this uncomfortable. He watched Sarah separate the bricks by size and color. His eyes sheened. He lowered until eye level with Billy. "Sarah, the doctor is waiting for us." He spoke calmly and slowly.

Billy shook his head.

"How about you bring some LEGOs with you?" Stu negotiated. "You can play with them on the drive over."

Billy pushed a brick with a fingertip, considering the request, then finally nodded. "I want to make two starships." Billy scooped LEGOs onto his skirt, then stood, holding the skirt hem in a makeshift bucket.

"Go wait for me at the car," Stu instructed. "I'll be there in a minute."

"I want a juice box."

Stu looked at the floor. "I'll get you a juice box."

Billy smiled and left the room.

Stu remained in his crouched position until Ian heard Billy go out the front door. His dad slowly stood, knees cracking. He roughly cleared his throat and walked to the door, where he stopped and turned back to Ian.

"So, that was Billy?"

Ian nodded.

"I think it best you understand that Jackie will never go away."

"Don't say that." Ian shook his head. "You lie. Mom will get better."

"I don't think she can. Billy isn't another person inside your mom. Neither is Jackie. They *are* your mom."

CHAPTER 19

IAN

Aimee faces me from the opposite side of our room. Rain pelts the glass door to the patio behind me. A single lamp casts a golden glow in one corner. The rest of the room sits in a shroud of shadows.

I watch her warily, my stomach queasy. I'll never forget the way she looked at me in the lobby. She'd laughed off Reese's comment. She thought it was a joke. Office humor, however sick it might have been. She'd glanced between us, and Reese groaned an apology. She held up both hands in a deflecting manner. "I thought you would've known."

Aimee looked at me. "Ian?"

I briefly closed my eyes, then forced myself to meet her gaze.

Her face drained of color. Her eyes told me everything. I'd lied to her. I'd betrayed her. I wasn't the man she thought I was.

I was no better than James.

That's when I acted. I got into Reese's face. "You and me, we're done with this assignment."

"I'm not on contract with you," she spat, appalled. As if I had the nerve to tell her what to do. At that moment, I was capable of more than ordering her around. I could strangle her.

"Then I'm off the assignment. Without my pictures, your article will be canned."

"You can't do that. You're on contract, too. You break it and you'll never have the chance to publish with them again."

I shouldered my pack and grabbed Aimee's roller case. "Come with me," I said. "Please." I was desperate.

I'm still desperate. I don't want to lose her.

She stands just inside the hotel room's door, cheeks void of color, mouth parted, and arms resting listlessly at her sides. She's quiet, too quiet. I can handle her anger, when her Irish gets riled and she's lobbing sock balls at me. I understand that Aimee. But this stunned, silent version? She confuses me. She scares me.

Will she leave me like she left James?

"Say something," I beg.

"I don't think I should."

"Then let me explain."

She shows me her palm. "Not yet. I need a moment." She goes to her roller case, lifts the luggage onto the rack, and unzips it.

Thank God. She's not leaving. Yet.

My knees buckle. I back up, leaning my weight on the table. I roughly run both hands through my hair and lock my fingers around the back of my head.

Aimee digs through her case and removes her toiletries bag. "I've been up for twenty-four hours. I'm exhausted. I can barely think straight. I'm going to . . ." She glances at the door, then the patio slider, and back to the bathroom. "I'm going to go in there." She points at the bathroom, then lets her arm flop against her side.

My joined hands slip to the back of my neck. "Do you know how long you'll be?"

"As long as it takes to figure out what I walked into."

"There's nothing between Reese and me."

Aimee glowers.

"OK." I nod. "I'll wait." I'd wait forever.

She walks into the bathroom and quietly shuts the door.

I listen for the shower, for the faucet to run, the toilet to flush. Anything to tell me she isn't in there silently crying. I picture her sitting on the closed toilet, elbows on knees, face in her cupped hands, her shoulders quaking. My heart splinters because I've probably broken hers.

My stomach clenches and makes a gurgling noise. I feel pressure at the base of my throat. The faucet runs in the bathroom and I blow out a long, even breath, relieved she's doing something other than sobbing. I shiver. Pushing away from the table, I cross the room to the thermostat and turn on the heat. My damp clothes are stiff and uncomfortable. They stick to my skin. Shedding my jacket, I proceed to strip. I'm down to my boxer briefs and stepping from my pants when the bathroom door opens. I look up from my hunched position.

Aimee's eyes narrow and I slowly straighten. Her gaze drops. "Sex isn't going to solve this."

"I wasn't . . . I'm not . . . ," I groan, exasperated, and kick aside my pants. I thrust a hand at the dirty clothes pile. "They're wet. I'm just changing." I put on jeans and a shirt, my torso shivering, skin clammy. I slide my arms into a hoodie and zip it to my chin.

Aimee frowns. "Are you feeling OK?"

"No," I snap, shoving my fists into the front pockets. "I'm standing on the edge of Half Dome wondering when you're going to shove me off." Lord knows I deserve it. "Would you please listen to me? I want to explain."

Aimee slowly shakes her head and returns her toiletries to her case. She zips up the luggage.

My heart knocks into my ribs. "Are you leaving?"

She turns around. "I'm not sure yet."

I close my eyes. "Don't go."

"Do you see what I meant the other day when we drove back from Nadia's? How I feel you've glossed over your history with Reese? It's like you were holding something back. Is she the reason you left in such a hurry?"

"No! I had no idea she'd be here, let alone assigned to the story. She was waiting for me when I checked in."

"It's true, then, you were married."

My shoulders drop. "Yes. For nine hours."

"Nine—*what*?" .

I cross the room to her. Only inches of air divide us. "It was a stupid decision during a drunken night full of them. You've got to believe me." I lift my hands to her face, but I don't touch her. My palms hover over her cheeks, hands trembling. "It meant nothing. She means nothing."

"It doesn't matter what it means. You should have told me."

"You're right." My arms fall to my sides. I back up a step. "You're right. I should have and that's my mistake."

"We've talked a little about your relationship with Reese. Why didn't you ever mention you were married?" She searches my face and it takes me a moment to answer. A very long moment.

"Before I met you," I begin, "I'd lost everyone important in my life. For years it was just me and my camera and the next destination. Then I saw you that night at the gallery. You were so beautiful in your black dress with your curls framing your face." I touch her hair. "I saw in you what I had felt for years after my mother left. I was alone and totally out of sorts with my place in life. I felt like I had no purpose and that made for one reckless teenager," I rasp, thinking of those hellish years. "But you smiled at me, and you let me buy you a cupcake, and I fell for you. I fell so hard for you. And for the first time in a very long time, I felt something important in here." I press a hand to my chest.

"When you'd left James and came back to me, I should have told you, but I didn't want to give you a reason to not want to be with me. Those nine hours with Reese are inconsequential to a lifetime with you. Those hours are an embarrassment. I didn't believe you'd take my feelings for you seriously—take *me* seriously—had you known. Bottom line? I was scared. I was afraid you'd leave me, too."

Aimee is quiet, her gaze turning inward. She's processing, kneading my words until she's molded them into a shape she can comprehend. Her lips pinch. She sharply exhales through her nose and lifts her chin. I recognize the look. "You're angry."

"Yes, but not because you didn't tell me Reese was your wife."

"For only nine hours."

Aimee's gaze broils and I clamp my mouth shut.

"No, I'm not angry," she corrects. "I'm disappointed you thought so little of me. That you thought a nine-hour marriage would scare me away. You should have told me."

"Yes, I should have, and I'm sorry. Can you forgive me?"

"That makes three now," she whispers.

"Three what?" I frown, confused.

"Three times someone important to me has kept something important from me because they think I can't handle it. James about his brother Phil. Nadia about how she's working *and flirting* with Thomas."

"Nadia's *what*?" I say with an unbelieving shake of my head.

"And you about your nine-hour marriage. I don't have a fragile temperament, Ian. I'm not a withering flower."

"You're right, you're absolutely right. You're a tree, with strong roots." I nod continually as I speak. "You can stand up to any sort of wind that tries to blow you down." I move my arms around for emphasis.

"Oh my God." She scrapes her hair back in frustration.

"Sorry, was that too much?" My mouth quirks.

She buries her face in her hands and cry-laughs. "This isn't funny."

I gently prod her hands away and dip my head to look up in her face, my own expression serious. I stroke her cheek. "You're right. It's not funny. I can't apologize enough for not telling you."

"I love you, Ian. I'm not going to leave you. But we are going to talk about this."

I briefly close my eyes, letting her words sink in, then cup her cheeks and rest my forehead against hers, amazed at how incredibly understanding she is. "I'll tell you whatever you want to know."

She nods and moves away. "Good. You can start by pouring me a glass of wine." She points at the complimentary bottle of Tempranillo on the bureau. "Then you're going to tell me how you got yourself hitched to Reese's Pieces."

"Reese's Pieces?" I look askance at her as I make my way to the bureau.

Aimee sinks into a chair. "Yes. She's a piece of work."

That she is. I uncork the wine and pour two glasses. I hand one to Aimee, which she downs. *O-kayyyy.* I show her the bottle. "Refill?"

"Please." She holds up her glass.

This time she swirls the glass and sniffs the wine. Then she takes a sip and sets down the glass on the table. She rubs her thighs. "I'm ready."

I'm not, but I don't have a choice. I don't want a choice. This is for Aimee. It's for us.

I don't sit at the table with her. I need to stand while I talk through this. It wasn't one of the best days of my life. In fact, it makes the top-ten list of the worst. I lean back against the bureau in a semistanding position, my legs crossed at the ankles. My mind tracks back to those years with Reese and my stomach curdles. I press my fingers into my abs and set the wine aside, my interest in drinking it gone.

"We'd graduated from college and wanted to celebrate so we went to Vegas. It happened to be the same day my mom was scheduled for release and Stu would be in town to pick her up. There were six of us from college, three guys and three gals. Reese and I were the only official couple. She was also the only one who knew about my mom."

I meet Aimee's gaze and she slowly nods, encouraging me to continue. Hugging my chest tight, I pace the room. Her gaze tracks me. I look at the floor as I talk.

"You know the story about how I found my dad drunk in his hotel room and that he told me my mom left before he got there. What I didn't tell you was what happened afterward. I drove around for hours, convinced I could find my mom at the bus station or waiting for a train. I even tried a few hotels to see if she checked into one. It was a waste of time. She was long gone. I finally met up with my friends on the Strip and proceeded to get really stinking drunk. We were all hammered, but I was a mess, and Reese was right there with me.

"I don't remember how it happened. Most of the night is a blur and several hours are flat out missing from the memory banks." I tap my forehead. "I only know that we woke up with rings on our fingers and our signatures on a marriage certificate I found in my suitcase."

"Holy . . . Wow. I can't imagine what was going through your head at that moment."

"Not much," I say with an unenthusiastic laugh. "Worst hangover ever."

"What did you do?"

I stop in front of Aimee. "We petitioned for an annulment. It was granted fairly quickly. We were both intoxicated. Happens all the time in Vegas."

"Technically, you weren't really married. The marriage was dissolved."

I sink to my heels and hold Aimee's hands in mine. "I know, but that doesn't excuse me from not telling you."

"You and Reese dated in college and were together for a year after. Did you wish . . ." She stalls, biting her lower lip. I squeeze her hands.

"Did I wish we didn't get the annulment?" She nods and I hum in thought. "Yes, for all of five seconds, right before I signed the paperwork. I loved her at the time, but she was adamant—we both were—that our careers came first. Marriage was not what either of us wanted at the time. What happened in Vegas was supposed to stay in Vegas."

"I can't believe Reese introduced herself to me as your ex-wife."

"I'm not going to say the b-word, but be my guest."

Aimee laughs, breaking the tension between us. "She's a royal—"

A wave of heat tumbles through me. Sweat seeps from my pores. My skin bakes. I let go of one of Aimee's hands and unzip the hoodie. The room feels like a furnace.

"You don't look well, Ian." Aimee touches my forehead. It's sheened in sweat. "You're warm."

"I don't like octopus. Promise you'll never boil octopus and make me eat it." My stomach pitches. I cover my mouth and rush to the bathroom and proceed to humiliate myself inside the toilet.

When I'm done, I fall back on my ass and slouch against the wall. Arms parked on my raised knees, I close my eyes and breathe through the nausea. I'm still tasting paprika. A cool washcloth touches my forehead, then my cheeks. I open my eyes and Aimee is there, kneeling beside me. "Thank you," I whisper hoarsely.

She hands me a glass of water, which I chug. "Slow down, you'll get sick again. Better?" she asks when I give her the empty glass.

"Much." Now that the slimy octo is out of my gut, my stomach has settled. But I feel a crushing weight on my chest and I need to get it off. I fix my eyes on hers. "There's something else I should have told you."

"Oh?" Aimee sits back warily.

"I should have told you before I left."

"But you didn't."

"I didn't." I roll my head from side to side against the wall. "We'd argue and I didn't want to do that before I left."

"What you have to tell me will make me upset?"

"Yes . . . maybe."

She pushes back her shoulders, which puts her eye level several inches above mine. She looks down at me. "Do I need to remind you I'm not fragile?"

"No. No, you don't." I smile weakly and wave a hand, my arm flopping back into my lap. "I'm tired of arguing."

"Me, too."

"I don't want to upset you."

"Spit it out, Ian, I can handle it."

"I talked with James."

"And you thought by mentioning this to me I'd accuse you of bringing up James again."

I nod.

She sighs, dismayed. "What happened?"

"He came to our house and he gave me Lacy Saunders's card. Remember her? She'd given it to him with the request to pass it along to me. That's why he wanted to see me. I called Lacy and—"

"Her number's disconnected. I know. But I got her new one and I talked to her."

"So did I. Aimee, her number wasn't disconnected when I called."

CHAPTER 20

IAN

"What did she tell you?"

"How did you find her number?" I ask at the same time.

Seven years ago, Aimee had tried locating her number with no success. She even hired a private investigator. Lacy never kept her numbers for long and seemed to constantly be on the move. She disconnected the number on her card immediately after we finished our call. So how did Aimee find it this time?

Aimee's gaze slides to the door. She stands, rinses out the cloth, and folds it over the lip of the basin. I push off the floor, feeling slightly woozy, but better than a few moments ago. I don't think I have food poisoning, though my stomach reacted to something. I grab my toothbrush and squirt on a strip of paste.

Aimee moves aside so I can use the sink. "Lacy mentioned that she spoke with you. She wants us to meet her at your dad's house on Tuesday."

I tilt my head back so I don't drool foam when I say, "*That's* why I left early. I wanted to get the assignment done before meeting Lacy. It wasn't because of Reese."

I spit out the paste, rinse my mouth, and tell her what happened.

After her text about Kristen being in labor, I drove home from the gym to shower before heading to the hospital. And there was Lacy's card, right beside my keys where I'd dropped them on the table by the door. I figured, what did I have to lose from punching a set of numbers into my phone?

The phone rang and I moved into the kitchen for a Red Bull. Long night ahead, what with Kristen being in labor and all. I expected to get the "This number has been disconnected and is no longer in service" recording and be on my way. But Lacy answered the phone.

"Hello, Ian," she'd said.

The back of my neck prickled. My pulse took a shot of adrenaline like a junkie. At the sound of her voice, I had an all-around bad-vibe feeling. "Why did you want me to call?"

"You've been looking for me."

"That was five years ago." Personal data is more accessible on the Internet than it was five years ago. I also had the funds now to hire a private investigator, assuming that's what I wanted to do. "I don't need you like I once thought I did."

"Maybe not, but you do need to listen to what your father has to say."

My father? The prickles on the back of my neck scampered like cockroaches across my shoulders. What did my dad have to do with Lacy? She was as much a mystery to him as she's been with me. "I haven't spoken with him in years. I doubt he has anything to say to me."

"He will."

I glanced at the kitchen clock. It was getting late. Aimee was waiting for me at the hospital. "Unless you have something to say, I'm hanging up." What a waste of time.

"I'm not wasting your time, Ian, so don't waste mine. Tuesday is a good day. It's my favorite day of the week. Mondays are the worst. Everyone's cranky and wants it to be Friday. But Tuesdays? People are more generous on Tuesdays. They give more to charity and they spend more money at stores. The stock market does very well on Tuesdays, too. We vote on Tuesdays. Change happens on Tuesdays. It also has cheaper airfares. I'll be at your dad's house on Tuesday. You should come, too."

"I can't. I'll be on assignment." The most important assignment of my life. Idaho is the last place I want to go.

"That's too bad. I have news of your mother." She hung up.

I blinked, pulled the phone away from my ear to confirm she'd ended the call. She had. I immediately redialed. It rang continually. I tried again after I showered. The phone rang; then it answered. "This number has been—" I disconnected.

"I called the airline to see if I could get a flight that night and then called Al. He signed off on me moving up the trip, so I decided I'd go to Spain and get the assignment done before meeting up with Lacy," I say to Aimee. "It hit me then why I'd been so irritable with you these past months."

"That's understandable. James threw us both for a loop."

"What happened last June hurt, I'm not going to lie. But there's more to what I'm feeling and it's not easy for me to admit." I stop and take a moment, lightly knocking my knuckles on the sink counter.

"What is it?" Aimee asks.

I take a breath. "I've resented you."

"Me?"

I nod. "I envied your bravery. You faced your worst fear when you found James after you thought he died. You not only let him go and moved on, you forgave him. You're a much better person than me."

"Don't say that, Ian. Don't think so little of yourself. Look at you and your success. You've come so far considering what happened to you."

I shrug. "It's how I feel. And I can't keep living this way. I need to put the anger and resentment I feel toward my dad behind me, and I need to deal with my guilt about my mom. That's why I'm meeting with Lacy. I don't know what I'm going to find out from her and I've got no clue what's up with my dad, other than my gut telling me something is wrong."

"And you always follow your gut."

"I trust that sucker," I say with a half smile. "I moved up my assignment so I could be in Idaho by Tuesday. Lacy's favorite day of the week."

"She's an odd woman." Aimee shakes her head, incredulous. "Have you tried reaching your dad?"

"I called him during my layover. He hasn't called back." My eyes search hers, so blue and vibrant despite how tired I know she is. "Why are you here? What about the café and your deadlines? You could have called me about Lacy."

She skims her hands under the unzipped flaps of my hoodie and pushes it off my shoulders. I let her tug the sleeves down my arms. The hoodie drops to the floor. "A long time ago, there was this girl and she was sad. She had lost her fiancé and was desperate to find him. But there was this other boy who loved this girl very much. So much that he traveled to the ends of the world to help her search for the fiancé she thought was her true love." Aimee lifts my shirt. I raise my arms and she pulls it over my head. The shirt lands on the sweatshirt. Cool air hits my torso and my skin puckers.

"What happened to this boy and girl?" I rasp, my eyes fixated on her fingers as she unbuttons her blouse.

"This girl found her fiancé, but he'd changed. The girl had to let him go, not because he changed, but because she'd grown up during his absence. Now a strong and independent woman with a clear head, she saw the imperfections in their relationship and acknowledged the damage they'd done. But in finding herself, she discovered she loved the boy as much as he loved her." She parts her blouse, exposing the black lace bra underneath. I groan.

"You're so beautiful."

The blouse floats to the floor. "Five years ago, you dropped everything to help me search for James. I want to do the same for you. I want to help you find your mom."

I steal a kiss from her and it tastes like heaven. My heaven. "I love you."

"I love you, too, Ian. You're my husband. We're a family. You don't have to do everything alone anymore."

I clasp her head, my fingers threading through her hair, pressing into her scalp. Emotion squeezes my chest. "I thank God every day you walked into Wendy's gallery and into my life," I say against her lips, my voice gravelly. I kiss her hard, and when I come up for air, my forehead pressed against hers, our breath hot and mingling, I ask her about Caty.

"She's fine. She's with my parents. They'll watch her as long as we need them to."

"And the café? Your plans?"

Aimee moves from my arms. "Can we talk about that over dinner?"

"Sure," I say, somewhat hesitant. "Everything OK?"

She smiles winsomely. "Everything's perfect. I'll tell you about it, but after I shower." She points at herself. "Travel scum."

I tap my chest. "Hiking scum. Shower with me."

She winks seductively, sending a zap of electricity straight to my center. "I thought you'd never ask." She shimmies from her jeans and I'm instantly on fire for her. She's wearing it, that swatch of lace that matches her bra and covers nothing.

I shove down my jeans and briefs and flip on the shower. Ice-cold water sprays the tiled walls. I rope an arm around her waist and haul her into the stall with me. She screams, ice water sluicing over her head and down her back.

"You jerk."

"You love this jerk." I laugh against her mouth, reaching behind her to adjust the water temperature. I unclasp her bra.

"More than words can say."

She kisses me and before I know it, I'm at a complete loss for words.

⁓

After we've showered and dressed and before we leave the room, I clasp Aimee's shoulders. "Are we good here?" I point from her to me. "About what happened between me and Reese?"

Aimee bites into her lower lip and her gaze turns inward. Then she nods. "I think so. Though, don't expect me to be nice to her," she says with a frown.

"After the stunt she pulled, you can be as nasty as you want."

She holds up her fist for a bump. "Deal. And, Ian? I do forgive you for not telling me about Reese."

I cradle her face and press my lips to her forehead, my eyes drifting closed. "And I forgive you."

"For what?"

I lean back and look down at her face. "For last summer, with James. In my head, I forgave you the moment you told me, but I never said it out loud to you. I'm sorry."

Aimee closes her eyes and nods. "Thank you," she whispers.

I kiss her lips, gently, lovingly. "We're good together."

She smiles. "Yes, we are."

I grin and open the door, standing aside to let her through. "Let's go eat. I think we've earned ourselves a warm meal." Alone, I hope, without Reese dining alongside us. I'd lost my lunch today. I didn't need to lose my dinner, too.

We walk to the inn's restaurant. When we pass the pool, I reach for her hand to stop her. She turns into me, chest to chest, and looks up. Wood smoke fills the air and the clouds have moved on. An obsidian sheet swathed in stars glistens overhead. Dishes clatter in the kitchen yards away and the colorful notes of a classical guitar ride the night air from an open window. Other than that, the countryside is quiet, settled in for the night.

"The sky is unreal," Aimee says. "I have to get out of the city more. It's been a long time since I've seen so many stars."

I hum, transfixed by the reflection of starlight in her eyes. She looks at me and I give my head a virtual shake before I get sappy and drag her back to our room.

"You didn't answer my question earlier. How did you get in touch with Lacy?"

Aimee lets go of my hand and backs away a step. I frown. That's not a good sign.

"Aimee?"

"Yeah . . . um." She twists her hands together. "I didn't find her. Thomas did."

My head snaps back. "You got Thomas involved?"

"James told me a little about how Thomas kept him hidden in Mexico. There's no doubt in my mind Thomas has connections. I figured if anyone could find a working number for Lacy, he could."

"So you called him." My tone has a hard edge.

"I met with him at his office."

White-hot rage plummets through me, coursing through my limbs like molten steel. Every part of me burns. I'm angrier than I've been in a long time, more than I felt toward Reese earlier or at James for kissing my wife. I inhale, nostrils flaring and lungs filling to capacity, and then I release a rope of the most unsavory, foul language I've probably spewed in Aimee's presence. Her eyes go camera-lens round and she backs up. Looking around, she moves her hands up and down, urging me to lower my voice.

I can't look at her. I turn around and walk away.

"I'm sorry, Ian, but I figured Lacy had something urgent to tell you and I didn't know who else to go to in such a short time."

Her apology rips me apart inside. Hands on hips, I turn to her. "Good God, Aimee. I'm not upset with you. It's me. I'm angry with myself. You went to see him because of me. I put you in that position. After everything he's done to you." Just thinking about Thomas makes her physically sick. "God, I'm sorry, baby. I should have told you about James and Lacy."

"Yes, you should have. But it's done and I survived. And get this, Lacy's real name is Charity Watson."

The name ripples through my head, its touch familiar, but unplaceable. "Thomas told you this?"

"Do you remember the café's soft opening and how I thought it weird that Thomas ended our conversation and left like that?" She snaps her fingers. "He'd seen Lacy in Mexico with Imelda. Then he sees her at my café. He dug around a bit and found out who she really is."

"I bet he threatened her."

"Most likely. That's probably why she shipped James's painting rather than try meeting up with me again. Anyway, Thomas knew her legal name. That's how he found her so quickly."

"I'm surprised he agreed to get it for you."

"I was, too, but I think he feels guilty about everything he's done. It's eating him alive. He looks horrible. I almost feel sorry for the guy."

"Almost?"

"Like this much." She holds her index finger and thumb a quarter inch apart. "The number is to a landline. Lacy lives in New Mexico with her granddaughter."

I pull Aimee into my arms and kiss her. "Thank you for doing this for me."

"I didn't think twice, and I did it for us. We're in this together, Collins. Now feed me. I'm hungry."

"Yes, ma'am." I link my fingers with hers, our hands swinging as we walk. I look askance at her. "Thomas and Nadia, eh?"

Aimee waves her hand in dismissal. "Don't get me started. But yeah, she's working on a project for him. And I got the impression from both of them it's more than business. She's on my bad-friend list right now."

"Then we won't talk about her." I kiss her cheek.

Alex seats us at a table under a window and immediately serves us the night's meal, salted pork shoulder with local greens and chickpeas.

"Are you serious about pulling from this assignment?" Aimee asks, cutting into her pork.

I set down my knife and fork and lean forward, my forearms on the edge of the table. "When Reese was a kid, she had a neighbor who neglected his dogs. He kept them tied up in the front yard."

"That's horrible."

"It traumatized her. She's taken it to the extreme and doesn't keep pets because of that. She's also opposed to animals being penned for whatever reason, but more so when the conditions aren't ideal."

"She doesn't see the Rapa as ideal?"

I shake my head. "I don't think so."

"How many horses are placed inside the arena?"

"Two hundred and for less than two hours. It's for the safety of the horses, and it's the fastest way the villagers can attend to them. They get the greatest number wormed in the shortest amount of time without causing too much stress to the animals and more extreme injuries to the handlers. The horses are wild. Given space to move, the vaccinations would never get done. They'd get sick and weak. The herds would eventually die off.

"The way Reese has been talking, I don't know . . ." I push food around my plate. "I'm concerned her bias will come across in the article. I don't want negative press. That's not what I signed up for. The villagers are passionate about their herds. The Galician horses are a rarity to them and the Rapa is an astounding event steeped in history and tradition. I want to share that through my photos, and I was hoping whoever wrote the article would express that.

"Reese was at the Rapa this past summer. She had to leave in the middle of it. She couldn't handle it. I took her up the hill today hoping she'd see they're free the other three hundred and sixty-four days of the year."

"You haven't seen them since you got here?"

I shake my head and put down my fork, appetite gone. "Tomorrow's my last chance, and after what happened out there this evening"—I tilt my head toward the lobby—"and on our hike today, I doubt she'll want to go with me. We came across a dead foal."

Aimee chews her food, thinking. "We have three more days before we have to be at your dad's house. You've come too far to give up. Text Reese's Pieces and apologize."

I laugh at the nickname. Then I laugh at the logic behind her suggestion. "You want me to apologize to her?"

"Yes, because you're going to be the mature one in this disagreement. You're also not going to let her, of all people, come between you and your dreams. Come on, Ian, *National Geographic*! Your photo could be on the cover." She stabs a chunk of pork, bites it off her fork, and grins.

"Is this your version of a pep talk?"

"It is, because you're taking us both. I want to see these magnificent Galician horses."

"Tomorrow ought to be interesting." Not awkward at all. I aim my index finger at the ceiling. "One condition. I'll give it another day. I'll ask Reese straight out what she plans to write. If I don't want my name in the byline, I'm calling Al and pulling out."

We finish dinner and afterward the cook invites Aimee into the kitchen to discuss Galician recipes and local delicacies. "Don't be surprised if I add a few Spanish items to one of my seasonal menus," she tells me.

I grimace. *Please, no octopus.*

"Dinner was amazing," she says.

Dinner *was* amazing. Because Reese wasn't here.

I draft a text to her that I'm leaving early in the morning on the same trail. One more shot to find and take shots of the herd.

I review the message, then swallow the maturity pill Aimee prescribed.

Sorry about earlier. No hard feelings. Let's make this work.

Satisfied, I send it off.

"Ready?" Aimee's back. She rests a hand on my shoulder.

"Yep, let's go." I push up from the table and we leave the restaurant, my hand on her lower back. "We didn't talk about the café during dinner," I say as we walk to the room. "What's going on with the expansion?"

"It's not."

"No?" I look down at her face, trying to read her expression.

"You were right about what you said earlier. I've lost sight of why I opened a restaurant in the first place. I'll admit, the idea of having three locations seemed cool. It was like I'd made it. I was better than Starbucks and Peet's because I'm thriving where other indies are closing. But what I really want is to be back in the kitchen. I want to bake for my favorite customers and concoct new recipes." She stops and I turn to her. "I don't want to be stuck in an office, running numbers and paying bills and managing three times the staff I currently have."

"Are you sure? You aren't doing this because I've been complaining?"

"You mean whining?"

I lean back, appalled. "I don't whine."

Aimee laughs. "No, you don't. You're very good at keeping me grounded."

"We balance each other."

"Yes, I love that about us. Because there's something else I want."

"Anything." I'd give her the stars and the moon, the whole freaking solar system.

"You and I both grew up as only children. I don't want that for Caty." She inhales deeply and grins. "I want us to have another baby."

My heart sinks and my shoulders drop.

She bounces on her toes and smiles so big because she can't contain her grin. I immediately wrap her up in my arms and bury my face in her hair. Because I can't smile with her. Not yet.

For the moment, I just hold her.

"Ian?" She wiggles in my embrace. I detect the note of uncertainty in her voice and my chest clenches. "You do want another child, don't you?"

I loosen my arms and clasp her face. My thumb skims her upper lip, a caress. Her eyes search mine. "What's wrong?"

"I do want to have more kids. But let's talk about this when we get home. Right now . . ." I stop and swallow roughly. "Right now . . ."

Her eyes close and she nods rapidly. "I get it. It's too much at once. I should have waited. I'm sorry for bringing it up. It's just . . ."

"No, no, don't apologize. You have nothing to apologize for. Let's get through the next few days. Then we'll talk." I kiss her forehead, then her nose and her lips. She looks so dejected and it breaks my heart to put off this discussion. But how can I return home and be the man my family needs—the one I committed to be when Aimee told me she was pregnant with Caty—when the mistakes I'd made in the past are still festering within me? I fear I'd only make more.

202

CHAPTER 21

IAN, AGE THIRTEEN

"Where's the film?" Ian leaned over his dad's shoulder. They were in his office next to Ian's bedroom. Stu was showing him a new type of camera he and some of the other professional photographers had received to test. He called it a digital camera. It was large and bulky and seemed unwieldy to Ian.

"There isn't any film." His dad pointed at the compartment at the base of the camera. "This is a built-in hard drive. The pictures are stored here."

"Like a computer?" Ian leaned closer, putting weight on his dad.

"Something like that. Pull up a chair. Let's have a look."

Ian dragged a wood chair around the desk. The same chair he sat in whenever his dad lectured him about homework and chores. He always seemed to be lecturing, Ian thought with a virtual eye roll. He plopped onto the seat.

Stu scooted his own chair closer. The tarnished brass casters squeaked and the leather seat creaked. He plugged the camera directly into the computer and clicked the mouse, opening a file that displayed ten icons, then double-clicked the first icon. On the screen appeared an image of Ian that his dad had taken only fifteen minutes before. Ian stood on the porch, grinning, his hair waving like a flag above his head, caught in a gust of wind.

"Whoa." Ian was impressed. There he was, on the screen, no darkroom needed. The quality wasn't great. There were features in the image that could be sharpened. "Why's it in black and white?"

"I don't have a color monitor. I guess I better get one." His dad leaned back in his chair, studying the photo, his hands clasped over his middle.

Ian picked up the digital camera and inspected the dials and buttons. "Will this be your new work camera?" His gaze dove to the professional Nikon his dad used for shooting ball games. Ian imagined the pictures he could take should he get his hands on that camera.

"Not this camera. The technology has a way to go." Stu took the digital camera from Ian's hands and returned it to the desk. "I predict in ten to fifteen years we won't use film, not like we do today."

"You think so?" Ian parked his elbow on the table and propped his chin in his hand. He reached for the digital camera again. He studied the casing. It was heavy with the additional compartment. Not convenient at all to lug around on a photo shoot.

"Put it down, Ian." His dad took the camera from him again and Ian huffed. "It's an expensive piece of equipment. Keep in mind, digital photography is the future." He leaned toward the monitor and clicked through the photos. Pictures of him and Ian around the property.

"Why didn't you take any of Mom?"

"I just didn't." His dad opened another icon. Ian hung upside down from a tree limb.

"She's pretty." Especially when Jackie doesn't cake Sarah's face in makeup or isn't getting into Ian's face. She'd get drunk and threaten to take his precious mama away from him. She never did. She always came back whenever she left.

But Sarah, when she was his mom, Sarah, was beautiful to Ian. "We need more pictures of her." He had too many of Jackie, and they weren't pleasant. He didn't like looking at those.

"Don't take pictures of your mom," his dad snapped.

Ian jerked back at his harsh tone. Where had that come from?

Don't take pictures of Jackie. That was the rule. Ever since Jackie drove them to the dive motel and met that biker, Ian had no problem whatsoever obeying it. There had never been a rule about not photographing Sarah. This was new.

"You take pictures of you and me all the time. We're family. Mom needs to be in those pictures."

"Just lay off the camera with her. She doesn't want her picture taken anymore."

"Why not?"

Stu dragged a hand down his face. "It's not important. Just don't do it."

"But—"

"End of discussion."

Ian hunched in his chair, simmering. He was thirteen. He didn't like being told what to do, and he especially didn't like not being given an explanation. What was wrong with taking his mom's picture?

Sheesh. Ian pushed away from the desk. He hated being treated like he was ten. If his dad were around more often, he'd see that Ian was almost a man himself. He was done hanging out with his dad. He had places to go, better things to do.

Ian stood, kicking the wood chair out of his way. It bumped into the wall.

"Ian. Put back the chair."

Ian ignored his dad and stomped to his bedroom. He pulled on a sweatshirt and cap, then stormed down the stairs. He'd spent the morning walking the perimeter of their property with his dad and Josh Lansbury, the man who farmed their land. Stu had invited Ian along to listen to their conversation about soil conditions and crop rotations. The land would be Ian's one day and his father felt he best understand how to work it even if he planned to lease it out like Stu did.

Ian wanted as much to do with the land as his father seemed to want to do with him and Sarah. His parents rarely spent time together, let alone in the same room. His dad slept on the couch in his office. When Ian had tried including Sarah on their walk this morning, she declined. She wanted to read. Ever since the motel incident, their marriage hadn't been the same.

Ian opened the front door, intent on going to Marshall's house. Better than hanging around home where no one wanted to be around the other people who lived there. He liked it at the Killions'. They sat together for dinner each night. They played board games and watched movies.

"Ian?"

He stopped short.

"Come here, please."

He closed the door and went to the front parlor. His mother sat in her reading chair in the corner. A knitted blanket covered her legs, which she curled underneath her. Stacks of books crowded the scuffed hardwood floor, surrounding her. There had to be more than a hundred books. She'd read each at least once. Several of them multiple times. An open book was facedown on her lap. He couldn't see the cover from where he stood, but guessed it was the latest Michael Crichton. She couldn't get enough of his sci-fi thrillers.

His mom smiled at him. "Where are you off to?"

Ian shoved his fists into his front pockets. It pushed his shoulders to his ears. "Marshall's."

"How's Marshall these days?"

"Fine, I guess." He hadn't invited Marshall over in months. He hadn't had any friends over the entire school year. Ian didn't trust his mom to be herself around them, and as ashamed as he was to admit, her alters' behaviors embarrassed him. Besides, his dad worried if anybody found out about his mom, they'd take her away. Or worse, they'd take Ian away.

His mom glanced out the window. "It's about to rain. Pick out a book. Read with me."

Ian's face scrunched up and she laughed. She pushed aside the blanket and stood, going to the bookshelf. "I'm sure there's something here that should keep the interest of a thirteen-year-old boy."

Ian snorted. Reading was the last thing he wanted to do. There were horses to be tended to in Marshall's barn and blueberry pie to eat. Mrs. Killion told him yesterday she planned to bake the pie this afternoon. She'd invited him to come over, but he'd gotten sidetracked with his dad's new digital camera.

"Why don't you like your picture taken?" he asked.

"It makes me uncomfortable," Sarah said, her back turned to him. She bent over to peer at the lower shelves. Her fingers trailed over the book spines. "Oh my goodness. Look what I found. Do you remember this one?"

The Black Stallion. She used to read passages to him every night until they finished the book and he asked her to start at the beginning.

"Read it to me."

He loved that book, like when he was seven. He made a face. "It's a kid's book."

"It's a kids-of-all-ages book. You used to beg me to read this to you every night."

Because he loved the way she read it to him. She'd get into character and make sound effects. Listening to her was better than watching the movie.

Sarah returned to her chair and patted the couch cushion beside her. "Sit with me. I'll read to you."

Ian glanced toward the staircase.

"I'll keep my voice low so your dad doesn't hear. I wouldn't want to embarrass you," she whispered conspiratorially.

Who cared if his mother was going to read to him like a little kid. What was the big deal?

"I'm not embarrassed." Ian crossed the room and flopped onto the couch.

His mom flipped the book open to the first page and started to read. Ian leaned his head back on the couch and closed his eyes. The soft cadence of her voice moved over him. Hearing her reminded him how much he used to enjoy this with her. No wonder he used to insist she tuck him into bed with that story. Every single night until her shifting became more frequent and he stopped asking her to read. He didn't know who would be tucking him into bed that night. And on some nights when Billy showed up, Ian was the one tucking his mom into bed.

Soon, his mom finished the first chapter and Ian lifted his head. She was looking at him. A tear beaded in the corner of her eye. She stood and grasped his chin, lifting his cap to kiss his forehead. "No matter what I do or where I go, never, *ever*, forget that I love you," she urgently whispered. "Whatever I do is because I love you."

CHAPTER 22

IAN

I pace the lobby, waiting for Reese. She didn't reply to my text last night or voice mail this morning. Hopefully she'll make an appearance.

I glance at my watch. It's after eight. We're getting a later start than planned, but I'm not complaining, too much. Aimee and I stayed awake late into the night because . . .

I missed her. Simple as that.

I missed my wife and that connection we have. So I took the time to show her just how much I missed her.

Carrying a brown paper bag, Aimee meets me in the lobby. "Any luck with Reese's Pieces?"

I snort a laugh and shake my head. "Whatcha got in there?" Pulling at the lip of Aimee's bag, I look inside.

"Paulo made us lunch."

"Who's Paulo?"

"The chef. I got the pulpo recipe from him. He's making us some tonight."

My stomach goes for a spin. "You're kidding, right?"

"Of course I am." She nudges my shoulder. "Let's go find some horses."

We make our way to the rental and settle into the car. As I sync my phone with the car's Bluetooth, a message pings from Reese. I glance at the notification. It's short and not sweet. She has other plans today.

In an effort to not think the article is a lost cause, I launch my Nathaniel Rateliff station on Pandora. "It's just you and me today." I kiss Aimee's cheek and reverse out of the parking lot.

"Sounds like a perfect day to me."

We drive to Sabucedo and hike the same trail Reese and I took yesterday. The hillside is muddy, but the weather is perfect. Wisps of clouds blotch the expanse of blue like the brown-and-white piebald coat of a horse. I don't point out the deceased foal when we pass the tree that sheltered Reese and me in yesterday's rainstorm. Instead, we pass the time talking about my last trip to Spain, my weeks traveling through the country, and the long weekend in Sabucedo and at the Rapa. We've been hiking for almost ninety minutes when we crest the hill and Aimee gasps.

"Look!"

Below us lies the rustic village of Sabucedo with its beige stucco walls and red tile roofs. On the hillside, about a hundred yards down from where we stand, is a small herd. I quickly count twenty-eight heads, a stallion, his mares, and several foals.

Slipping off my pack, I pull out my Nikon and the 70-300 mm lens. It's light and compact with a sharp autofocus. Perfect for moving around with as the animals graze and wander. It's also the ideal lens to capture them in action should they decide to gallop away. I also unpack my stand and the camera's remote so I can capture some stills of the countryside.

"They're right there," Aimee exclaims. "So beautiful."

I glance from the herd to my wife. "*This* is what I came to see." I grin, grateful we found them. Reese should be seeing this.

Turning on the camera, I check the battery and add a backup battery and chip to one of the gazillion pockets lining my pant legs. Maybe we can catch up with Reese this evening and show her the pictures.

"I count about thirty of them," Aimee says. "Is this all?"

"It's only one herd. Over two thousand were recorded roaming the hills throughout northern Spain back in the 1970s. There are just under five hundred today."

"That's tragic. What happened to them?"

"Poachers, predators, poor economic conditions." I zip up my pack. "The villagers do manage overpopulation because there's a lot of competition for grazing land with farmers. But right now, all they want is what's left of the population to thrive."

Aimee shields her eyes from the sun's glare. "They look different from regular horses."

"They've adapted to their environment." I take in the herd, their hardy frames and shaggy chestnut coats. Through my lens, I see that some of the mares have longer, thicker hair around their muzzles, telling me they're older than the others. I point at a thick hedge. "See those gorse bushes over there? They love to eat them. The hair on their faces protects them from the bushes and their thick coats insulate them from the weather. We're less than fifty kilometers from the coast. It gets cold and misty up here."

"Are we a safe distance from them?"

I do a visual estimate and guess we're about fifty meters from the herd.

"We'll be fine. Just don't get any closer." I glance around. "Let's set up here."

Aimee shrugs off her pack and takes out a blanket. She lays it on the ground.

"I'm going to walk around, take some photos."

Aimee makes an OK sign with her thumb and index finger. "I'll have lunch ready when you're done."

I spend the rest of the morning walking the perimeter of the herd, framing shots and snapping photos. I play with angles, the composition, and the light. The horses let me get within thirty-five meters of them before they flick their manes and tails, fidgeting at my nearness. Backing off, I wait for them to settle so I can take more pictures. I then set up some panoramic shots, using my stand and remote to minimize any vibration that would blur the pictures.

After a while, feeling light-headed, I return to Aimee, sinking beside her on the blanket. She gives me a sandwich of marinated vegetables and cut meat. I bite off a mouthful, and flavor explodes. "This is incredible." I chew and swallow. "The horses are amazing. You're amazing."

Aimee tosses her head back with a laugh. "Hungry?"

"Starving." I take another bite. Dressing leaks from the corner of my mouth. I thumb it off.

"You're just happy because I fed you."

I chuckle. "Good call on the sandwiches. My stomach thanks you." Had it just been me up here, I would have survived the afternoon on RXBARs and nut packs. Boring squirrel food compared with the gourmet lunch Aimee brought along. "You can travel with me anytime if you bring food like this."

She nibbles her sandwich. "Do you realize I've never watched you work?"

"You've seen me work." Plenty of times. She's witnessed me spend countless hours tweaking photos in my home office, or work the floor at my showings as I schmooze clients and upsell new buyers.

"I mean, I've never been on-site with you," she clarifies. "Your focus is intense."

"So is yours when you're baking."

She props her chin on her knees, hugging her shins, and smiles. I'm downhill from her on the blanket so I lean back on my elbow and rub her calf. Flies buzz past. The air smells of damp dirt and pine.

"Do you remember what you told me in Mexico?" she asks.

"I told you a lot of things in Mexico."

Her eyes sparkle and I know what she's thinking, how I told her that I loved her. But the next move had been hers, and she'd left me.

I could have gone with her, but I'd decided to stay an extra day. Yes, I was curious about Lacy and her connection with Imelda and the possibility of finding my mom through her. But Aimee's quick departure from the country confused me. I didn't know what happened between her and James the previous night, and I wasn't entirely sure Aimee felt the same for me. Asking her to stay meant risking her rejection, and I'd been burned once too often.

"Do you remember comparing my baking to an artistic craft? You said I was an artist because 'true artists elicit an emotional response.'"

"I did say that." I nod slowly. "I still think that."

"Me, too, about you and your work."

"Thank you." I sit up and kiss her leisurely; then I lie back down and sigh. Folding my hands behind my head, I close my eyes, letting the sun warm my face. This is what life is about, these slivers of time when my mind is a blank slate and I don't think or worry. But there's too much traffic in my head today. I wonder if Reese and I can meet halfway and make the feature happen and I wonder about Lacy. Dread falls over me, a blanket that covers me from head to foot. I feel as though we've been in Spain one day too long.

I sit upright and look at the space on my memory chip. "I should take some more photos."

"Do you think your pictures will change Reese's mind about her feelings toward the Rapa?"

"I certainly hope so." I switch out chips and put aside the camera. "She asked me yesterday why I was so taken by these horses. She pointed out that they're more semiferal than wild. I told her that I see the relationship between the villagers and the herds as symbiotic. It fascinates me. But that's only part of the reason."

Aimee wraps the remains of her sandwich and returns it to the paper bag. "What's the other part?"

"My favorite book as a kid was *The Black Stallion*. Don't laugh," I say when Aimee's mouth twitches.

"I'm not. I guess I imagined something different."

"I've read my share of Christopher Pike novels and Superman comic books. But that's beside the point. My mom loved *The Black Stallion* as a kid, too. She used to read a chapter a night to me until we finished the book and I'd beg her to start over. I swear we read that book over a hundred times. She would get into character and the story came alive. She could have read that book to me forever."

"Why'd you stop?"

"I stopped asking." I tug up a clump of weeds and chuck them. Beyond us, the horses nicker. A foal ambles to its mother. "After Sarah was imprisoned, I spent more time at Marshall's. I could tend to his horses and forget how shitty life was back home. I guess, in a weird way, I feel closer to my mother around horses."

Aimee studies me with cool fascination. I pull my legs in, resting my elbows on my knees, hands hanging loose between. She smiles sweetly.

"What?" I ask, cracking my own smile.

"You're her Galician knight and her aloitador. In a way, she was wild and you tried to manage that wildness the best you knew how for your age. And when she wasn't the most willing or cooperative subject, you watched over her. You took care of her. And then she left you and you didn't know what to do. You probably felt like you didn't have a purpose. It's probably how these villagers would feel should they lose these herds."

"Huh. Interesting. I never thought to look at it that way." I yank off a blade of grass and chew on the end.

Aimee makes a face. "*Eww*. Horses walked on that."

"Yeah, probably." I toss the mangled blade and grin. "That was deep, Aimee. What should we talk about now? Politics, clean energy, babies?"

Aimee lifts a brow and I sigh.

"I know," I acknowledge. "I said I wanted to table our discussion, but . . . you want another one? For real?"

"I do."

"This isn't a residual feeling from seeing the burrito-wrapped bundles at the hospital?"

"Those bundles reminded me that I've been feeling this way for months. I wanted to talk about it with you last summer when you got back from Spain, but . . ." Her voice tapers off. She picks off burrs clinging to her shoelaces.

"But what?" I give her calf a squeeze.

"Things happened."

My chest feels heavy. "You mean James happened."

Aimee nods.

I breathe deeply. "Tell you what. How about we get back to focusing on us rather than what's happening around us?"

We watch each other for a long moment. My heart beats for her and I reach for her hand. Our fingers entwine. She watches my thumb caress hers.

"I'd like that, very much," she agrees.

I give her arm a gentle tug. "Come here."

Aimee scoots down the blanket. I lie back, pulling her down with me so that her chest is on mine. Her hair spills over her shoulders, framing her face. I trace her cheekbone. "I just remembered something."

"What?" She dips her head and kisses my jaw.

"We forgot to Skype Caty last night."

Aimee trails her lips along my jawline. I feel the press of her breasts with each breath, the gentle rush of air from her parted lips through my whiskers. It makes my blood thrum.

She kisses my chin, then lets her lips hover above mine. "We were a little busy last night."

"Yeah, we were." I laugh the words. My body heats at the memory.

"We'll call her when we get back to the inn."

"Good idea. Now kiss me," I demand, memories of last night lingering in my brain.

Her mouth crushes mine and my arms loop around her back. We spend the afternoon like this, kissing and embracing, relaxed and sun warmed. The horses graze nearby, their nickers and whinnies background music. It's late, the sun sinking lower on the horizon, when the herd starts to wander toward the next hillside. Deciding to trail the horses for a bit, I slip my arm from Aimee and grab my camera. I've wandered off a bit when I turn back to her. I point at my watch and flash five fingers two times, asking her to give me ten minutes.

She waves and packs up the picnic.

A short while later, my memory chip loaded with images, I join Aimee. I show her some of the photos on my camera display, unable to contain my excitement at capturing them.

"It was a good day," Aimee says when we start walking downhill. "I'm glad you found what you were looking for."

Not everything, not yet. But maybe that'll happen on Tuesday.

I wrap an arm around Aimee's waist, ready to embark on the next leg of our adventure.

Early the next morning, I check out of the inn while Aimee chats with Catherine on the phone, updating her on our plans. We're driving to the coast for breakfast and will catch our flight this afternoon, landing in Boise late the same day. We'll spend the night there before venturing to my dad's place. Lacy didn't give us a time to meet, just said that she'll be there on Tuesday. So we'll be there. Early. This will be my first visit home since before I graduated from college. It'll also be the first time I've seen my dad since Las Vegas.

Aimee ends her call and pulls up the handle on her roller. "Ready?"

"Yes." I pick up my bags and, leading us to the front door, catch Reese sitting alone in the dining room. She waves for us to wait.

"Hold on a second," I tell Aimee as Reese makes her way over. I left her three text messages and two voice mails last night. I apologized for threatening to pull the photos to sabotage her article. I told her we'd found one of the herds and that I wanted to show her the pictures. She should have been there. She would have loved them. She never replied, which told me her heart isn't in this feature, not like mine is. I worry the article won't capture the essence of the relationship between the village and the herd, and that it may cast a negative light on the ancient festival.

"Hi," Reese says in greeting. Her gaze slides from me to Aimee and back. She hitches her hands in her back pockets. "I was hoping to catch you."

Aimee crosses her arms and inches closer to me.

"What's up?" I don't bother to put down my bags or ask whether we should sit.

"You found the horses."

"We did." I take the car keys from my pocket and jiggle them.

"When's your flight?"

"Late afternoon. Why?"

"Would you take me there? If you don't mind." She glances at Aimee.

"Can't. We have plans today," I reply.

"No, we don't." Aimee uprights her roller.

I look at her. "We don't?"

"He'll take you," she says to Reese, then rests her arm on my elbow. "Go work on your assignment. Get the story you want." She looks at me and I catch her meaning. I have three hours to pitch Reese my perspective. Three hours to win her over. Aimee pats my arm. "I'll wait here."

I make a show of looking at my watch. "If we're doing this, we do it fast."

Reese nods. "Thanks." She looks at Aimee. "Thank you."

"You better make it worth his while." She kisses me. "See you in a few hours."

Reese and I hike hard. I have my camera out, telephoto lens, stand, and remote attached. I'm ready to go. The herd wandered off yesterday so I'm anticipating we'll capture them at a distance.

We quickly reach the crest of the hill where Aimee and I spotted the herd yesterday. They aren't nearby or where they ventured off toward yesterday evening. It's cool and misty. Sunlight pierces the white veil, and given any other day, it would make for some cool photographs. But, no horses.

I shove back my sleeve and glance at my watch. I've got two hours before I need to be back at the inn. "Sorry, Reese. I have no idea which direction they've gone; otherwise, I'd walk you that way."

"You don't owe me an apology. I'm the one who's sorry. That wasn't the most brilliant introduction I made with your wife."

I press my mouth into a flat line. "It wasn't one of your better moments." I turn around to head back downhill.

"Hey." She reaches out to stop me. "Let me make it up to you. What can I do?"

I can only think of one thing. The article. I want it unbiased and for the pictures to speak for themselves. I'm about to tell her when her eyes go wider and brighter than the sun. She points west. "Over there."

On the next ridge is a herd of Galician horses at full gallop. Filtered sunlight highlights their chestnut flanks. Dust raised by their pounding hooves cloud the ground, lending the herd the appearance of running on air. It's the perfect cover shot. The perfect two-page spread.

Scrambling, I extend the stand's legs and position my camera. I adjust the settings to stabilize the camera's vertical movement and look through the lens, bringing the horses into focus. With any luck, the herd will be in sharp focus and the background blurred. I can see them galloping off the pages in the magazine. Taking a deep breath, I press the button on the camera's remote. The shutter fires in rapid succession as I pan in the direction the herd flies across the hilltop.

"Look at them go." Reese's voice is filled with wonder.

My lens follows the herd. "They belong here."

"I never said they didn't."

I glance over at Reese. Her aviators shield her eyes but she's smiling. I can't tell what she's thinking. But she's transfixed on the horses. They disappear over the rise.

"There they go."

"I guess I had the impression you didn't like the horses," I say as I check the view screen, making sure I got the shots.

She looks at me oddly. "What gave you that idea?"

"You said you didn't like the Rapa."

"No, I didn't. I just didn't like watching. And I didn't understand why they had to put so many horses in such a confined space. Just because I get squeamish over a dead foal and have a hard time with animals penned up doesn't mean I'm going to work my opinion into the feature. I'm here to tell the village's story."

I cap my lens and start to pack my gear. "Which is what?"

"The village and the herds need one another."

I stop what I'm doing and look at her curiously. "What changed your mind?"

"Talking with the villagers. I spent the entire day with them yesterday. Look, um." She checks the time on her phone. "Do you still write?"

Other than an article here or there to accompany my photos, my writing amounted to nothing more than a picture caption of a few sentences. "Infrequently, why?"

"We're short on time, but I want your perspective. You're the only one I know who was on the floor who wasn't a villager. I want to know what that felt like. And I want to know why you're enamored of these horses. What's your connection? Let me try to write the story you envisioned when you submitted your pictures."

The corner of my mouth pulls up. "You're insightful."

"I'm a journalist. I study people. Not much gets past me. Do you think you can have something for me by late Tuesday?"

"Tuesday?" I meet with Lacy on Tuesday, and hope to be on my way in locating my mom.

Reese nods. "I got an e-mail from my editor. The magazine's moving our article up an issue. She needs my draft by Wednesday."

I feel my eyes bug. "Wednesday." I swear under my breath.

"Al didn't tell you?"

I shake my head. There are more than ten thousand photos on my memory chips. With the shortened deadline that means I have to whittle those down to several thousand and edit my top ones, the images I think they should print, by Thursday, whereas I thought I'd have a week. How am I going to accomplish that when I'm also writing an essay and meeting with Lacy on Tuesday?

Change happens on Tuesday.

"Is that too soon? I might be able to push back my deadline a day or two, but no promises."

I shake my head and shoulder my pack. "Nope, I'll manage." Because I'm determined to have it all. Find my mom and nab the *National Geographic* cover. To get that cover, I have to stick to the deadline.

"One more thing," she adds when I start walking. I turn around. "I have a confession."

I quirk a brow. She looks at the ground, then off into the distance. She absently pats her leg, then slides her fingers into her back pocket as though she doesn't know what to do with her hands. "You don't have to tell me."

"I do. You're a good man and entitled to the truth." She takes a reassuring deep breath. "I did still love you."

"Then why did you leave?"

"I got scared. You were trying to fix me—"

"Fix you?" I interrupt, flabbergasted. "What the hell does that mean?"

"—and I didn't want to be fixed," she says at the same time.

"What are you talking about?"

"Me and my animal issues. That cat you adopted for me? It wasn't the first time you tried to give me a pet. Remember the stray dog we picked up in the rainstorm on the roadside? You wanted us to take it home and adopt it. You were convinced if I had a pet to love that I'd get over my aversion to having one. We argued big-time until you finally agreed to take him to the animal shelter."

I grind my teeth. That night had been one of our biggest arguments. It was the first night since we'd started dating that she'd insisted on sleeping alone. I spent a long night on the lumpy couch.

"Rather than talking to me about it, you ran?" I ask.

"I did try talking to you. You wouldn't listen. You were too fixated on trying to solve my animal issues."

"I wasn't trying to solve your problems," I say, hating how defensive I sound. But she's hammering a nail that's hitting a sensitive mark.

"Braden saw that picture of your mom you kept on the mantel and pointed out the similarities between me and your mom's coloring and facial structure. Funny, but I never saw that until he mentioned it and then I couldn't get it out of my head. The idea that I looked so much like her and that you'd date someone who physically resembled her creeped me out. It hit me that you would keep pursuing me on the pet issue the same way you kept taking photos of your mom even after both she and your dad insisted you stop. I feared your obsessive mission to resolve my animal issues was just the beginning. What would you try to fix next about me? My issues with animals are mine alone, and I've learned to cope with them. I manage just fine."

"Did you take on this assignment just to tell me this?" My face is hard, my voice tight.

Reese tosses up her hands. "I don't know. Maybe?"

"And it's been sitting on your chest for over ten years. You just had to get it off." Aimee's right. Reese is a bitch. I shake my head at her and start walking downhill again.

"Ian, wait." She rushes to my side, keeps pace alongside me. "You're a good guy. I did love you. And I loved you when I left you."

I stop suddenly and turn to face her. "Love isn't running out on someone. It's working through your issues, fixing them together."

"That's not the way it always works. Sometimes, the only way a person can be fixed is for them to do it themselves. And other times, a person can't be fixed. But they can learn to cope with their issues the best way they know how, even if that means leaving the one person they loved most at the time."

She looks at me pointedly and I sense that what she's talking about goes beyond us.

CHAPTER 23

IAN

Five months or so after the Ian Collins installment of *The Hangover* when I'd married Reese under the influence, I'd downshifted from the hostile and infuriated stages of anger and was revving in frustration over my father's lack of *Find Sarah* ambition. I figured I should give the old man a call and give our relationship one more shot.

Unlike the years I lived under his roof where he had two defined seasons, baseball and football, with schedules that informed me what hotel he'd be at and in what city, my dad was then doing freelance assignments between games. His work kept him out of state and in a perpetual state of movement. He lived in hotels and socialized at airport bars. I had no idea where he was or when he'd be home. Mobile phones weren't as commonplace then. He might have had one, but I didn't have the number.

It took him ten days to return the message I'd left on the dated machine at the farmhouse that still played the greeting I recorded my freshman year in high school. *You've reached the Collinses' house. Leave a message.* I'd copied the greeting my mother had recorded when she purchased the machine, except I replaced "family" with "house" because we weren't a family. Not anymore.

When I answered the phone, my dad had said hello, heavily cleared his throat, and asked, "You're moving to Europe?"

"We're thinking about it." Reese and I had been planning an eight-week trip. We'd travel through Italy and France, working odd jobs in between her writing and my photography, earning money to extend our time overseas. Should we fall in love with the vibrancy of the big cities or the intimate pace of a quaint village, we'd consider staying. Perhaps indefinitely. At that age, life was about adventure. We'd live it one day at a time at maximum capacity.

"You're going with that girl you've been dating?"

"Her name's Reese. Yes, we're traveling together."

"She come from a good family? No funny business?"

No one slammed it into the outfield like Stu. I caught his meaning like a fly ball landing smack in the middle of my glove. He wondered if Reese had a normal upbringing, nothing sick happening between family members that might have left her with a screwed-up head. I reassured him there weren't any skeletons in her closet except the one she brought out on Halloween. That was one scary mother. It looked more like a medical school study aid than a holiday prop.

Through the phone receiver came the flare of a match. The short, rapid puffs igniting a cigarette. A long, deep inhale. "She sounds like a nice girl," my dad said through a tight throat, his words carried on smoke.

Ripping a page from Pop's get-straight-to-the-point playbook, I asked, "What's going on with Mom?"

"How the hell would I know?" he said, irritated.

"You haven't heard from her?" Disappointment nose-dived into my gut. I'd had hopes he would have come to his senses after I left him in Vegas and he sobered up. "Have you even tried looking for her?"

"She's gone. She left us. End of story."

"She's sick, Dad. She doesn't realize it, but she needs us."

"I'm not discussing her with you. Come to think of it, you bring her up again, I'm hanging up."

I beat him to it. I hung up, and other than leaving a brief message that I was getting married and to give him my cell number, I hadn't called him since. He texted a reply, twice. First, his congrats on marriage, and second, on fatherhood, after I messaged him that Aimee had given birth to Sarah Catherine.

I never understood why he gave up on my mom—his *wife*—so easily. Or me, for that matter. He discarded me like an overexposed, blurry image. But I'd done the same, I think as I drive with Aimee toward the old farmhouse I haven't seen since my early twenties. My last visit had been the summer before my final year at ASU.

It's midmorning Tuesday. Aimee sits beside me, her gaze on passing storefronts. Old, run-down Americana. The town hasn't changed and surprisingly, I don't miss it. Aside from my dad, I can't think of anyone here worth keeping in touch with. Mrs. Killion passed a few years ago and Mr. Killion sold their farm soon after. Like me, Marshall left after he graduated from Boston College. There isn't much to do around here unless you go into ranching or farming. Last I heard, Marshall was married with three kids and living in the Boston suburbs as a financial adviser.

"I'm nervous about meeting your father," Aimee says for the second time this morning.

I rest a hand on her thigh. "He'll be fine," I say to reassure her and myself. I'm feeling apprehensive. A growing sense of concern keeps me rigid in the driver's seat. It kept me up all night. "I doubt he'll be home, though. It's football season."

"Lacy seems to think he will be."

I see the roofline of the house above crumpled stalks of corn, dried out from the sun. The front fields still haven't been plowed. Flipping on the signal, I slow and turn into the driveway, and then I brake, coming to a full stop. I reverse the car and stop again. "I think we have our answer." I nod at the mailbox. The flap is open, exposing the overstuffed interior. Random-size letters and circulars scatter the ground like fallen leaves.

Putting the car in park, I get out and Aimee joins me. She collects the mail strewn along the roadside while I clean out the box.

"I'll take those," she offers, and I hand over the mail.

"Thanks." I look around, lifting my face to the wind. Barn manure, wet grass, and the acerbic tang of nutrients. "I forgot how strong fertilizer can smell."

Aimee's nose crinkles. "That's really unpleasant."

"Welcome to farmland. Let's go see if my dad's home, and if Lacy's there." I hold the door open until she's settled in her seat. She balances the mail on her lap. I close the door and walk around the car and sink into my seat. I take in the house at the end of the drive, the white siding sun faded and dusty from the fields. The rain gutter upstairs has pulled away from the roof. Screens on some of the windows are ripped. One of the porch columns leans precariously off to the side, causing the overhang to sag.

"Did the house always look like this?"

"Not this bad." I coast slowly up the gravel drive and bring the car to a stop beside my dad's old Chevy truck. He sold the station wagon when I was sixteen, exchanging it for a beat-up Toyota 4Runner, which I used to get around.

Folded, dried-up newspapers litter the front porch, spilling down the steps like coffee beans poured from a canister. I kick aside the papers so Aimee doesn't trip, and walk the length of the porch, which wraps around the side of the house. My boots leave prints in the dust, fine soil carried by the winds that come through here. I peer into the parlor and dining room windows. The interior is cast in gray light. "I don't think he's home."

Aimee looks around the front yard. "Lacy isn't here either. There's no car. Think she'll show?"

"No clue," I say, nudging boards along the porch edge with the toe of my boot. Bending over, I try lifting a few.

Aimee comes to stand over me. "What are you doing?"

"When I was ten, Jackie locked me out of the house one night. It was storming and the rain was pouring by the bucketload. I was too scared to run to Marshall's house, and I couldn't see. I didn't want to risk twisting my ankle running across the fields, so I slept on the porch. Curled up right there on the doormat like a dog." I lift my chin in the direction of the front door.

"Ian." Emotion weighs down my name.

"Hmm." I look up at Aimee. Anger hardens her features. Her blue eyes smolder. "I can't believe your mother—"

"Ancient history, darling. Mom couldn't help what she did when she shifted. And Jackie can't hurt me now."

I tug a board. It doesn't budge. I move to the next one and pry it open. "Jackpot." Reaching inside, I fumble around the porch framework until I find what I'm looking for. My fingers touch metal. Grinning, I show Aimee a weather-tarnished key. "I stashed this inside here after that night. Never said a word about it to my parents."

"Let's hope your dad hasn't changed the locks."

I straighten and look around. "He hasn't changed a thing." The porch furniture is still in the exact spot it was when I left for college. Sarah's pots bookend the front steps, partially filled with hard dirt left over from the plants she once cherished. Even the heap of a truck my dad refused to give up and continued to drive was in its usual spot.

Sliding the key into the lock, I turn it and the tumblers release. The door creaks open. I nudge it farther. Aimee comes up next to me, her side pressing into mine. Her warmth soaks into me. I rest my hand on her lower back as we stand in the doorway and stare down the narrow foyer that opens up to a wider hallway running the length of the house. It ends at the kitchen in the rear. Dust particles dance in ribbons of sunlight. The rest of the house drowns in sepia, like an old, faded photo. I cross the threshold and Aimee follows. Floorboards give way, creaking through the house's quiet solitude. On our left is the front parlor, the bookshelves empty. At some point, my dad must have packed away my mom's books. The dining room on our right is also void of her belongings. The embroidery machine that had been left untouched throughout her prison term is no longer there.

The house is warm from being sealed up, the air stale. Aimee lifts her chin and her nose twitches. She makes a noise in the back of her throat and looks at me. Our gazes meet and hold. Worry clouds her brilliant blues.

I grimace. "Yeah, I smell it, too."

The putrid, foul odor of a decomposing body is unavoidable. My heart pounds and my mouth suddenly goes dry. There might be another reason the mail has piled and the newspapers have collected. Given the smell, the way it clings to the walls and seeps through the house, whoever died has been deceased for a while.

Wouldn't someone have come looking for him? Surely Josh Lansbury would have been by at some point during the last month to check in with my dad.

I should have come.

I should have visited years ago.

Guilt is a vicious beast in the land of retrospect and hindsight. I scrub my face with both hands and pinch away the unexpected burn in the corners of my eyes. I blink rapidly.

Aimee adjusts the load of mail in her arms and reaches for my hand. I clasp hers in a tight grip.

"Do you think Lacy knew?" she asks.

"I don't know what that woman thinks." Let alone what I think of her at the moment. How thoroughly morbid and disrespectful to get me back to the house this way. Why not tell me over the phone? Why not warn me, soften the blow?

I can't believe this is how it ends with my dad, my calling the morgue to pick up his remains. All the time I thought we had, when one of us would see past our thick heads and apologize, to forgive and forget, lost.

I draw my gaze up the staircase. "Wait here. I'll have a look around."

"I'll put these on the dining table."

I watch her go into the room and set the mail on the table. The pile slides to the side and Aimee grabs it before envelopes spill to the floor.

Moving down the hallway, I follow the stench into the kitchen. Countertops are clear of dishes and food. A thin layer of dust drapes the furniture and surface tops like a bride's veil. I turn to the closed laundry room door where the odor is the strongest and pull up my shirt collar over my nose and mouth. Bile thickens in my throat and my gag reflex wakes up with a nice stretch. I grip the doorknob, reluctant to find what's on the other side, but understanding I don't have a choice. It doesn't matter what age or the dynamics of the relationship, no kid should have to come across a parent's dead body.

"This is fucked."

Heart pulse thumping in my throat and sweat drenching my arm-pits, I shove open the door where it stops halfway, blocked by whoever is on the floor. Forcing myself to look behind the door, my gaze drops to the floor.

"Oh shit." I jump back, my shirt pulling off my face, and bend over, gasping, hands on my knees. "Oh shit, oh shit. Oh thank fuck."

Aimee comes running into the room. "Are you OK?" She rests her hand on my back. "Ian, talk to me," she urges when I don't respond right away.

Straightening, I turn to her, cupping my palms over my mouth and nose. A sick laugh escapes, muffled in my hands. I lower my arms. "Dead possum."

She tries to peer around me. I grasp her shoulders, backing her away from the laundry room. "It's not pretty."

Aimee presses a hand to her chest. "For a moment . . ."

"Me, too." I briefly close my eyes, urging my insanely beating heart to chill out.

She hugs me, resting her cheek on my chest. My eyes burn. I turn my face up to the ceiling and squeeze my eyes, staunching the flow of tears I don't want to deal with, because right now, I need to deal with the mess in the other room.

Aimee releases me. "Let me help you clean up."

I shake my head. "I'll take care of it." Opening the lower cabinets, I search for garbage bags.

"I'll go sort the mail, then."

She turns to leave and I stop her with her name. "Thank you for coming."

We share a sad smile and she leaves the room.

Locating the bags, I pluck out a few, using one as a makeshift glove. The animal doesn't go neatly into the trash bag and I have to stop every minute or so to leave the room and gulp fresh air.

This is not how I expected to spend the day. Al sent an e-mail this morning, confirming the new deadline Reese told me about. He wants my photos by tomorrow morning. I've narrowed ten thousand down by three. Seven thousand more to go and I'm beyond exhausted, thanks to jet lag and the lack of sleep. Lacy better get here soon.

I dump the remains in the outside trash and mop the floor.

Aimee returns and glances around the small room. "How did the possum get in here?"

"I'm not sure." I inspect the walls, looking behind the washer and dryer, and find a hole. "Back here." I show Aimee. "He must have chewed his way through and couldn't figure how to get back out."

"Poor guy."

I put away the cleaning supplies and wash my hands.

"I tossed the newspapers and swept the porch," Aimee says.

I close the supply-closet door. "Any word on Lacy?"

She shakes her head. "I just got the answering machine at her house. What now?"

I glance at my watch. "I guess we wait."

Raking both hands through my hair, I walk down the hallway and out the front door. The screen door slams behind me, banging against the frame before it settles. Planting hands on hips, I stare down the empty drive. A random car passes on the road every couple of minutes, but none slow and turn down the drive.

I might as well make use of the time and fire up my laptop. There are images to edit and an essay to write. I turn back to the house.

"Hello, Ian."

I jump. "Shit."

Sitting on the old wicker chair is Lacy Saunders. I blow out a long stream of air. She scared the bejesus out of me. Where did she come from and how did she get here?

She smiles and her lavender eyes sparkle. "Lovely day for a chat, isn't it?"

CHAPTER 24

IAN, AGE THIRTEEN

Ian woke up in the station wagon's front passenger seat groggy, disoriented, and with drool smearing his right cheek. The car coasted along the highway under a midnight-blue sky. Yellowish-orange road reflectors winked under the headlamp beams. He could barely make out landmarks beyond the swatch of triangular light, and what he did see was unfamiliar.

Ian sat upright, adjusting the grip of the seatbelt across his lap. He wiped off the saliva from the side of his face with the back of his hand, and in his mind, played back the day's events. He'd been at an invitational track meet in Boise. His dad hadn't made it. Shocking, Ian knew, but this time Stu had a legitimate excuse. His flight had been delayed, so his mom picked him up after school and they drove straight to the meet.

Everything was going fine. He medaled in the 400 m and 1600 m. His mom seemed happier than her usual self, almost normal as she cheered him on from the sidelines. Afterward, she treated him to a celebratory dinner before heading home.

But they didn't seem to be headed in that direction now.

It had been dusk when they returned to the car, his belly full and quads aching from the record-setting race he'd accomplished. They should have been home by ten. The digital numbers on the dashboard clock glowed an aquamarine 11:56.

A cold sweat broke out across Ian's body, adding another layer to the crust that covered him from the meet. He didn't have to wonder who was driving the car. The music blaring through the speakers gave her away. His mom didn't listen to the Eagles. It must have woken him up, and as the lead singer crooned, Ian feared this night would be one of those crazy nights, like the one last year when Jackie met the biker at the motel and Sarah had to drive them home, shaken and disturbed under a cloak of starry-skied darkness.

Ian covered a yawn. He'd stayed up late studying for a test, then spent the late afternoon at the meet. Take his exhaustion from both, top it off with a full belly and the gentle vibration of the station wagon's tires on the road, and Ian had conked out before they exited Boise's city limits. He'd missed when his mom had phased out. He'd missed his opportunity to have Jackie drop him off at home.

He watched the road, waiting for a signpost to appear. He wanted to know where they were and the direction they were driving. Luckily, he didn't have to wait long. A skinny post flashed by on the roadside. Ian swiveled in his seat, following the sign until it faded in the night. **93 SOUTH.** They'd been driving for almost two hours. They had to be in Nevada by now.

He settled back into his seat. "Where are we going?"

"You're awake. About time."

"The music woke me up. It's too loud."

"It's been loud," Jackie scoffed.

"I was tired. I stayed up late studying last night."

"Not my problem." She huffed exactly like Marshall's older sister. This wasn't the first time it occurred to Ian that he and Jackie bickered like siblings, even more so as Ian grew older. Here's the thing about his mother's alters: they didn't age. Jackie would always be seventeen. One of these days, Ian would be the adult and Jackie still a teen. He doubted Jackie would ever respect his authority.

"I have a test tomorrow. Take me home," he said at the same time it hit him that they were in Nevada. The state that never slept. "Never mind, just drop me off at the next town." They passed a sign a bit ago. Wells was sixty miles ahead. He'd find an all-night diner and call his dad. He should be home by now.

"No can do." Jackie shook her head. "I need you."

Ian crossed his arms tightly over his chest. "You don't need cow dung from me."

"I do this time. You have to keep me awake." She opened her mouth on an exaggerated yawn.

"Pull over and sleep in the car."

"We don't have time."

"Scared you won't be you when you wake up?"

She blew out a puff of air in annoyance. "Don't be a dumbass. Sleep has nothing to do with me being here or not."

"Then what's the big deal? Go to sleep . . . or, I know, let's turn around and go home. What a concept."

"The big deal is that we'll miss him. He won't be there when we get there. Since I can't control this"—she tapped her head—"I don't know when there will be another chance to go after him."

Traces of fear tiptoed across Ian, leaving his hands and feet chilled. She better not be meeting that bounty hunter again. "Go after who?" he risked asking.

"My stepfather."

His hands fell onto his lap. Ian's mom never discussed her childhood. Her years at home with her parents were a mystery to him. "I didn't know you had a stepdad." A stepparent was like a real parent, wasn't it? Surely tonight couldn't end up the way it had last year with that bounty hunter forcing himself on his mom.

"There's lots of things you don't know about me. But here's the only thing you need to know about Francis—that's his name, by the way. He can't stand it when I call him that. He gets real mad." She let out a low whistle of dismay. "Francis"—she said the name through her nose, sharp and nasally, snickering—"had a deranged way of showing me how much he detests that name. He said he did it out of love. But Frank"—her voice drops, deep and guttural—"is what he wants me to call him; he's not a nice man. You best remember that, Ian, no matter what goes down tonight, Frank is a bad man."

In the shadows, Jackie shivered. She drove them for another fifty minutes before taking the exit at the interchange in Wells. From there, they drove east on I-80 for two hours.

Throughout the drive, Ian pinched his arms to keep himself from falling asleep. He fretted about the science test he'd miss in the morning and his father not finding him in bed when he arrived home tonight. He was probably there by now. Ian thought of Mrs. Killion and what she would assume about him when he didn't show up after school tomorrow to help Marshall clean the horse stalls. She'd invited him to stay for dinner. Ian worried about his mom and what Jackie was getting her into. He needed to stay awake for Sarah. When Jackie subsided and his mom resurfaced, he'd need to show her the way home.

His concern for his mom kept him rooted to the seat rather than sneaking to a phone booth when Jackie stopped for gas. It kept him engaged in idle conversation with Jackie as they drove, not because she'd get upset if he didn't do as she asked. Rather, he didn't want her falling asleep at the wheel either. She'd kill them both and that would suck.

Mostly, though, it was his love for his mom that kept him alert in the passenger seat. She'd recently told him that no matter what she did or where she went, she did it because she loved him. She would always love him. Ian had memorized her pledge as though the words had been tattooed on his forearm. He felt the same for her.

It was almost three in the morning when Jackie slowed and turned into a truck stop in West Wendover. For the past hour, Ian had been fighting to keep his and Jackie's eyes open. The change in speed and engine tone woke him as though he'd guzzled a can of Mountain Dew. Adrenaline poured through him. He blinked at the flashy neon signs lining the boulevard he swore could be seen from outer space. This was Nevada, after all. He'd never been, but his dad had regaled him with stories.

Jackie coasted through the large parking lot, weaving around rigs parked for the night, and backed the station wagon into an empty slot that afforded them a view of the entire lot as well as the road. She turned off the ignition and unclipped her belt.

The engine settled with a few pings and a sigh, and the vinyl seat creaked as Jackie shifted, stretching her arms overhead.

"Now what?" Ian asked.

"Now we wait. He should be here soon." Jackie yawned, but she didn't settle back and close her eyes. She leaned forward, her chest pressed into the steering wheel, and kept her gaze on the lot's entrance.

"How do you know he'll come?"

"We found out he stops here every time he makes the drive to Reno. He sleeps for three hours, then hits the road so he's in Reno by nine."

Ian wiped his damp palms on his athletic shorts. He bounced his knees and cracked his knuckles, pretending boredom to hide the nerves. What did Jackie have planned? He'd asked earlier and she wouldn't tell him, simply replying, "You'll see."

He reached for his backpack in the rear seat. Intent on distracting himself, he removed his camera, set it on the seat between them, and took out his science textbook.

"What are you doing?" Jackie asked, annoyed.

"Studying."

"Now? How can you focus on that?"

Ian jutted a shoulder. He flipped the pages to the periodic table and glanced at Jackie from the corner of his eye. She gnawed on her index nail. "Are you scared?"

Jackie blew a raspberry. "No."

Ian didn't believe her. He looked at the book on his lap and tried to study.

Twenty minutes later and not one more element memorized than he knew, the air inside the station wagon thickened with tension. Jackie leaned forward, squinting at a large rig pulling into the truck stop, her lips moving. Ian glanced from Jackie to the truck and back and realized she was mouthing the license plate number.

The truck cruised around the lot, gears low and rumbling, and pulled into a space that gave them an unobstructed view of the rig, about thirty yards from where Jackie had parked the station wagon.

"Is that him?" Ian whispered.

"Yes," Jackie said, reaching under the seat.

Ian shoved the textbook off his lap. It thudded on the floor. He picked up his camera, shouldered the strap, and turned it on. The camera whirred to life, the lens expanding and retracting as it set itself on autofocus, the noise loud inside the car. But it was another sound that froze Ian, chilled him to the bone. Beside him, Jackie checked the magazine chamber of a semiautomatic pistol. His dad's gun. The one that should have been locked up inside the safety box in Stu's desk. The one Jackie should not have known about.

"Wha—What are you doing?" Ian choked on his words.

"Fulfilling a promise."

She slammed the magazine into the well in the handle. Sweat sheened her forehead. Her hands trembled, making the gun shake. She settled the weapon on her lap and looked coolly at Ian. Under her tough, hard-as-steel exterior, Ian saw her fear. But he also noticed her resolve. Whatever she had planned, she'd see this through. He had to stop her.

"You don't want to use that, Jackie."

"Yeah, I do."

He tried another tactic. "Mom, please. You'll get arrested."

Movement outside caught their eye. The driver had opened his door. He lumbered down from the cab, muscles stiff from sitting for long hours. He stretched his hamstrings, then his quads. For a guy with a sedentary job, he appeared to be in good shape, his physique lean and defined. Twenty years ago, Ian bet he'd been built like his dad.

Jackie opened her door and got out of the car. She didn't bother closing the door or hiding the gun. She marched straight toward the trucker. Whatever was going to happen would go down quickly.

Ian brought the camera to his face. He shot photos in rapid succession, the shutter clicking as fast as his heart pounded. He might not be able to talk Jackie out of her plan, but he could use the photos as evidence. Somehow, Ian would prove Sarah hadn't brought him here tonight. It had been Jackie.

Ian leaped from the car and jogged after her. "Mom!" he shouted, giving it one last attempt. "Don't do this. This isn't something you want to do."

Jackie swung a one-eighty, arm raised, and pointed the gun at Ian's forehead.

He gasped and skidded to a stop, hands raised. A whimper escaped and a tear fell. "Please, Mom," he whispered. "Don't do this."

"You can leave now. I don't need you anymore."

Her expression, the way she said the words—she looked and sounded like Sarah.

Ian shook his head. Tears blurred his vision. This woman was not his mother. "You told me once that whatever you did it was because you loved me. This isn't how you're supposed to show me that you love me. You have to stop." Ian pointed at the trucker. "Killing that man is not what you want to do for me."

"I'm not doing it for you. I'm doing it for Sarah. Know why?"

Ian violently shook his head, his lower lip trembling. He dragged a forearm across his face to clear his vision.

"Sarah's weak. She's a coward."

"Sarah?" The trucker looked at her, mouth agape. "Is that you?"

Jackie held out her arms. "Here I am, *Francis*." She sneered the name. "Miss me?"

He looked left and right, then pointed a finger at Jackie. "Don't say that name around here. Now tell me, Sarah, why are you here?"

"It's Jackie, you sick prick." Her arm flopped against her side in exasperation over their name battle. She groaned with exaggerated irritation, then raised the gun again.

Frank parked his hands on his narrow hips. He smiled into the barrel of the pistol aimed at his chest. "You still using that hooker name? Fine. We'll play it your way. Why don't you put that gun away and join me inside? You can call me whatever name you like in there." He thumbed at the cab behind him. "It's nice and cozy, plenty of room for two people." He held his palms a few feet apart and smiled, a thin spread of lips. "I have a big. Wide. Bed."

Jackie fired the gun. Ian jumped, his hands covering his ears. Sparks and asphalt splintered in all directions at Frank's feet. He danced out of the way. "What the hell is wrong with you?"

Ian's hands shook as he brought his camera back to his face. He clicked away, the camera's bulb flashing.

"Stop with the photos," Jackie screamed over her shoulder.

Frank leered at her, making Ian's skin crawl. That was his mom the trucker had in his sights.

"I still have all those photos I took of you, sweetheart. Trucking's a lonely business. Someone's got to keep me company on the long haul. Those pretty pictures make my nights seem—"

A shot fired and Frank screamed, jerking back against the truck. Blood splattered the side.

"Shit," Ian said to himself. *Shit, shit, shit.*

He dropped his camera. It swung from his neck and smacked him in the chest. The lens would have shattered on the ground had he not thrown the strap over his head and shoulder when he got out of the car.

Frank clamped a hand over his bloody shoulder. "You bitch," he shrieked.

Sirens pierced the air in the distance. Jackie fired again. Tremors racked her body and the shot misfired, blowing out Frank's knee rather than his head. He collapsed, screaming like a gutted pig.

A trucker in a rig off to the right laid on his horn. It blared, waking other drivers. Headlights and spotlights flared on around the parking lot. Jackie turned and shot out the nearest truck's headlight, the bullet zinging over Ian's head. He dropped to the ground, panting, and covered his head.

The sirens grew louder, drawing closer.

Ian looked up from under his arms. Jackie's face had gone white. The anger and loathing replaced by panic. She stared at the gun in her hand as though she couldn't believe she held it. She tossed the pistol and ran to the car.

"Mom!" Ian chased after her.

Sarah started the engine and floored the vehicle. Tires squealed. Ian tried to jump into the open passenger door, but the door knocked into his hip, throwing him off-balance. It slammed closed, trapping his camera. Sarah peeled away, jerking Ian against the car, his head and shoulder stuck in the camera strap. He screamed for his mom to stop. He tried to stay on his feet, running alongside. But the car swerved and he lost his balance, stumbling, his upper body hanging on the door, as he was dragged across the parking lot, his track shorts no protection against the asphalt.

Sirens blared. Gravel sprayed Ian's face. Asphalt tore up his thighs. The car swerved again and jerked to a stop. Ian twisted his head to see that three police cars blocked their way. Then his head fell forward and he passed out.

CHAPTER 25

IAN

Lacy sits across from me at the dining table, hands folded on the worn pine surface.

"You said a friend dropped you off?" I reaffirm, looking for a logical explanation to her sudden appearance on the porch, like a ghostly apparition.

She smiles, humming an affirmation. It's conceivable I walked past her without registering her presence. More than once I've walked into the front room at home and stared out the window, deep in thought while drinking my coffee, without realizing Caty is sitting on the couch near me until she pipes up with a "Hi, Daddy."

But I should have heard Lacy's arrival. The crunch of gravel under the weight of a car. The porch cracking and popping when she walked up the front steps. This house doesn't hide visitors. It announces them.

Lacy traces the divots on the table's surface, scars left from my mom's work. A dropped stack of embroidery books, the pointed tip of a pair of scissors, the weight of equipment. As I watch Lacy touch each mark, I get the sense she's reading them, learning their memories. Her smile fades, she frowns, and then she murmurs, the words indecipherable to me. When I realize where my thoughts have taken me and that Lacy is visualizing my mom, I shift uncomfortably in the chair.

"Did you fly in this morning?" I ask, and the image of her on a broom wielding a wand gels in my head. Thank you, Harry Potter. I silently curse my imagination. That's what I get for reading the book to Caty.

"Your father will be here soon."

"When?" I look out the window.

Before she answers, Aimee appears with refreshments. "I found Crystal Light mix and ice cubes. It's not fresh-squeezed lemonade, but it's better than the scotch I found in the cabinet."

I wouldn't turn down a finger, or three, of the hard stuff. She moves by me to set a tray on the table. I catch a whiff of her perfume. It's all Aimee. Playful and sensual at once. Familiar and grounding. Calming. Needing to touch her, I rest my hand on her lower back as she stretches across the table to give Lacy a glass.

"Thank you." Lacy sips her drink.

She hasn't changed much from my memory from when she found me in a ditch on the roadside, or the photo from the café's soft opening. Just an older version of herself. Her hair is more silver than the platinum it used to be and is cut into a bob. Those mysterious lavender-blue eyes that have both fascinated and haunted me since I was nine have faded, as eyes do with age. They are a light shade of blue. A spiderweb of fine lines edges her eyes and mouth. Her hands are weathered.

Aimee pulls out the chair beside mine. I thread my fingers with hers and hold her hand in my lap when she's seated. She pushes a glass in my direction and I drink obediently, finishing off half. What I wouldn't give for that scotch. I can't pinpoint why, other than there are too many unanswered questions where Lacy's concerned, but she makes me nervous.

Aimee looks at me, her expression questioning. I squeeze her fingers reassuringly.

"I was right about you two."

Aimee and I turn in unison toward Lacy.

"You're meant to be."

"What do you mean? Like soul mates?" Aimee asks.

Lacy lifts her shoulders and makes that affirmative noise again behind a closed-lipped smile. She looks at me, then through me, and I inhale deeply against my rising sense of anxiety. My knee bounces. This soul mate stuff is fun and all, but I want to get to the heart of this meet and greet. What does she know about my mom, and what's so important my dad has to tell me? The man's not even here.

"You have a lot of questions, Ian. You both do."

I lift my brows, ignoring the uneasiness her comment incites, and invite her to elaborate.

"You wonder why I had you go to Mexico," she says to Aimee and turns to me. "You wonder how I found you all those years ago. And you both wonder how it's all connected." She draws her hands in the air around an imaginary globe.

I resist the urge to quip about tarot cards or show her my palm when Aimee says, "A smidge." She spreads her index finger and thumb an inch apart.

"Have you heard about the Red String of Fate?"

"No," Aimee says as I inwardly groan. Did we really come all the way to listen to this?

"It's an ancient Chinese myth about soul mates," I explain. "The red string connects two people destined to spend their lives together."

"You're right, Ian, but it's more than that. The string connects us for all sorts of reasons. It connects two people who are destined to meet under extraordinary circumstance and it connects people destined to help each other. Some of these connections are stronger than others, and I sense them."

I glance over at Aimee, wondering if she's buying this. She doesn't look at me, her expression intent on Lacy.

"I met Imelda Rodriguez while on vacation with my daughter and son-in-law. I knew right away I was meant to help her, but I didn't know why or how. Imelda and I became good friends, and one night she confided in me her arrangement with Thomas. She was miserable. She hated deceiving James, but she was financially strapped, and Thomas scared her. I couldn't *not* help her, and the only way I knew how was to eliminate Thomas's need for her. To do that I had to get rid of James, and make it look like Imelda had nothing to do with him going back home."

"That's when you found me."

"Exactly." Lacy points her finger at Aimee. "I told Imelda I tried talking with you at James's funeral."

"I wouldn't call it talking."

I nod my head in agreement. Lacy had chased Aimee through the parking lot. She spooked her.

"That's true," Lacy laments. "Looking back, I should have waited for a more appropriate time."

I want to agree with Lacy, but had she waited, I wouldn't be the guy sitting beside Aimee. This conversation wouldn't even be happening.

"It took months for me to convince Imelda to allow me to approach you again, and only on the condition it couldn't be traced back to her." She looks at the table. Her finger traces a groove.

"What happened, Lacy?" I ask.

"Thomas saw you at the café's soft opening. He figured out what you were doing."

I look at Aimee, wide-eyed, then look at Lacy. She's nodding. "Something else happened at the café. Fate is a mysterious, fickle woman who loves to play practical jokes. Imagine my surprise when I saw you." She snares me in her gaze. Her words are cubes of ice dropping from a freezer dispenser through me. My limbs chill. "I saw your connection to Aimee, and I saw again, my connection to you. There's a red string that binds us. I realized, once again, I was destined to help you. That's when I decided to speed up the process, Imelda's fear be damned. I shipped James's painting to Aimee. She had to see for herself that the red string didn't link her to James. It links her to you, Ian."

Aimee and I share a look. Soul mates or not, psychic meddling or not, I didn't want to spend my life with anyone but Aimee. But something else occurs to me and I frown. "You might think you helped me, but what about Imelda? James didn't go home."

"But I did help her. She no longer had to lie to James. That's the secret that was making her miserable." She sips her lemonade.

"Huh." I look at Aimee, wondering what she thinks about all this. She shrugs a shoulder and I make a show of looking under the table for the string that attaches us. A short laugh escapes her and she shushes me to stop messing around. Red strings, soul mates, fated connections, oh my! I've mentioned to Aimee on several occasions that I've seen and experienced some surreal things during my travels that I couldn't necessarily explain. There was that out-of-body experience I had after a night of hookah smoking in India. There were three of us—me, Dave, and Peter—and we'd just finished a three-day photography hike in Manali. I had an insane dream of running back up the trail we'd just come down because I wanted to take more photos. The kicker is that the temperature at night dropped into the tens and I was shirtless. Dave, who didn't smoke, and I had a good laugh when I told him the next morning about how Peter was in my dream and he wasn't. Peter didn't have a shirt on either or his shoes. Thank God, it was a dream, else we'd have frozen our asses off. Anyway, it was a good laugh until Peter woke up and told us he had the same dream. Then he showed us his feet. They were cut up, bruised, and caked with dirt. The ridiculous thing is, Dave was up most of the night reading. He said we never left our mats after we'd passed out.

I don't have a logical explanation for that night, other than we were too high to remember, and Dave had to have fallen asleep for several hours for Peter and me to slip past him on our way to be idiots. As for Lacy's "red string" theory, she can call it what she wants. I think her connection to Aimee and me is nothing more than an it's-a-small-world coincidence. Serendipity.

Lacy looks around the dining room, studying the crystal chandelier overhead and satin curtains, the hems dirty from years of dust. "I always wondered what Sarah's house looked like."

I sit upright in the chair. She said my mom's name with the familiarity of a friend. That's not something I expected. "How do you know my mother?"

Lacy smiled tenderly, her sadness evident in the gentle curve of her mouth. "She's my stepsister."

Aimee gasps. My back slams into the chair. I feel the blood drain from my face, and my fingers reflexively squeeze Aimee's hand. The woman sitting across from us, sipping lemonade from my father's glass, the one I welcomed into his home, is Frank's daughter, the man Jackie shot. I read about him in my mom's court transcripts. He'd sexually abused my mom since she was twelve, around the time her mother, my grandmother, married him and he moved into their home. He continued to abuse her until the day she ran away. She'd been eighteen.

My mom had taken on odd jobs to survive, doing what she could to remain invisible to Frank until the day she met my dad. She saw a protector in him, the one man who could keep her safe from Frank. Move her far away from the stepfather, which made sense to me once I connected the story my mom told me of how she met my dad to her testimony at the trial.

Something clicks inside me and I make another connection. The legal name Thomas gave Aimee for Lacy. Charity Watson. *Charity.*

"Impossible," I murmur to Aimee. "She can't be her stepsister."

"I don't understand," Aimee whispers back.

"I'll explain later."

"My father was abusive. Sarah wasn't his only victim," Lacy acknowledges.

"Oh dear," Aimee says.

"We should all be thankful that man is locked away."

My mind takes an excursion to that night. I hear the gun blast, feel it reverberate in my ears, see it blow out Frank's knee. My skin itches the way it had when it healed from the asphalt abrasions. I scratch at my thigh.

"As Ian recalls it, you met Stu at a diner and offered to help find Ian, but that's not what happened, is it?" Aimee asks, and Lacy slowly shakes her head. "I'm going to venture to guess you didn't use 'psychic powers' either." She draws quote marks in the air.

I peel my hand from Aimee's and look at her in question. "What are you saying?"

"If she really is Sarah's stepsister, I think she was told where you might have been, which would have made it easier to locate you."

"Is that true?" I ask and Lacy nods. Damn, my wife is perceptive. "What happened?" I demanded, needing answers to all the questions I had as a kid.

"Sarah showed up at my house. She wasn't acting herself. She insisted her name was Jackie. I didn't know then that she had a personality disorder. I thought she was on something. Her behavior was erratic."

"That was Jackie."

"And she was looking for Frank. Sarah had left Jackie a note on where to find me. She thought I'd know where he was. I didn't at the time, of course. And I didn't want to look for him. My parents had joint custody when I was a kid. I hated the weekends I spent at Sarah's house with my father. But that's beside the point. Jackie bragged about what she'd done to you. She was betting you were stupid enough to listen to her and walk home. Then she left. I assume she eventually returned here." She looks around the room. "I called your father and he confirmed you were still missing. Together we found you based on what Jackie told me."

My hands fist under the table. "Did Stu know who you were?"

"That I was his stepsister-in-law? Not at first. I think Sarah eventually told him."

I shoot up from the chair. It falls back with a thud. Hands gripping my hips, I pace the room. Aimee gets out of her chair and leans over to right mine. I'm at her side in two long strides. "Thanks, hon, I've got it." I pick up my chair for her and brace my hands on the seat back. "You've got my attention. What's going on? Why'd you bring me here?"

"Your father won't listen to me. You must talk to him. You have to convince him to tell you the truth about your mother."

"Do you know where she is? Why not just tell me?"

"It's not my place. That's Sarah's request, not mine. This is between you and your father. Get him to talk. Listen to him and keep an open mind."

"Give me one good reason I should give that man my time when he never gave me his."

"He's dying."

CHAPTER 26

IAN, AGE FOURTEEN

Ian sat on the front porch waiting for his dad to get off the phone with Mr. Hatchett, his mom's attorney. Ian hadn't seen her in months, not since he testified at her trial.

A lot of good that did. She was still sentenced to nine years. He'd be in college by then, or graduated with a degree and a job. Where would he go if she wasn't here?

Somewhere close so he could visit her. He missed her something fierce.

Ian picked up a rock, hefted the stone, then threw it hard. The rock hit the rear fender of his dad's truck with a loud ping.

The abrasions on his legs had healed; his skin was pink where the scabs had rubbed off. The doctor said the scars would fade. Ian wondered if the same could be said of the dark cloud building inside him. His dad didn't know, and he'd die if his friends found out, but Ian cried himself to sleep like a baby most nights. Under the privacy of his covers, he'd bite into his pillows and sob.

Jackie had done what she'd threatened to do. She'd taken his mom away for good.

Ian folded his arms on his knees, dropped his head, and let the dark cloud billow. It thickened and expanded, growing angry. He hated Jackie.

But today, they were visiting Sarah. Ian could finally apologize for losing the pictures he'd taken that day. When the car door slammed on his camera with him stuck in the shoulder strap, the casing had popped open, exposing the film. Gone were the images he believed could have proved her innocence. Jackie had fired the pistol, not Sarah.

Tired of sulking, Ian lifted his head and clicked through the settings of the new digital camera Stu had purchased as a replacement for the one permanently damaged that night. It was an expensive camera, and still a rare find in electronic stores. But his dad had connections, and Ian figured he gave it to him out of guilt. He should have been home to take Ian to the track meet.

Ian lifted the camera to his face and squinted through the viewer. Tulips bloomed in his mom's pots. Corn sprouted in the fields, the stalks low enough so he could see the road and the mailbox at the end of the drive. Ian zoomed the lens and snapped a photo.

Inside, behind the screen door, his dad paced the long hallway. The farmhouse's old walnut floor snapped, crackled, and popped under the weight of his boots. He stopped just inside the doorway and within hearing distance. Ian picked up snippets of his dad's conversation.

"There's nothing we can do to change her mind?" he asked the attorney. "Uh-huh . . . uh-huh . . . how long?" Ian pictured Mr. Hatchett in his office in Nevada, his Santa Claus paunch giving him no choice but to lean back in his chair as he stared at the ceiling, patiently answering Stu's questions. The same questions Ian bet Mr. Hatchett heard from every client.

Ian's dad fired a round of curse words. They pelted the air like firecrackers and Ian cringed. Something had his dad fired up.

"Fine . . . Yes . . . I understand . . . Call me if she changes her mind or shows improvement. Thanks."

His dad retreated farther into the house. He slammed down the cordless phone and swore. From where Ian sat, the phone sounded like it had shattered. Behind him the screen door opened and slammed shut. His dad settled on the porch steps beside Ian.

Ian clipped on the lens cap and shouldered the strap. "Ready?" He stood, eager to get on the road. They had a ten-hour drive to Las Vegas with plans to camp overnight halfway. They'd fish for their dinner this evening and Ian wanted to leave so they'd get to the campground by late afternoon. He was also antsy to see his mom. Excitement kept him in motion. He bounced from foot to foot.

Stu reached into his breast pocket and withdrew a cigarette and, rolling onto his hip, leg extended, dug a lighter from his jeans. He made a show—all in slow motion, in Ian's opinion—of lighting the cigarette and taking a few deep sucks until the end flared orange. Cigarette hanging from his lip, he stuffed the lighter back in his front pocket and patted the space beside him. "Have a seat, son."

"We're late." Ian glanced at his dad's truck. He'd packed the cab with road-trip snacks and drinks. The cooler in the back was full of ice and food for the four-day trip. Two there and two back. A mini-vacation, his dad had said. Preseason football started in a month. Best for them to get in some father-son activities before the three months his dad would juggle time between football and baseball.

Ian had also wrapped a gift for his mom, a book of poems by T. S. Eliot. She loved poetry. She said the words soothed her. Ian had purchased the book with his allowance from the used bookshop in town. He could see the present on the dashboard, floral printed wrapping tied with a yellow bow.

Stu took a long draw on his Marlboro. "We're not going."

Ian's heart plummeted into his stomach. "What do you mean?"

"How do I put this?" his dad muttered. He rubbed his forehead with the hand holding the cigarette, then looked at Ian. "She doesn't want to see us."

"You're lying."

"Wish I was." Stu sucked on the cigarette like his life depended on it. Ian watched the smoke veil his dad's face. Deep grooves bracketed his mouth. Shallow creases marked his father's forehead like yard lines on a football field. His dad had aged these past months. The trial had been difficult. He'd spent a lot of time traveling between home, Nevada, and his games. He still had to make a living, he told Ian. Someone had to put food on Ian's table and keep the roof from collapsing on him.

"You said we could see her as soon as she could have visitors." Ian had been waiting for months.

"We're not on her list."

"Then get us on it." Ian clenched his hands and took a threatening step toward his dad.

Stu's eyes narrowed in warning and Ian shrank back. "I can't. It's not that simple."

"Why not?" He was her son. How could she not want to see him?

"She's sick, Ian." Stu sucked at the cigarette. "She's lucky she's getting any treatment at all in there."

"The doctors will fix her."

"They'll try, but there's no guarantee." He flicked the cigarette with a thumbnail. Ash dropped in the dirt. "Until she's stable, no visits." With the edge of his boot sole, he buried the ash.

"Do the doctors know why she's sick?"

"Yes."

"And?" Ian pushed. He wanted answers. He needed to make sense of why his mother's behavior was so erratic.

"It's confidential." Ian held his father's gaze, pleading for more information. Stu broke contact and looked at the ground. He scratched his lower lip with his thumb. "She had a rough childhood. Her stepfather wasn't . . ." He stopped abruptly and cleared his throat, rubbed his eyes. "He wasn't nice to your mother. She shouldn't have married me. She probably shouldn't have had a kid either."

Ian stumbled back a step. "What's that supposed to mean?"

"Nothing. Listen, I've got to make some calls." Stu pushed off his thighs and stood. "Unpack the truck and get your chores done."

"What about Mom? She's waiting for us," Ian protested.

"Dammit, Ian. Your mother doesn't want to see you."

Ian moved his head in a slow, disbelieving shake. "Liar."

"She asked for space, so we've got no choice but to give it to her."

"Liar!" Ian screamed. "I took care of her. She needs me." Ian smacked his chest, and to his humiliation, the tears he tried hard to hide from his dad boiled over. "She loves me. She said she would *always* love me. I want to see her. I have to make sure she's all right."

"She's not your responsibility, Ian. Not now, not ever." Stu retreated into the house.

Ian watched the screen door slam. His legs shook and a sick feeling twisted inside his stomach. He'd failed his mom at her trial, and he'd failed her with his life.

His mother had lied to him. She didn't love him.

She hated him.

He never should have been born.

CHAPTER 27

AIMEE

Ian and I watch Lacy traipse along the drive. She ambles along in a straight line, one foot in front of the other, hands out like a gymnast on a balance beam. It's almost childlike, the way she wobbles from time to time. She's in no hurry, moving at a reluctant pace as though she wants to stay, to linger over mint tea and afternoon gossip. But she insisted on leaving to allow Ian the chance to absorb the impact of her words. If Lacy can be described as anything, I'd say she is a stealth bomber. She appears from out of nowhere, drops her payload on the unsuspecting citizens below, only to disappear as her targets try to make sense of—to survive in—the surrounding rubble and devastation of their lives.

I can't imagine the guilt Ian must be feeling about his father. All the years he could have reached out to make amends.

A gust of wind cuts a path across the yard. We feel its impact on the porch. Air fills my ear with a pop. Ian's arm hugs my waist a little tighter. I see Lacy's skirt billow like a sail. She staggers, then does a quickstep to keep ahead of the current so she doesn't stumble. Another flurry lifts and swirls the dried, crackly leaves at her feet. She's in the vortex of a red, gold, and yellow dust devil. Everything is flying, ruffling in the wind. She shields her face with an arm and lets the eddy carry her along. I see Lacy as chalk marks on a board, and the swirl of wind, an eraser, expunging her from our lives. On to the next lesson. Time for a new chapter. As I watch her dance around and around with the wind the last few yards to the oak-tree-shaded mailbox on the edge of the road, I know in the way that I know my own heart that this is the last time Lacy's path will intersect with ours.

"I forgot to ask why she gave the card to James," I say, regretful.

"I didn't. I asked when I called her."

"And?"

"Serendipity."

"What?"

"Serendipity. Coincidence. She told me she was vacationing with her granddaughter in Hawaii. Hanalei Bay is a popular beach. She recognized James."

I scrunch up my lips. "I'm not sure I believe that. Do you?"

Ian shrugs; then he points his chin toward the road. Lacy has reached the mailbox.

"Does she have a ride?" I ask.

"She said a friend dropped her off. I assume she's picking her up."

"She doesn't have a purse on her."

"Or a phone."

"How does her friend know when to pick her up?"

"Maybe she sent her a telepathic message."

I look at Ian. He keeps his eyes ahead. His cheek twitches. He leans his head toward me and says, "They probably arranged it ahead of time."

"You're probably right," I agree.

Several cars pass. A truck blares its horn.

"She's still standing there."

"So are we." He removes his arm from me and grips the porch rail with both hands. He straightens his arms and leans his weight into it, using the rail as support. "Do you want to go inside or wait until she gets picked up?"

"We're waiting. I want to see her get into a car and drive away like a real person. Don't you? Do you believe she's psychic? And what about the red-string myth? Do you think she can sense connections like she says?"

A little smile lifts Ian's mouth like the wings of a butterfly. It looks sad. He seems sad. "You're just full of questions."

"Aren't you?"

He shrugs. "I believe in you. And I believe in us," he answers, kissing my forehead, and my heart makes a swirly dive.

Because he's right. The two of us are what matters.

As for Lacy's psychic abilities, I guess it doesn't make a difference anymore. She accomplished what she set out to do. She led me to Mexico to find my way to Ian, and she lured Ian to Idaho, which leaves me to wonder. Did she lead him here to find his way to Sarah or back to Stu? Maybe she's only showing him the road home, back to where it all began. Back to where Ian can make amends.

Ian sighs. He sounds tired, worn down and depleted, when he says, "My mom's defense attorney had her plead not guilty on account of her DID. He argued that she was mentally ill and shouldn't be held accountable for her crime."

I rest my hand over his on the rail. Ian looks at our hands and briefly closes his eyes before continuing.

"All the prosecution had to do was disprove she hadn't been aware that it was, in fact, premeditated. It didn't help her case that Jackie never surfaced during my mom's deposition or trial. There wasn't much of a paper trail of treatment either. My dad tried for years to get her to regularly see a psychiatrist and go into therapy. He wanted her to do anything that would help her work through whatever it was that damaged her mind. She fought him. She canceled the appointments he'd make or she just wouldn't show up. She threw away her pills. Then there were the pictures I took." He swallows roughly. "All those pictures." He deepens his bend, popping his shoulders, then rights himself and turns to face me. He leans his hip against the rail, crossing his arms, and looks at his shoes. I tuck my hand in my front pocket.

"When I was a kid, I thought the pictures I took of Jackie would prove Sarah wasn't herself. I don't know why I kept it up all those years. Reese seems to think I obsess over wanting to help people, that I want to fix their issues, like I did with my mom. I guess I tried to do that with Reese, too. Who knows, maybe I do. And maybe I knew Jackie would get my mom in trouble and my mom would need them one day. So I kept at it, and I hid all of them from Jackie, just like my mom told me to do. I could see the difference in the photos: her facial expressions and her eyes, especially the eyes. They weren't the same. Surely anyone else could see it, too. It wasn't until after I graduated from ASU and read the trial's transcript . . . Hell"—he shoves his fingers into his hair—"it could have been sooner and I was in denial, but I realized how stupid I'd been to take those pictures. The prosecuting attorney subpoenaed years' worth of photos. He used them to prove his point. My mom was unstable and violent. In her defense, she'd suffered years of sexual abuse. Her stepfather, Frank Mullins, broke her. It also helped her case when the cops arrested Frank. They found pictures of underage girls in all stages of undress in his truck cab. His browser history was drowning in a thick soup of child pornography. My mom's attorney bargained for a reduced sentence when she admitted her intention was to keep Frank from harming other girls. It also helped that Frank didn't die. The judge and jury sympathized with my mom."

"Ian, I can't even . . ." My stomach churns. What Sarah had gone through as a child? I think of Caty. I want to rush home and hug her.

Ian glances at Lacy, still waiting by the mailbox. "Here's where it gets strange. A portion of my mom's deposition was filed with the court. There was mention of a stepsister, Frank's daughter from his first marriage. Her name was Charity Mullins. She was two years older than my mom and came to stay with them on the weekends. My mom confessed that her stepsister was the one who told her about Frank's trucking routes because Jackie's bounty hunter was useless. She said Charity showed her where and when to locate him, and my mom would pass along the details to Jackie in notes between them in the top middle drawer of my mom's vanity table. My mom was tired of living in fear her stepfather would find her. She worried there were other victims. She thought the only way to solve the Frank problem was to get rid of Frank, but she didn't have the courage to go through with it. Only Jackie had the guts to pull the trigger."

"That's not strange. It's tragic. Your story makes me sad." My eyes feel misty and I brush them with the back of my fingers.

Ian swings his eyes to mine. "My mom's stepsister died when she was seventeen. She wandered off while on a hiking trip with friends in Tahoe."

The fine hairs along my forearm rise. I shiver. "What are you saying?"

"I looked it up, Aimee. The articles were there. They never found her. Just her shoes and purse and dried bloodstains in a steep ravine."

"Then who gave your mom the tip on Frank?"

Ian nods his chin in Lacy's direction. "If Lacy is my mom's stepsister, I bet he abused her, too. I think the authorities presumed she'd died, but she really just ran away and changed her name to Charity Watson. I can't tell you whether she's psychic, if that's really a thing, but I think she keeps up the disappearing act, initially because of Frank, and later, because of Sarah. She's an accessory to Frank's attempted murder. It's right there in the transcript. Charity—I mean, Lacy—has never wanted to be found. She can't be found."

"Then why would your mom call out her own sister after she helped her?"

"Think about it. Records show Charity is dead. Blaming her further supports my mom wasn't right in her head. I doubt her attorney, let alone the prosecution and jury, have an inkling Charity's alive. And considering how Charity believes she's connected to people out of duty and obligation to help them, she may have felt she had no choice but to help my mom. She may even have convinced my mom to run away from home when she did."

We look at Lacy. She bends over and swipes dust off her shoe. She ties the laces, then stretches her arms overhead, then lets them flop back to her sides.

Ian's expression clouds. He frowns and seems to weigh something in his mind, something big. He reaches for my hand. "There's more, Aimee. I read something else. I found out that I did something wrong, terribly, horribly wrong, to my mother. My dad tried to stop me, but I wouldn't listen. I was young and cocky with false confidence. I was convinced what I was doing would help my mom. Frank used to take pictures of her and with her. The sessions they had were so disturbing that it fractured her mind. Jackie surfaced during those years. Sarah couldn't cope so Jackie took her place. That's what the psychiatrist who evaluated my mom stated pretrial. The defense brought her in as a witness. It was all right there in the transcript. I didn't break my mom, but I didn't help her condition either, not in the least. All those pictures I took, every snap of the shutter, they were probably triggering her shifts. Just the sight of me with my camera, I don't know. It must have done something to her." His voice is thick with anguish.

"You didn't know. You were a kid. There's no way you could have known."

"You asked me once after we married why I haven't put my full heart into finding my mom. I denied to myself that's what I was doing. But you're right. You're spot-on. My attempts have been half-assed. You know why? I'd have to face her and I'd have to face what I'd done to her. I'd wronged her. I'm the one who drove her away, long before she tried to murder her stepfather. I'm the reason she didn't put me on her visitor's list, and I'm the reason she ran away after her release. Me and my stupid camera. Ironic, isn't it? She hates being photographed but married a photographer and had a son who aspired to be one."

Ian's eyes are damp. His hand shakes in mine. I close him in my arms, my ear pressed to his chest, absorbing the wild thump-thump of his heart, my face turned to the road. That's when I see what I didn't want to miss. Lacy is gone. How, I don't know, and right now I don't care. Ian's in my arms and he's hurting.

CHAPTER 28

IAN

A silver compact turns into the drive, gravel popping like Bubble Wrap. Aimee's arms slip from me and we turn to watch the driver approach and slow to a stop, facing us, in front of the house. He cuts the engine but doesn't get out of the car. He stares at us from under the sun visor and behind his dark glasses.

"Your dad?" Aimee asks.

"My dad." I haven't seen him in sixteen years, but the box jaw, defined chin, and wide fingers curled around the steering wheel are unmistakable. So is the wave of hair lifting off his face, one uncooperative lock dividing his forehead. They're the same as mine. What doesn't sit well with me, though, is that I'm having a hard time digesting the sunken cheeks and the color of his hair. He's gone completely gray.

Stu cuts the engine and opens the door.

I clasp the back of Aimee's head and, tucking her under my chin, speak into her hair. "Will you give me a minute with him?"

"Take all the time you need."

I kiss her head and go down the steps to meet with my dad, to get the truth from him about my mom. To find out what's going on with *him*.

His movement from the car is slow and labored. When he finally stands, bracing a hand on the door while reaching the other into the backseat, my step falters. A clear tube wraps under his nose and winds over his ears and dips into the cab of the car like an umbilical cord. With some effort, Stu hauls out a portable oxygen tank. The wheel catches on the runner and drops to the ground.

I rush to his side. "Let me help."

He stops me with a raised hand and a stern, and slightly uncomfortable, expression. I back up, realizing he's embarrassed. And I'm ashamed. I should have been around earlier, years earlier, to help him. His frame is a wasted, wan version of himself, a dried corn husk of the robust man he'd once been. He cautiously bends over, never letting go of the door, and uprights the tank, balancing the cart on its wheels. He keeps a tight grip on the handle, shuts the door, and turns to me. We watch each other for several moments, each assessing the other. I'm taller and wider. He wheezes as he breathes. I can't see his eyes behind his shades, but whatever sickness he has, it's been dining on his body for some time.

"How long?"

He smiles, exposing a row of yellow-tinged teeth. "The prodigal son returns."

"Surely you have a better line than that."

He nods once. "Long enough. Who told you I was sick?"

"Lacy Saunders. You probably remember her as Laney. Or better yet, Charity Watson, or Charity Mullins? Any of those ring a bell?"

He nods ever so slightly.

"Did you know she was Mom's stepsister? Back when she helped you find me?"

He shakes his head. "Not at first. Your mother told me later who she was. Charity's a meddlesome woman." His words come abbreviated and breathy, and I have to turn my ear toward him to hear over the sound of the tractor working the field next to ours.

"That story of her finding you in a diner with the police you told me as a kid?" The one I'd told Reese when we dated and Aimee while we were in Mexico. "Was any of it true?"

"Some of it. You were asking too many questions then." He lifts his head. "That your wife?"

I look back at Aimee. She raises her hand in a short wave but her eyes hold mine. I feel her love and it gives me the strength I need to keep my anger at bay. Stu never shared anything with me about Lacy, about the source of my mom's condition, so I'd have a better understanding. About his own disease.

"You should have told me."

"Probably." He drops the car keys in his pocket. "Let's take a walk."

I follow him around the house to the ash tree with the trunk that's thickened, its web of branches filled out. A mixture of burgundy, yellow, and green leaves dance and shimmer like jewels. A blanket of them covers the ground.

The oxygen tank bobbles over dirt clods and stones. I consider offering to buy a cart with larger wheels. It would be easier to manage over the property's uneven ground. But making the offer would force my dad to answer, and talking while walking is an effort for him. Just walking seems too much.

We stop at a new-to-me wood park bench under the tree. The painted wrought-iron scrollwork is peeling and the wood stain is worn away on one side of the seat as though someone sat there often, looking out over the property. One could see quite far, as we can today, when the cornstalks have been removed and the soil is tilled in preparation for the oncoming winter.

My dad eases onto the bench, using the oxygen-tank handle like a cane. He invites me to sit down.

"I'm dying," he says without preamble when I take up the spot beside him. No warning. No *I've been diagnosed with*. Just *I'm dying*. Well done, Stu. Let the sharing begin. Thankfully, Lacy had warned me, else I don't know how I would have handled that blow, no better than an uppercut from the right.

"From what?" I ask.

"Lung cancer. It's a bitch." He coughs.

My knees are spread and I clasp my hands between my legs, rest my forearms on my thighs. I inhale deeply and close my eyes, allowing his words to make their impact. His life is over, and no thanks to my stubbornness, I missed so much of it. Then I let him speak, and I listen, something I should have done a long time ago.

"I'm selling the farm. Never wanted it. Your grandfather insisted. I had to give the dying man his last wish. Looks like I've come full circle." He chuckles. It turns into a coughing fit. I wait it out, looking at my hands, hands shaped like my father's. Funny how I never realized that before, and today it's the first thing I noticed.

My dad wipes his mouth with a soiled handkerchief he dug from his pocket and continues. "I didn't lease the land until he passed. I didn't want him to know I had no interest in it."

Grandpa Collins passed before I'd been born. I'd never met him. "You never told me about this."

"I didn't tell you a lot of things. Seemed the right thing to do at the time."

"And now?"

"'To regret deeply is to live afresh.'"

I look at him. I never took my dad to quoting Thoreau, or reading poetry. But my mom had stacks of books, from Frost, to Wilde, and plenty of Thoreau. Why this quote? What is he trying to do right by this time? I don't have to wait long. He finally catches his breath.

"I have a buyer. Half will go to you and the other half into a trust I'm going to ask you to manage."

"For whom?"

He quickly glances at me, then looks at the ground. He pushes dead leaves with the toe of his shoe.

At first, I think he plans to give half the money from the property sale to his tenant, Josh Lansbury, but he turns his gaze to the horizon. His throat ripples. He wipes his nose. And he takes a deep, fluid-filled breath where the air moves through him like water thick with mud around boulders and it dawns on me who will get that other half. My own breath leaves in a whoosh and I look at him, shocked to my core.

"That night in West Wendover nearly destroyed your mother. She didn't know your camera was stuck in the door. She didn't know she was dragging you. She couldn't hear your screams. She was on suicide watch the first couple of years until a psychiatrist took interest in her case. She helped your mother manage her condition. It was your mother's decision not to come home. She'd almost killed you twice. She couldn't risk a third time. She left you because she didn't trust herself around you. She left you because she loves you. She gave up her right to be your mother to keep you safe. And I agreed with her decision. I couldn't let something else happen to you. I couldn't leave you alone with her again."

It takes him a while to explain this, with plenty of starts and stops along the way. When he's done, he sounds like he ran a 5K at race pace. His chest rises and falls deeply. He doesn't look at me and that's when I realize he has known. He has known all along what happened to Sarah.

"You saw Mom when she was released."

"I set her up in her apartment. I found her a job as a seamstress."

"And you've been supporting her ever since. That's why you need me to manage the trust. After you're gone."

He nods. "Her term came up and she made me agree not to tell you. She didn't want you to come looking for her. She thought it best for you to believe she didn't care. That's why I stayed away when I should have been your father. I thought you'd see right through me."

"You knew what her leaving did to me. How could you agree to such a thing?"

"I swore that I'd keep her safe and you safe from her. I love her, Ian." His eyes sheen and hands clench tighter on the cart handle. "I did it because I love her."

I feel my face heat. I'm sure it's as red as the leaves scattered around us. I want to punch him. How could he let her take herself away from me when I needed her most? My teen years were more confusing without her than my youth had been with her.

But as I stare at him, seething under my skin, something happens. An epiphany of sorts. That damn lightbulb goes off like a camera flash and frames the picture. I recognize something else of me in him. No matter what my wife does, or has done—yes, that includes kissing James and keeping his damn paintings on display at the café—I would always love her. Had Aimee been in my mom's place, I would have done the same as my dad. I love her that much.

"I know you blame yourself. It's not your fault, Ian," he says. "Your mother's leaving has never been your fault and I'm sorry I made it seem that way."

Emotion wells and I can no longer contain it. I bend at the waist, a tree giving in to the wind, and I do something I haven't done since I was fourteen. I weep.

CHAPTER 29

AIMEE

When Ian first told me about his mom's arrest and imprisonment, he explained that he wanted to be up-front with me. James hadn't been open and honest about his family history and Ian respected my need to know about his childhood, and why he was estranged from his dad. Over dinner one evening, he relayed the sequence of events, from being abandoned on the roadside to being dragged in a truck-stop parking lot, with the detachment one used as though talking about someone else. I listened in stunned silence, my heart going out to the young boy he'd been. My soul ached for the man he'd become. That detachment spoke volumes. His past was as much a part of him as the humor and carefree spirit that made up his character. And he hadn't moved on from it.

Ian had told me previously his mom didn't physically abuse him, but emotionally? I couldn't understand why he wanted to find her after the years of turmoil he endured. His love for her, though, was unconditional. He didn't blame her for how she was. It wasn't her fault her mind fragmented. But after hearing the full story today, I better understand his pursuit, and his guilt. He believed he owed her an apology for taking the photos the prosecution subpoenaed—the photos he thought would help her case, not imprison her. He blamed himself for why things were the way they were with his parents. That's an enormous burden to be carrying all these years.

I watch him talk with his dad, head bowed and hands on hips. Their voices are low and Ian keeps his face averted from mine. I can't hear them so I don't know how Ian's taking everything in—seeing Stu for the first time in a long time, Stu's sickness, and whatever Stu's telling him—until he turns to me. They both look my way. While Stu's expression is curious, Ian's demeanor is all sorts of anger, confusion, and hurt.

I want to go to him. Everything inside me is pushing me his way. But other than waving, I don't move a muscle. I give him the space he asked for.

Ian's eyes latch onto mine. We watch one another for a long moment, and when I smile, a smidge of the tension straining his face eases.

They walk off together and talk under a large tree behind the house, a bench and leaf-sprinkled ground giving the yard a parklike setting. They talk for a long time, and I wait. I'd wait for as long as Ian needed me to, for he'll need me when it's over.

I catch up on e-mails. I call Kristen and ask about the new baby. Theo is nothing short of perfect. He's a good eater and sleeper and isn't fussy. It's Kristen's third child. I figure she has a good handle on motherhood by now and anything Theo does will seem like a stroll through peppermint frosting compared with the first child. Short of the usual exhaustion that accompanies a newborn, life is grand for the Garners.

I call my mom, dodging her questions about Idaho and Stu. This is Ian's story to tell, and perhaps he will share it with her one day during our Sunday lunches at my parents'. For now, I let her know we're flying home in the morning.

I'm reading a book I'd brought along with me when Ian settles on the porch chair beside me some ninety minutes later. His face is drawn, the conversation with Stu, jet lag, and the *National Geographic* assignment taking its toll. He takes my hand, kisses each knuckle, and asks if I don't mind spending the afternoon at the house, which I don't. Finding my way into town, I buy us lunch, deli sandwiches and sodas. Ian spends the next five hours working himself to exhaustion. He patches the hole in the laundry room and repairs the porch. He's sweaty and dusty by the time he's done and I get the sense he's making up for lost time by cramming as many odd jobs around the property as he can in these few hours.

We learn that Stu moved into an assisted-living facility five months ago. He makes it out to the farm every few weeks to check on the house. He collects the mail and papers, and when he agrees to my offer, I go online and arrange for both to be forwarded to his new address, little things he never got around to doing when he moved out.

It's late afternoon when we say our good-byes. Ian reassures Stu he'll call to schedule a date to sign the paperwork, for what, I don't know. He's quiet on the drive back to Boise, lost in his thoughts. I hold his hand so that he knows I'm here for him when he's ready to find his way back.

We check in to a hotel near the airport and Ian immediately shuts himself in the bathroom and takes a shower. When he's done, his hair still damp and jaw overdue for a shave, his skin smelling of soap, he settles at the table with his laptop.

"Al moved the feature up an issue. He wants my pictures tomorrow morning." He powers up the laptop and types in his password.

"Did you just find that out?"

"He e-mailed this morning."

"That doesn't seem right. He isn't giving you much time to edit your work."

Ian shrugs.

"Does he expect you to edit them?"

He shakes his head. "He wants the raw images. His team narrows the selection to support the article and edits them. But that's not how I roll." They're his photos, his work and reputation on the line. I don't blame him for putting in the extra effort, but after sailing in a similar boat, I worry he's taking on too much. Squinting at the computer, he opens his apps and gets to work. He barely registers when I kiss his cheek and tell him I'll pick up dinner.

I walk across the street to Applebee's and order dinner to go. The hostess hands me a pager and I slip outside to make a few phone calls. I explain to my banker that I'm certain I want to cancel the loan application and I tell the property owners of the two sites I'd been considering that I'm no longer interested. When I finish, gone is the desire to conquer the coffee world, as Ian once described to me. In its place blossoms the same excitement and nerves I felt when I first opened Aimee's Café. It makes me eager to get back to milk-and-butter basics. Baking cakes and breads and delicacies. Crafting new specialty drinks to add to my ever-growing menu. Taking down James's paintings.

Yeah . . . that.

I should have removed them years ago. Good thing James is expecting to receive them.

I'll take care of it this week, I decide, adding a note on my calendar to pick up packing material, and the Applebee's pager vibrates.

After I get our food and start back toward the hotel, Nadia calls me. I stop at the sidewalk and stare at the image on my screen, the two of us at the Garners' ugly sweater party last Christmas. Time to change that photo, but I'm not sure I'm ready to talk with Nadia. Still, I answer the phone.

"Hey, are you OK?" she asks after I greet her.

"I'm fine."

"I've been trying to reach you. Did you really go to Spain?"

"I did, but we're in Idaho now."

"Idaho? What in the world are you doing there?"

"Visiting Ian's dad. Hey, can we talk later? I just picked up dinner and Ian's waiting."

"Yeah, whenever you want. But, Aimee, about Thomas. I'm sorry."

At the sound of Thomas's name, I slow down and turn around, spotting a bench off to the side of the hotel entrance. I sit down. The stale odor of nicotine clings to the air. Cigarette butts litter the receptacle beside me, ends sticking out of the sand like rotted dock pilings on a beach.

"I went to see him."

"Thomas? You went to his office? About me?"

"Another matter, but yes, your name did come up. I'm still having a hard time understanding why you took the job."

There's a long pause on the other end of the line before she comes on to say, "Do you remember Thomas in high school? He used to be funny and real."

"And then he changed."

"Yes, he changed," she agrees, her voice quiet, reflective.

"Now he's cold, calculating, and manipulative," I point out. "You can't forget that."

"I know, you're right."

"So, you didn't go to dinner with him the other night?" I ask, recalling their text message exchange.

"I did, and . . ." Her voice trails with remorse.

"Please don't tell me you slept with him."

"Jesus, no. We didn't even kiss."

"What did you do, then?"

"We ate, Aimee. And we talked. He's lonely. He has a lot of regrets."

"Nadia." I drag out her name. "Do you have feelings for him?"

"I don't know if I'm attracted to him, or just got caught up with the man he used to be. The guy sure can turn on the charm."

"I repeat. He's manipulative." I don't say anything further, and for a moment we're both quiet, lost in our thoughts. I'm not sure I can handle Nadia dating Thomas, but I don't want to lose her as a friend either. "Are you still working with him?"

"Yes, but not for much longer. I send off the plans next week. Unless he makes any changes, my contribution to the project will be done."

"Are you going to see him again after that?"

"I won't if you don't want me to. Our friendship is too important."

"I can't tell you who you can or can't date. Just know that I don't trust anyone in the Donato family, especially Thomas. You shouldn't either. Be careful around him. I care about you too much."

"Don't worry about me. I will."

"Good. Now I need a favor from you. Meet me at the café Thursday evening."

"Why?"

"You'll see. I've got to go. My dinner's getting cold."

I end the call, and on the way back to the room, I purchase two beers in the lobby bar. Ian's still at the table upon my return. He briefly looks up when I set his dinner and open beer beside him, but he doesn't touch his food. I quietly eat mine so as not to disturb him, then take a shower. When I'm finished, dewy and wrapped in the hotel's terry-cloth robe, I return to his side. He's turned off the lights and shut down his laptop. He faces the window, which he opened in my absence. The sheer curtain billows like an ocean surface. Our room is on the second floor and the soft glow of the parking lot lights cast Ian's profile in muted grays like an old black-and-white movie. He still hasn't touched his food.

"Ian?"

He doesn't look at me. "Al won't contract me again if he doesn't have the shots by morning. I'm not even halfway done."

"They seem to be in an awful rush for this feature. Can you get an extension? Tell him you've had a family emergency."

"Oldest excuse in the book. He won't buy it."

"It's the truth."

He looks at his hands and runs a nail around his thumb cuticle. "Stu knows where Sarah is."

My breath catches in my throat. "Did he tell you?"

He nods. "He bought a condo in Paradise and set her up there after her release. He found her a job, too. She's a seamstress at a dry cleaners in Las Vegas."

"Ian." I can't even.

I sink to my heels, looking up at him, and grip his hand with both of mine.

"He's been supporting her and he expects me to take over when he's gone. Thing is, I can't see her. Unless it's a medical or financial emergency, or she reaches out to me, I'm not fucking allowed to contact her." He snatches his beer and downs half.

"Why not?"

"Jackie was violent. My mom doesn't trust herself around me. She doesn't want to hurt me."

"But that was a long time ago. Surely she's had time to better understand and manage her condition."

Ian shrugs. He finishes his beer and sets down the bottle. "She has a companion. She's a nurse or something like that, and she lives with my mom. She helps her with her schedule and accompanies her when she leaves the condo. I'm expected to communicate through her." He looks down at me and smiles. It comes across as a sneer. "It all makes sense now, why my dad took on those extra assignments. He was saving money. He and Sarah hatched the plan long before her sentence was up and he kept everything from me. He let me believe my mom needed distance and that she didn't love me. Turns out that's why she left. She loved me too much to risk hurting me again. All these years I thought she hated me and all I wanted was to tell her, 'I'm sorry.'"

My heart breaks for him. I kiss his hand, turn it over, and kiss his palm. I press his palm against my cheek.

"I don't think I can do it, Aimee. I can't make financial and medical decisions on her behalf and not see her."

Crawling into his lap, I wrap my arms around him, threading my fingers in his hair, now dry and wavy. He lowers his forehead to my shoulder and ropes his arms around my back. He sighs, a long exhalation full of sadness.

Ian, my Ian.

I kiss his head and he murmurs something incoherent. His hair tickles my nose as I inhale his scent. Tea tree shampoo and hotel soap. I want to absorb his pain, take it all away from him.

He murmurs my name and lifts his head. We look at each other. His eyes are dark and full of anguish. I want to comfort him, but he has other things on his mind. As the sheer curtains surge with a breath of night air, Ian takes my breath. He kisses me and kisses me again, deeply. His hands move to my front and untie the belt at my waist. He parts the flaps and cool air moves over my skin like morning mist over water. Slowly, gently, his hands trace the lines of my waist, the edges of my breasts. His thumbs carefully outline my nipples, and still, he kisses me.

I meet his kisses, take in the lingering taste of hops on his tongue. Then everything changes, happening fast. My robe is off, I'm in the air, the muscles in Ian's arms twisting and cording underneath me as he carries me to the bed, his lips never leaving mine. My head has barely settled on the feather pillows before he's stripped and covering me, his flesh on my flesh, his hips between my legs. I close him in my arms and open for him, and he moves against me as though he can't get enough. He can't keep still. His hands are everywhere and it's exquisite.

Our lovemaking has ranged from sensual and seductive to wild and rough, leaving us sore and exhausted. But his fervor, it takes us to a whole new level. It's lewd and beautiful, dirty and glorious.

He stirs everything inside me as he kisses me, as he flips me over, as I take him deep, and deeper still. Only then does he consume me, his fingers biting into my skin. He moves in a way that makes me hunger for him, and makes me aware he's exorcising years of pain and unrest. And I take it. I take it all. Everything he has to give me, and when he's spent, our breathing erratic, his forehead drops to rest between my shoulder blades. We lie like that, in the quiet, enveloped in darkness, until our heartbeats slow. I start to drift off to sleep when I feel a drop on my back followed by another.

Ian.

I roll over. He lifts his head and I cup his face. His jaw is tight and the skin is tense around his eyes—his beautiful, soulful eyes.

"Ian." *My love.*

I kiss the moisture from his cheekbones, then hold him to my breast, where he falls into a fitful slumber.

CHAPTER 30

IAN

Don't look directly into the sun. You'll burn out your retinas. My parents had the good sense to warn me. It's what we've taught Caty. She listens, and in that matter, I did, too. But sometimes, looking at the sun is unavoidable. I'll catch a glimpse of a reflection off the window of a passing vehicle. Or I'll stand under a tree and look up into the skirt of branches to take a photo. A leaf bends and twists, the sun appears, and *bam!* The outline of the leaf or shape of the car window is seared on my eyeballs. And man, does it burn. I blink, and continue to blink, and eventually the bright spots go away.

I have two clear images of my mom that have left an impression on me. I carry them with me, a virtual keepsake. But rather than a shape captured by the sun that fades and disappears, they are branded in much the same way an image is recorded when light passes through the camera aperture and photons strike the film. Like a photo, the memories have faded over time. They aren't quite as sharp, but they're permanent. I can't blink them away. They haunt me.

I remember my mom, gun in hand, the moment she looked at me, face stricken, as the awareness of what she'd done set in. The look of horror that actors portray in motion pictures doesn't come close to the real deal. Genuine fear consumes you. It's palpable, even to an observer. It tastes of dust and asphalt and oil. I can still taste her fear. I can still see the moment she realized she was lost to me. She'd accepted she couldn't be the mother I needed.

My second memory is of the three of us, my parents and me, on a lakeside picnic. I was eight and my dad had a rare Sunday off work. We spent the afternoon fishing under my mom's watchful gaze, her back against a tree, a book of poems open on her lap. We took a break for lunch, and I asked what she was reading. Walt Whitman's "O Me! O Life!" She offered to read it to me and I said no. I was an eight-year-old kid more interested in cramming a PB&J sandwich into my mouth and washing it down with a Coke so I could get back to my fishing pole. I didn't want to listen to my mom recite romantic prose. It wasn't until a college literature class that I read the poem. The professor had us dissect it line by line. Had I known then the meaning behind the poem, I would have asked her if she was questioning her own existence. Did she wonder if her life had meaning? Was she feeling helpless? Had she known then the road she intended to travel, the one that led her away from me? I would have taken the time to listen. I would have made sure she was all right.

What I do know about that day is how content she seemed. How she couldn't not smile when she talked with my dad. How they shared a laugh, their foreheads bent as they whispered to each other. How my dad's lips lingered on her cheek when he kissed her before joining me at the shore. To the outside observer, we might have appeared to be the perfect family on a Sunday outing. It was the calm before the storm of my life. It's my last good memory of the three of us.

When Aimee and I arrive at the Tierneys', we descend upon a similar scene in their backyard. Catherine rests with her back against the giant sycamore that shades the grass, a book open and facedown on her lap. Hugh sits cross-legged on a plaid blanket drinking from a plastic teacup. His shirt has grease stains and his chin is smudged with oil. He was probably in the garage working on his Mustang. But he keeps his pinkie up when he lifts the cup to his lips as Caty instructs. As I watch them, I can't help thinking of that Sunday afternoon long ago.

Aimee senses I'm drifting. I'm not quite in the moment, and she clasps my hand. I look down at our linked fingers, then up into her eyes.

"Time," she says. "Give it time. The pain will lessen, it really will."

I believe her. She would know. But right now, I'm still too raw to make that step forward. "I'm not sure what to do about my mom."

"I know you aren't, and that's OK. You'll figure it out. Trust your instincts. They're good to you. They led you to me." She smiles, and for the moment, I'm lost in her, who we were on our own and who we have become together and where we're going. Then Caty squeals and the moment is shattered.

"Daddy! Mommy! You're back!" She runs straight for me. I lift her in my arms and she smothers me with kisses. "I missed you," she coos, resting her head on my shoulder.

"I missed you, too, Caty-cakes."

"Did you see your daddy? Mommy said you went to your daddy's house."

I look at Aimee over our daughter's crown of curls. She shakes her head. Caty doesn't know he's sick.

"I want to meet him," Caty says.

I want her to meet him, too. Instead, I showed my dad pictures of Caty on my phone. He had asked about her, but he doesn't want her to visit. Her one and only impression of her grandfather would be of him on the brink of death hooked up to an oxygen tank. His words, not mine. I don't agree with him, but if I've learned anything, it's to be respectful of another person's wishes.

That's when it hits me. My eyes burn as though I've looked into the sun, and in a way, I have. It's all so clear now. I know what I want, what I've wanted all along. I pinch my face to keep myself from falling apart in front of my in-laws. Aimee takes Caty from my arms.

"Hey, you OK?"

I nod stiffly. "Do you mind if we skip lunch here and go home? I have some things I need to take care of."

"Sure," she says.

The next day, after a long conversation with Erik about how Al Foster wouldn't be doing what he did as *National Geographic*'s photo editor if he weren't damn good at his job, I send off thousands of raw images to him, noting the ones his team should consider for the feature. Trust him to make your images look good, Erik had advised. It's his reputation, too. I also e-mailed my essay to Reese. Then, late in the evening, after Aimee left with Caty to meet Nadia at the café to discuss redecorating the walls, I book a ticket to Las Vegas for the following morning. I'm gone before my wife, daughter, and the sun are up.

Swift Cleaners is open when I arrive. Customers carry in soiled clothing and walk out with plastic-covered pressed suits and shirts. Each time the door opens, I can smell the kerosene-like vapor of hot fabrics and solvent. I don't go inside. I watch the activity through the window because on the other side is the seamstress's table. The sewing machine is covered, and rainbow rows of thread are neatly aligned. A rack of clothes is nearby, hems cuffed and pinned. My mom pinned those cuffs. She touched those pants, and she's sat in that chair, the leather stretched and worn from years of use. This is where she spends her days, has spent every day since the day after her release from prison.

How often did my dad visit? Did they talk about me? Did my mom ask about me? Did she ever think about me? Has her mind settled? Is she at peace with the choices she made about her life? Is she happy without me?

My questions are endless and I'm so deep in thought that I don't at first hear the question posed to me.

"Excuse me?" I ask.

An elderly man, his pants buckled at his ribs, the short-sleeve plaid shirt tucked inside, smiles. "Are you coming in or not?"

I turn around. Across the street is a coffee shop. Tables line the windows. "No, thanks," I tell him and jog across the street, dodging cars and a bicyclist.

I order coffee, black, no sugar, and keep an eye on the tables. When a mother and her two toddlers vacate one, I slide into the seat, pushing aside crumpled napkins and muffin crumbs with my arm.

From where I sit, I can see out the window, back across the street, through the dry cleaner's large front window to where the seamstress sits. The sign posted in the door notes she'll arrive by nine.

I remove my jacket and fold it over the chair beside me. I set my phone on the table, glance at my watch, and sip my coffee. And then I wait.

∞

"Ian."

I pull myself away from the window and glance up at Aimee. Caty smiles beside her. I blink, feeling a rush of confusion. "You're here."

"I got your note."

"For you to call, not . . . You flew here?" I still can't make sense of her and Caty standing there.

"We took the plane, Daddy. Mommy let me sit by the window. We flew into the clouds."

"Lucky for us there's a flight out of San Jose to Las Vegas every ninety minutes. I hope you don't mind we came," Aimee says, looking

nervous. I'm sure she's wondering if she made the right decision to follow me here.

At first, I thought I wanted to be alone. But now that they're here?
I'm relieved. I don't want to do anything without Aimee by my side. I
stand and rope my arms around her. I hug her tightly. "No, not at all.
I should have asked you to come. I'm sorry I didn't."

"Have you seen her?" Aimee whispers so Caty won't hear.

I nod and point out the window. My mom sits in her chair, hunched
over her machine. I feel Aimee's slight intake of breath.

"Have you talked to her?"

I shake my head.

"Have you been sitting here all day?"

I nod. "Since eight thirty." It's now after five. My mom works
until six.

Aimee leaves my arms and seats Caty at the table. She takes out
paper and crayons from her large shoulder bag and gives them to Caty;
then she orders a chocolate milk from the counter.

I sit back in my seat beside the window and drink my coffee. My
fourth one for the day. It's gone cold.

"Did you go to school?"

Caty shakes her head. She pushes a piece of blank paper toward me
and hands me a brown crayon. Fuzzy Wuzzy. It makes me laugh and I
show Caty the label.

"Mommy said you were sad. I always hug Pook-A-Boo when I'm
sad, but I didn't bring him."

"Where is your bear?" I ask.

"On my bed. He was still sleeping when we left." She points at the
crayon. "You should draw a bear. Maybe it'll make you happy."

"I think that's a fine idea."

Caty grins and together we color. Aimee returns with Caty's chocolate milk. Caty pushes a blank sheet toward Aimee. "Color with us,
Mommy."

"In a moment, sweetie, after I talk with your daddy."

Aimee sits beside me, her eyes imploring. "You scared me, Ian. You've been holed up in your office for two days and when I woke up this morning, you were gone. You left so suddenly. What's going on?"

She didn't straighten her hair this morning, probably didn't have time. I touch a curl. It feels like silk. "I'm trying to fix it, what I did wrong."

"Which is what, exactly?"

I look out the window at my mom. She's helping a customer. "She cut her hair. It's short."

"She's beautiful."

I nod. "She smiles a lot. I don't remember her smiling much."

Aimee rests her hand on my thigh. I feel the heat of her through my jeans and turn back to her. "I didn't listen to my dad when I should have. For once, I'm going to do as he asked. I'll manage her finances. I'll keep her books; I'll pay her damn bills. And I won't contact her. I'll stay away like he asked and she wants. But first . . . first I needed to see her. All these years I thought I needed to apologize to her. I kept taking those damn pictures. But really, I just want to know she's OK. I want to know that she's happy."

"But you won't go talk with her?"

I shake my head. "She doesn't want that."

Aimee is quiet. She watches me for a long moment. Eventually, I turn away, drink my cold coffee and twiddle the crayon, spinning it on the table. Still, Aimee watches me. Then suddenly, she stands and removes her sweater. It's missing a button and there's a tear near one of the holes.

"I'll be right back."

Caty looks up, surprised. "Where're you going, Mommy?"

Aimee glances from Caty to me and back. She reaches for Caty's hand. "Come with me. We have a very important errand."

My heart rockets into my throat. "What're you doing, Aimee?"

She rests a hand on my shoulder. "Trust me," she says, then leaves the coffee shop.

I swing around in my chair and watch her and Caty wait for the light at the corner. It changes, and they cross.

"What are you doing?" I murmur.

What are you doing? What are you doing?

My palms sweat. I rake my fingers through my hair.

Aimee pulls open the glass door to the dry cleaners, stands aside for Caty to enter. The door swings shut behind them. Through the window, I see them approach my mom. Envy ricochets through me, heating my arms and legs. I want to be the one to talk with her. Does she sound the same? Do her hands still flutter when she talks? Does the left side of her lip still pull higher than the right when she smiles?

But I can't go to her, not if I want to respect her wishes, to honor my dying father's request.

I see my mom lean down to talk with Caty and I want to weep. *She's your granddaughter. She looks like you. Do you see it, the honey color of her hair, the dimple in her chin?*

Aimee points at a blanket folded on a shelf and my mom shows it to her. They talk for a bit until my mom folds the blanket and puts it back. Aimee then shows my mom her sweater. She points at the missing button and the small tear where the wool has unraveled. My mom nods and smiles.

I want to shout, *I'm over here, Mom. I'm OK. I did all right.*

She takes Aimee's sweater and gives her a receipt. She waves good-bye and I shake my head. Not yet, not today. I'm not ready to say good-bye.

Aimee and Caty leave the dry cleaners and my mom sits back in her chair. I want to ask her what she thought of my wife. Did she enjoy meeting my daughter? Could she love my family?

It pains me I'll never know the answers.

Caty settles back in her chair, grinning. "That nice lady over there and I have the same color eyes. And she knows all about coloring with crayons." She picks through her crayons. "If I put these three together— brown, orange, and yellow—I can make my eye color on paper." She shows me the crayons. Mango Tango, Sienna, and Goldenrod.

When did she color? In prison? Was it part of her therapy?

"That's great." My voice cracks. I look at Aimee, expectant. *Tell me everything!* Her eyes glisten. She rests her hand over mine on the table.

"I didn't tell her who we are, but I asked about her job, and I asked what she likes about living here. She loves to sew. She showed me a quilt she's working on. It's beautiful. The stitching is intricate with a complex pattern. She's an artist, Ian. She complained about the oppressive heat, but wouldn't think of living elsewhere. People are kind to her here. She was kind to me and she adored Caty. She's doing OK, Ian." She squeezes my hand. "She's doing more than OK."

My throat constricts. I close my eyes and nod. Then I feel Caty's hand cover ours.

"Are you happy now, Daddy?"

A sob barges its way into my throat and I disguise it with a rough laugh. "Yes, Caty-cakes. I'm happy now." I clasp Aimee behind her head, my fingers digging into her scalp, and press my lips firmly to her forehead. "Thank you," I whisper harshly into her hair. I kiss her temple, her ear. "Thank you."

Overcome with emotion, I keep my face buried in her hair as I hold her, this woman I love who has given me so much: her hand in marriage, a family of my own, and in a way, through her, she's brought my mother back to me. I kiss her lips. "I love you."

"I love you, too."

"*Eww*, no kissing in public."

Aimee and I laugh, and together we turn to the window. We stay that way, her hand over mine, my arm around her shoulders, Caty coloring, until my mom leaves. A few minutes before six, a blue Honda pulls up to the curb in front of the dry cleaners. A brunette with large-framed sunglasses sits behind the wheel. Within moments, my mom packs up her station and leaves the dry cleaners. She smiles at the Honda's driver and settles into the passenger seat. The driver glances over her shoulder and eases into traffic. I watch them drive away until they disappear, turning a corner one block up. I've seen what I came here to see today.

I scrub my face with both hands and rest my forearms on the table. "Whad'ya think? Time to go home?"

Aimee taps her chin. "I don't know. We *are* in Vegas."

"Think we can find a suite with two bedrooms?"

She grins. "I like your line of thinking, Collins. I bet we can find a dessert buffet, too."

Caty's face lights up like a Vegas hotel. She claps. "Oh, yes, please. Can we stay?"

"As long as my two best gals are with me, I'll stay anywhere."

CHAPTER 31

IAN

Three Months Later

"Many outsiders do not understand the relationship these villagers have with the herds, and I admit, I had a hard time understanding myself. Why would a village expend such effort and expense to herd these wild horses into pens only to wrestle them, sometimes to the ground, to clip their manes and tails, administer medication, and then let them go? It's about love. It's about preserving history. And it's about tradition. The Rapa das bestas is an ancient festival that showcases the symbiotic relationship this village has with the animals that run wild and free through their hills. And it was through the words of our photographer, Ian Collins, that I finally saw the beauty of the Rapa das bestas. 'To love someone unconditionally is to let them thrive, even if that means letting them go so they can run wild and free.' I'm not sure if Mr. Collins was referring to the Galician herds or someone else—who, I do wonder—but to me, his words eloquently sum up the relationship between the villagers and the horses they manage."

Erik finishes reading the excerpt from this month's issue of *National Geographic* and grins at me. "Reese wrote an incredible piece. And these photos? Stunning." He shows me the foldout in the middle of the article, the wide-angle shot I took on the last day of the galloping herd on the neighboring hillside. Then he closes the magazine and points at the cover, grinning and nodding at the two stallions rearing up in the packed curro. I remember the smell and the noise, the flies buzzing. I remember how the Galician horses moved like schools of fish, their coats drenched in sweat, a shimmering mosaic of chestnut, mocha, and sable. But I remember most the incredible feeling after Al Foster's phone call three weeks ago. My photo had been selected for the cover.

It's early evening and we're at Aimee's Café, the after-party from this afternoon's opening at the Wendy V. Yee Gallery. Wendy covered her walls with not only my recent work in Spain, but a history of photographs since I first picked up a camera. A study of my life's work. She'd included photos of my parents, from the viewpoint of a child. They were the good ones, like the picture I took of my mom standing in the middle of the pond, her skirt skimming the surface, the sun bathing her face. I titled it *Beautiful Sadness*. Wendy intentionally left a blank wall symbolizing my future work. I have more stories to document. The show is in celebration of my first *National Geographic* assignment, the first of many, God willing, and will last for three weeks. Wendy managed to get a two-column feature in last week's Arts & Entertainment section of the *San Francisco Chronicle*. Today's opening was packed.

Erik raises his champagne glass. "Congrats, my friend. Here's to more epic shots."

"And glossy covers," I add.

"I'll drink to that."

And drink we do. Erik finishes his glass and glances around the crowded café. "Any chance of finding a beer in this place?"

"I happen to know where the owner keeps a secret stash." I lead him into the kitchen and grab two Anchors from the fridge, popping the tops. I give one to Erik.

"Thanks," he says, and takes a long draw from the bottle. "Have you heard from Reese?"

"She texted her congrats when she heard about the cover. You?" Tonight's the first chance Erik and I have had to catch up since his assignment with Reese in Yosemite. He's been traveling and I've been making frequent smaller trips of my own.

"Not recently, but we're going on assignment together in January."

"That's great. Where to?"

"Morocco. She's writing a piece about camping in the Sahara and requested me as the photographer." He sets aside his half-empty beer and scratches his lower lip. "She tells me you have history."

I nod slowly. "It was a long time ago." When he doesn't immediately acknowledge what I said, I raise an eyebrow.

"She's talented."

I slowly grin. "She feels the same. She wouldn't have requested you if she felt otherwise."

We share a smile and I clap his shoulder. "Come on. Let's join the others before my wife finds me hiding out in the kitchen, drinking beer. She spent a pretty penny on the champagne."

When we return to the dining area, I look around. Aimee has my photos everywhere, including on the wall once dominated by James's paintings. She cleared it off last October and shipped his work to him in Hawaii. She did keep one, a miniature of her parents' house James had painted when he was seventeen. It hangs in her back office, a reminder of where she came from and how much she's grown since then.

Everyone is here. Erik and a few of the guys from the gym. Lance and Troy, two buddies from ASU I've kept in touch with over the years. Even Marshall Killion and his wife, Jenny, managed to get out here from Boston. Nadia's off to the side chatting with friends and some new guy she brought with her. He dotes on her like a young pup. His eyes track her everywhere. She keeps sending him off to fetch her cocktails. *Yeah, that relationship won't last long,* I think, laughing to myself.

Caty's at a table with Kristen's two oldest, eating cake and drinking sparkling cider. Kristen stands watch over them, rocking Theo. My gaze swings left until finally, across the room, I find the woman I'd been searching for. Beautiful in a black shift dress with a cascade of ruffles along the neckline, Aimee talks with Catherine and Hugh. Nick joins them, offering Aimee a glass of champagne, which she declines.

My gaze narrows. Excusing myself from Erik, I cross the room.

Nick eyes the champagne glass I take off his hands. I sip the bubbly. "Tee time's seven thirty. Gonna make it?"

I set aside the glass. "Wouldn't miss it. I'll wager a hundred dollars you don't shoot a single eagle this time." Nick is by far the better player between us. There's no way I'm betting I can beat him. When we play, I wager he will outperform his previous game.

Nick clutches his chest. "You wound me." Then he grins and grabs my hand. "You're on."

"See you on the course."

"Great show," Hugh says.

"Congratulations, Ian." Catherine kisses my cheek.

"Thanks." I clasp Aimee's hand. "Would you excuse us for a moment?" I say to them.

"Everything all right?" Aimee asks, her expression one of concern as I lead her to the back office.

"Everything's great." I close and lock the door, pull her into my arms.

"Ian, we have guests."

"I know, baby, but this can't wait." I cup her face and kiss her. I kiss her and kiss her, look at her, and kiss her again. Then I smile, my forehead pressed to hers.

Winded, she asks, "What was that about?"

"I just wanted to show you how much I love you. And to say thank you."

"For what?"

I rest my hands on her hips and back us up to the desk. Sitting on the edge, I pull her between my legs, our eyes level. I trace her hairline along her cheek and over her ear. "The past couple of months haven't been easy on us." I've been taking frequent, short visits to Idaho to make sure my dad's receiving the treatment he needs. He's deteriorating fast and the inevitability of losing him has affected me harder than I expected. "But I have some good news."

Aimee's eyes sparkle like cider. "You do?"

I bite my lower lip and nod. "My wife's pregnant."

She frowns, the ivory skin between her trimmed brows folding. Then those brows lift and her eyes go big. "How did you know?"

"You turned down a glass of Dom Pérignon. Who does that?"

She laughs. "This gal," she says, pointing at herself.

I rest a hand on her flat stomach and Aimee covers mine with both of hers. There's a life growing inside there. Caty will be thrilled when we tell her. And I want to tell my dad, before he goes. "How long have you known?" I whisper the question, my voice intimate.

She skims her fingers up my chest, under the lapel of my blazer, and hooks her hands behind my neck. "A few hours. I was planning to tell you tonight, after the party."

I lean in to kiss her, my lips within a whisper of hers, when there's a knock on the door. I groan.

"Aimee?" It's Trish.

"Tell her to go away." I run my tongue along her lower lip.

She twists her head toward the door. "I'll be out in a moment."

"There's someone here asking for Ian. Is he in there?"

I run my hands up the sides of her rib cage. "Shh. I'm not here," I tease and kiss her jaw, lingering on the soft indentation below her ear.

I just want these few minutes alone with her. I've been shaking hands, meeting new people, and fielding questions all day.

"She's from out of town. Says her name is Sarah Collins."

My hands squeeze Aimee's waist and I freeze. A tightness forms in my chest, spreading outward. I slowly lift my head. Aimee looks at me and our gazes hold. She smiles, and it's full of love.

"Did you know?" I ask.

She slowly shakes her head. "But I was hoping. I didn't want to say anything in case she didn't show."

I frown. "I don't understand."

"I left my first name and the number to the café on the ticket at the cleaners. I figure if your dad and mom do talk about you, she'd know about me, and Caty, and the café. I wanted to give her the choice to call. I hope that wasn't too presumptuous of me, but I wanted to know if she still felt the same way she did about her condition when she left you. If there's one thing I've learned these last seven or so years, it's to not assume things are the way they appear."

"When *did* she call?"

"It took her a while. She called last week. I mentioned your show and invited her and her companion to visit. She doesn't go anywhere without Vickie. Your mom explained to me that Vickie keeps her grounded. She helps her when she shifts midconversation or is out and about so she doesn't run off or get lost."

Trish knocks again. Aimee quirks a brow. "Should I tell her to give us a second?"

I'm stunned and elated and nervous and in awe. I clasp Aimee's face and, without taking my eyes from hers, call out to Trish. "Bring my mother back here."

"Your mother?" Trish exclaims. "Will do." I hear her walk away.

"Have I told you lately how much I love you?"

"Yes, but feel free to say it again," Aimee says with a smile.

"I love you." I kiss her. "You're amazing."

"I know."

I laugh and hug her tightly. When I let go, her face sobers. She fiddles with a button on my pressed white shirt. "A *National Geographic* cover and your mom. Two dreams come true in one day."

"Make that three." My hand slides to her stomach; then I grab hers. "Come with me."

"Anywhere. Always."

We cross the room and I unlock and open the door. To an even brighter future. The future we've hoped for.

ACKNOWLEDGMENTS

This book is dedicated to my readers who've journeyed with Aimee, James, and Ian through the entire Everything series. Thank you for reading, thank you for reviewing, and thank you for loving my characters as much as I do. I have many more stories to share and hope you stick around.

As with my previous books, *Everything We Give* involved a bit of research. I wanted to send Ian on a unique adventure and knew that I found it when I stumbled across an article about the Rapa das bestas. Since I have never attended the festival, I contacted the only person I know who lives in Spain. As luck would have it, she's been to the Rapa not once, but three years in a row! Thank you, Barbara Bos, for sharing the sights, sounds, smells, and tastes of the Rapa. Thank you for walking me through your experiences and sharing your emotions as you watched the event unfold, from herding the horses downhill with the villagers to the "shearing of the beasts" in the curro. Thank you for sending me photos of your adventures in real time! Barbara is the managing editor of *Women Writers, Women's Books*. If you're a writer, I encourage you to explore her website at www.booksbywomen.org. It's a wealth of information.

I also must thank Barbara for introducing me to Claire O'Hara, documentary and adventure photographer. I have to credit Claire for sharing with me the extraordinary connection the village of Sabucedo has with the Galician herds that roam their hills. She eloquently explained their symbiotic relationship, how without one, the other wouldn't survive. It is through Claire's eyes, experiences, and photographs that I managed to craft Ian's adventures in Sabucedo. Her photos from the Rapa das bestas are breathtaking, and I invite you to view them at her website, www.claireoharaphotography.com. Thank you, Claire, for breathing life into Ian's travels.

I delved deeper into the emotional and psychological aspects of mental illness with this book than I did with the previous two Everything books. While there is plenty of information available about the causes, symptoms, and treatments of dissociative identity disorder (DID), I wanted to capture what it's like to grow up with a parent who suffers from this condition. I needed a child's perspective. I owe a debt of gratitude to bestselling author Annette Lyon for directing me to Tiffany Fletcher's memoir *Mother Had a Secret*, a true account of growing up with a mother who had multiple identities. Thank you, Tiffany, for inviting me into your world so that I could make Ian's more real. I'd also like to thank Rachel Dacus for sharing with me her own experiences of growing up with a parent with mental illness. I'm in awe of your bravery and candor. Thank you, Dr. Nancy Burkey, for your insight on treatment, therapy, and the types of medication that can be prescribed. With regard to the condition itself, any inaccuracies in the portrayal of dissociative identity disorder are mine and for the purpose of making the information work within the story.

Thank you, Kelly Hartog, for your tips on court transcriptions, and to Matt Knight for, once again, answering my legal questions.

To my top reader group, the Tikis. Thanks for your advance reads and honest reviews, your ongoing support and enthusiasm. Your love for my stories keeps me writing, and your comments and posts in the

Tiki Lounge keep me entertained. A special shout-out goes to Letty Blanchard, who gave Ian's childhood friend his name: Marshall Killion. I have heaps of gratitude and respect for Andrea Katz, whom I've come to think of as a dear friend, for her enthusiastic support of me and the publishing community through her Ninjas and Facebook group, Great Thoughts' Great Readers. Thanks to the book bloggers, reviewers, and Instagrammers who read advance copies and shared your thoughts and photos across social media.

Usually, a manuscript's fast first draft comes easy to me. I can crank out a book's skeleton within eight weeks. But after a year of writing, revising, and editing not one but *three* manuscripts, I started writing *Everything We Give*, my fourth book, only to hit a wall three chapters into the story. Writer's block is a real thing, and it's scary, especially when you're mentally exhausted and there's a looming deadline. I stared at my monitor's blank screen and empty Word document for six weeks until I finally got my act together and made a phone call. I owe a huge thank-you to bestselling author Barbara Claypole White, who, after a forty-five-minute pep talk, cleared the fog in my head. After that call, I powered out Ian's story in seven weeks, typing THE END the night before I left for Paris. Lesson learned: call Barbara sooner.

To my first readers, Barbara Bos, Emily Carpenter, and Rachel Dacus, each of you read the draft for a specific reason. Thank you for your honest and insightful feedback. You helped make *Everything We Give* a more powerful and genuine story.

To Danielle Marshall, Christopher Werner, Gabriella Dumpit, Dennelle Catlett, and the entire Lake Union Publishing team for making the Everything series soar. You are such a joy to work with, and I look forward to collaborating on many more projects. I couldn't ask for a better team. To Kelli Martin, my developmental editor through the entire series, thank you for your editorial savviness, your fun texts during your read-throughs, and your friendship.

Gordon Warnock, my agent extraordinaire who always seems to know what I want before I do, thank you for watching my back and for your ongoing support. Your ideas, advice, and expertise are always spot-on.

Hugs to my husband and our kids. I love each of you to the moon and back and then some.

Finally, I love connecting with my readers. Stop by my website, www.kerrylonsdale.com, and say hello. Let me know what you think of Ian's story.

BOOK CLUB DISCUSSION QUESTIONS

1. *Everything We Left Behind* ends with Lacy Saunders giving James her business card with the request to pass it along. Did you suspect the card was intended for Ian? Were you surprised that James gave the card to Ian? What do you think about the way James introduced himself to Ian?

2. How do you think Ian handled the news about Aimee kissing James when James first returned to California earlier in the summer? How do you think Ian handled James's return the second time around and Aimee going to visit with him? Are you satisfied with the way Aimee and James said good-bye and the reasons why?

3. Ian first mentions his desire to find his mom, Sarah, in *Everything We Keep*. What did you think had happened to her when you read about her disappearance in the first book? What are your thoughts about Ian's reluctance to search for her in recent years?

4. What do you think of Lacy's role in Ian's life, first when she helped Stu find him, and again when she helped Sarah track down Clancy? Were you surprised at Lacy's connection to the Collins family?

5. What do you think of Reese Thorne? Should Ian have confided in Aimee the details of his relationship with Reese?

6. Discuss Ian's childhood. Are you amazed by Ian's resilience and ability to love? What thoughts went through your head as you read his backstory?

7. Discuss the similarities and differences between Ian's and Aimee's journeys of confronting their traumas, letting go, and moving forward. How did they help each other?

8. Many themes are presented in this novel: longing, maturity, sacrifice, secrets, family, letting go, and love in all its forms. Which theme resonated the most with you? The least?

9. In the end, Stu reveals he's kept Sarah hidden from Ian at her request. Did his actions surprise you? Sarah gave up her chance of being a mother to Ian. Was she right to leave him?

10. Ian finally follows his dad's orders and doesn't contact his mom. But he does spend a day watching her from across the street. What emotions did you experience while reading this scene? Should Ian have contacted his mother, or was he right to keep his distance? How would you have handled yourself in a similar situation?

11. The Everything series ends with James living in Hawaii with Natalya and his sons, a possible relationship developing between Thomas and Nadia, and Sarah Collins showing up at Ian's *National Geographic* celebration. What do you think happens next for these characters?

ABOUT THE AUTHOR

Photo © 2013 Deene Souza Photography

Kerry Lonsdale is the *Wall Street Journal*, Amazon Charts, and #1 Amazon Kindle Bestselling author of the Everything series—*Everything We Keep*, *Everything We Left Behind*, and *Everything We Give*—as well as *All the Breaking Waves*. She resides in Northern California with her husband and two children. Learn more about Kerry at www.kerrylonsdale.com.

Made in the USA
Middletown, DE
07 May 2020